A
BLACK BEAR
KILLER
IN CASTAWAY COUNTY

By the Same Author

A Cold Snow in Castaway County

A
BLACK BEAR
KILLER
IN CASTAWAY COUNTY

JOHN LINDSEY
HICKMAN

This edition published in 2023 by Loony Moose Publishing

2nd Edition

ISBN Paperback: 979-8-9882533-2-7
ISBN Ebook: 979-8-9882533-3-4

A catalogue copy of this book can be found in the Library of Congress.

Published with the help of Indie Authors World
www.indieauthorsworld.com

To my mother and father, who adopted me at only five days old and provided me with the love, care, and development every child dreams of having. My mother ensured that I gained a knowledge and love of music and books, and she educated me in the proper use of King's English. My father challenged my imagination and creativity to ensure they developed freely. You were both, truly, the best!

ACKNOWLEDGMENTS

I would like to thank Liane Paulson, Gloria Gaudreau, John Gorman, and my wife, Jennifer Hickman, for serving as the initial editors for this book. Without their kind help, many more errors would likely have appeared upon these pages.

I also thank Chief Deputy Shawn Donahue of the Washington County Sheriff's Department, Machias, Maine, and former Chief Deputy Michael St. Louis, both for being so kind as to provide technical information about investigative procedures in a Maine sheriff's office.

And thanks again to Richard L. Skinner for making a final review of the book as both a former deputy sheriff in Maine, as well as one who loves reading a good book on a cold winter night.

Thanks also to Stanley and Ellen Wills for reviewing the final draft.

I am grateful to Carrie Foscato Design for the wonderful job she did on designing the cover for this book. It came out exactly as I had hoped!

I also want to acknowledge Louise Hector, who kindly reviewed my first novel in the Dell Hinton, Sheriff series and suggested a change in the writing style to better accommodate my writing and personality. I'm sure the change has improved this sequel.

And thanks to Geri and staff at IndieBRAG, who honored my first book with a BRAG Medallion and have so kindly supported me, as well as the entire self-publishing world, through their organization.

And lastly, my thanks to my wife, Jennifer, and my son, Branden, who make my writing possible by keeping me happy and sane (for the most part) and putting up with my temperament while I am going through the creative writing processes. You are the best!

1

It was early in the morning. I had gone to bed late after watching an old Western movie on TV and had been careful not to awaken Suzi, as she was sleeping comfortably on her side of the bed. I was in the middle of an all too familiar nightmare, one that seems to haunt me on occasion with a restlessness and aggravation I can't seem to shake off.

In my dream, I'm back on the Boston Police, and I've responded to a break-in call in one of the warehouse districts. It's a cold, rainy night as I walk around the south end of a huge warehouse and see an open window toward the rear of the building. I have my gun drawn and my flashlight pointed toward the window. The beam of the flashlight is broken by the heavy rain and the distance between us, so it doesn't fully illuminate the suspect as he begins to exit the building through the window.

As he steps down on the pavement underneath the window, I yell for him to stop and put his hands up, and I identify myself as a cop. The suspect turns toward me, and in that split second I see a small twinkle of light shining off a dark metal object in his right hand. My mind reels, and I'm sure it was a reflection off the barrel of a gun, which is now pointed in my direction. I immediately squeeze the trigger on my gun, firing two shots toward the suspect, and he, in turn, falls to the ground in a heap.

As I walk toward the motionless suspect, I call on my portable radio that I have shots fired and one suspect down. I get to the suspect, and, while covering him with my gun hand, I use my other hand to roll him over so I can check his vital signs and recover his weapon. As his body turns, I look at the face and realize the suspect is a youth, not a grown man, probably fifteen or sixteen. I quickly glance at his hands and find that the metal object I saw gleam in the light was merely a black metal flashlight.

I immediately begin sweating and start having convulsions as a precursor to puking. I can hear sirens in the background as I fall to my knees.

As this horrible scene was taking place in my dream, a loud ring broke my concentration. I immediately sat up and began to reach for my phone beside the bed. I was soaked with sweat and still trembling.

That instant, when the ring of the phone interrupts a deep sleep, is one of the hardest things about being a law enforcement officer, especially one who's in an administrative position. You have to train yourself to be able to go from deep sleep to totally awake in an instant. I know that such morning calls are always ones where the caller is seeking some definitive direction or solution to a major problem. I have to be ready to focus on the problem and give them the correct answer, so I have to be wide awake. That's my job. I'm the sheriff: Dell Hinton, sheriff of Castaway County, Maine.

I looked over at the digital clock on my bed stand and read the time to be 3:07 a.m. and simultaneously picked up the phone and said hello.

"Hi, Sheriff, it's Polly. Sorry to wake you." The caller was Polly Hand, a night dispatcher for the Maine State Police who also provides my office with coverage when we don't have our own person on duty.

"Oh, hi, Polly. What do you have?"

"Well, it looks like you have a multiple homicide out at the old Irving Truck Stop. We have a trooper on the scene and another on the way to help."

She called it the old Irving Truck Stop because, although it was so owned in the past, and the Grohe Corporation now owned it, many long-time citizens still referred to it by the Irving name. Mr. Thurston Grohe IV, who owns a huge all-year cabin on a hill above the head of our lake and is the current CEO of the corporation, had decided to purchase the truck stop. He had since renamed it the Black Bear Truck Stop in homage to the local citizenry. I'm not sure the name change and purchase helped his image with locals much. Last year, Mr. Grohe had called us to his big house because some kids had thrown a couple of eggs at his front door. He's the type of guy who wanted us to take fingerprints from the eggshells left behind so we could catch the kids. Like it was a heinous crime. Anyway, he had become known as someone who had entirely too much money and too little community spirit. Maybe he thought buying the truck stop and renaming it would help his image some. Who knows.

"Okay, has anyone called my chief deputy yet?"

"Yes, sir, he's on his way as well. I'd expect him to be there in about fifteen minutes."

"Okay, Polly. I'll get dressed and be right over there. I'll call you when I get to my Tahoe."

I hung up the phone and rolled back over toward Suzi. Even at that time of the morning, she was a beautiful picture. Her lovely skin, beautiful face, and, lucky me, she slept without clothes most of the summer months. Hey, even a blind squirrel finds a nut now and again! While I was wishing I had more time, I knew that my duties called and I needed to go.

She took a look at me and asked if I had had that nightmare again. I told her I had, but this was the first time in six or eight months, so it wasn't recurring as often as before. I just hoped it would eventually cease to exist in my nights at all. I told her I would be okay and that I was leaving to go in to work.

As I gave her a kiss on the cheek and told her to go back to sleep, her cell phone began to ring.

"Well, Dell, it must be a big crime. I expect they're calling me to come into the studio."

Suzi's station, Channel 4 News, wanted her to come in so she could coordinate with the onsite team they were sending to the crime scene to ensure she broke the story on her 6:00 a.m. broadcast. They would have a truck on the scene sending photos and reports via satellite to her production office and staging area, and it would be her responsibility as the lead news anchor to review it, consolidate it into a reasonable three- or four-minute piece, and prepare it for final tape presentation. And she would have to discuss with the onsite reporter if they were going to provide a "live" segment to augment the taped portions, which I suspected they would. In more metropolitan areas, there would be various production managers and editors who did these jobs, but in rural Maine, Suzi had to do a lot of that stuff herself. They were lucky to have the mobile report truck in the first place. I think it was a grant or donation from one of our more wealthy summer homeowners.

We showered quickly, grabbed a coffee and a stale donut from the kitchen, and ran out to our vehicles in the driveway. I gave her a quick peck on the cheek, wishing it could have been a lot more, and got into my police package Tahoe, while Suzi got into her gold Rav4 and headed for the studio. I radioed State Police Dispatch to tell Polly I was on my way and that I would be there in about twenty minutes or so. After I exited the deep woods around my cabin and got onto Route 121 headed toward Daphine Crossroads, I turned on my blue lights but kept my speed down. There was no need to race to get to the scene; there were already troopers there, and most likely, my chief deputy, Berkley Smith, was there as well. I used the lights to scare off moose and deer as much as anything, especially when rounding some of the sharp curves in the road on Route 121 and Route 7 heading toward the scene. That time of the morning, the biggest traffic threats were moose, bear, and deer in the roads, and maybe an occasional porcupine.

While they were all hazards, moose could be downright problems. Moose have a propensity to charge lights. If you're driving down the road and run up on a moose, you should immediately turn off your headlights to avoid the moose charging your vehicle. A friend of mine once told me about this very thing happening to her and her sister one night. They rounded a corner, and there in the road was a big bull moose. They remembered having been told by their father about moose and headlights, so they turned theirs off right away. As there was a nearly full moon that night, they were able to still see the moose quite well. It charged toward their vehicle, scaring them quite a bit. Just short of their bumper, he stopped, turned around, and gave a kick of his back leg toward the vehicle as if flicking away a fly, then trotted back into the heavy forest alongside the roadway. In the old west, moose often charged locomotive engines because of the large headlights on them. You really have to be careful on backwoods roads, especially running at higher speeds responding to a bad call.

As I turned north on Route 7, I could see the flashing red and blue lights at the Black Bear Truck Stop up ahead. I pulled into the lot and parked away from the crime scene on the south portion of the paved parking area. I told Dispatch that I was on the scene, grabbed a pair of latex gloves from the box I keep in the Tahoe, and exited my vehicle.

While I was walking toward the building, I found the scene to be the usual chaotic mess. There was a state trooper, a game warden, an Eagle Ridge Town police officer, and a Bureau of Indian Affairs police officer from the Indian reservation just across the county line, from Washington County. This is often the case with crime scenes in our community. Although there are few officers in each agency, there are quite a few police agencies in the area, so we all provide backup on calls. This creates a mismatch of uniforms and policies, which can make for a confusing scene, but it provides great protection for each of us in the long run. That's part of living in a smaller community, and, generally, it makes all of us work together in a more cohesive way with fewer "turf battles."

As I was walking past the game warden, I noticed he had watery eyes. As I continued to walk, I put on the latex gloves I was carrying so that I would be sure not to corrupt anything at the crime scene by leaving my fingerprints or smudging those of others. I knew that the best thing for me to do was to keep my hands in my pockets unless given other direction by one of our trained investigators. There's nothing worse for a crime scene than a sheriff or chief to walk into it and begin contaminating evidence because they haven't had the technical training their staff has been given. Then the officers in command of the scene, who know better, often find it hard to tell their boss to stop what they are doing. I knew this from my experience as an investigator in Boston, so I was not about to put any of my guys in that awkward position. At least not if I could help it.

As I continued walking toward the door of the Black Bear, I recognized the partially covered body near the front door by the green uniform pants, and I knew why the game warden had been crying: the body was that of a fellow game warden. Just behind his body lay another covered object almost at the edge of the doorway, in front of a poster in the window for cigarettes. Before I was able to enter the building, a state trooper called out to me as he was stretching out a large piece of crime-scene tape. He was tall and slightly gangly looking; he was clearly a country boy, and he didn't try to hide that fact. I'd met him before, and he had a real Southern hospitality about him.

"Sheriff Hinton. Over here, Sheriff."

"Thanks for the call out. Has Berk arrived yet?"

"Yes, I think he's already inside the truck stop having a look around. I'm roping off the scene outside so we can be sure to keep all the rubber-neckers and any press that may show up away. Just want to be sure no one messes up this scene."

"Great, Trooper. I'll go in and see where Berk is on this thing so far. Who's the game warden?"

"It was poor Paul Windom. I think he had about six more years to retirement. Bad way to get it. Looked like he caught one right in the head."

"Aw, he always seemed like a good guy to me. Any ID on the other victim?"

"One of the clerks, I'm not sure of the name. There was another clerk inside. But they transported her. Not sure she'll make it though."

"I'll check in on Berk. Is the crime-scene investigation truck en route?"

"You bet, Sheriff! I'm glad this won't be my investigation. Guess Lieutenant Bell will get primary on this one. Looks like it's gonna be a long one!"

Trooper Henderson was referring to the chief investigator at the Maine State Police, Lieutenant Franklin D. Bell. By code in Maine, the state police have primary jurisdiction over homicide cases out in the counties of the state. Though in reality, they usually asked for a person from the local sheriff's office to be assigned to assist. It was my immediate guess that Lieutenant Bell would want a couple on this case. At this point, our job was to secure the scene, prepare the initial crime-scene report, and await the state police response from Augusta.

I turned away from Trooper Henderson and muttered that I agreed with his point about this investigation. And I hated one that involved a police shooting. It always made tempers flare more and often caused people to jump to quick conclusions in an effort to realize some reason for the tragedy. Families want answers, and the police family is very large and quick to expect them. Unfortunately, objectivity could often be lost in the rush to pass judgment in a case like that.

After surveying the outside of the building again, I walked through the front doors and looked around for Berk. My chief deputy, Berkley Smith, is my height, about six feet two, a little shy of forty, but has this cherubic face that sometimes makes him look about twenty-five. When he smiles, you'd swear you were looking at Opie Taylor all grown up as a young adult, except that Berk has dark brown hair.

I found Berk over by the far end of the counter area for gas payments. He had his gloves on and was making notes in his police 007 notebook. This is a slim profile notebook that can be easily carried in the hip pocket of a law enforcement officer's pants. He had a frown on his face as I came up to him.

"Hey, Berk. You got this one all figured out already?" I asked with a smile.

"Oh, hi, boss. No, there's a lot here to process, even in the mind."

"Well, give me a brief overview then."

"One clerk, Mary Watson, was found here behind the counter with a gunshot in the chest. She's alive but may not make it; she was hit pretty near the heart as far as I could see before they took her to the hospital. She wasn't conscious, so I couldn't get anything from her.

"Another clerk, Betty Dillon, was found dead just outside the front door. She's out there just behind the game warden and near the front window. She caught a bullet almost dead in the forehead. I'm sure she never knew what hit her at all, thankfully."

"That leaves the game warden, Berk."

"Yeah, he didn't even get to fire his gun; he had just cleared leather when he took a shot in the head as well. His wound was on the right temple area, though, not directly in the forehead. None of the holes look to be very big; I'd say maybe a .25 or .32 at the biggest, definitely not any large rounds."

"So, was money taken?"

"Well, the first cash register was open, and the money was missing. The second one was ajar but had money in it and didn't look like it had been touched."

"Okay, working theory or is it too early?" I wanted to have something in mind to give Lieutenant Bell when he arrived.

"Boss, right now I'd guess that this was a robbery, and the game warden just walked in on it. But we'll know more as we go, so I guess we can start from there."

"Good work, Berk. You keep working up the initial crime-scene report. I'll stick around outside so I can handle the media with the trooper while you and Alec work on the scene. Let me know if I can help you with anything on this, okay?"

As I walked outside into the fresh air, one of my other deputies, Alec Wardlow, came near me bagging some initial items for evidence. I also passed by Dink Abernathy, a clerk at one of our local stores who specializes in photography. I had made an agreement with the store in my first six months as sheriff to allow us to use Dink as a crime-scene photographer. Dink was always great using a camera and developing film and such, and it seemed natural to use him for that purpose until we got better training for our own staff. In the meantime, we had few big crime scenes, and he did the job on a case-by-case payment basis.

Before I could get over to Trooper Henderson's location, I saw a young woman charging over toward me. It was one of the junior reporters for Suzi's station, and she was clearly looking for someone to give her the story. *Oh well*, I thought, *here we go with the media circus!*

2

It was about seven thirty when I left the scene at the Black Bear Truck Stop in the capable hands of my chief deputy and Trooper Henderson. Lieutenant Bell had called and was not expected to arrive at the scene with the crime lab unit for another hour or so. The sun had finally begun creeping over the tree line as I drove south on Route 7 toward Weaverton and my office. As I was driving, I suddenly realized that I was quite hungry, so I decided to stop for some breakfast at the Woodburn Diner. Driving along Route 7, I could smell the crisp wind coming over the saltwater mingling with the intense pine bough aroma. It served to remind me exactly why I had fallen in love with Maine's coastal area so quickly a couple of years ago when I first moved here with my second wife, Liz.

We had moved to Castaway County mostly because my high school friend Dexter Delaney had been living here, working as pastor for a local church, and he had regaled us with story after story of the simple life he was living in Maine. I guess in some ways it reminded me of all the Westerns he and I used to watch on Saturday morning television: all good and bad, with good usually winning out, set in a more simple time. Dex and I used to love getting caught up in those movies and then wishing we had been born a century earlier. As we got older, though, we realized that the movies romanticized the Old West, and life in those days was even harder than today. But it was still fun for us both to dream!

After we moved to Maine, Liz and I grew distant as a couple and finally went our separate ways. By that, I mean she flounced off to find her gold mine, and I stayed in Castaway County and tried to put my second failed marriage behind me. Seeing Liz go wasn't too bad, but getting on with my life seemed a little harder to do. But now

I'm in a great relationship with Suzi Parks, the primary anchor at Channel 4 News, and I'm the duly elected sheriff of Castaway County. *Who would have expected that?*

As I pulled up on the street in front of the diner, Dr. Myron Clopper, our town's family doctor and part-time coroner, came down the sidewalk with his German shepherd, Ben.

"Hey, Doc. How are you and Ben doing today?"

"A whole lot better than you, I'd guess, Dell!"

"Oh, yeah, Doc, we haven't had a bad one like this since I've been here. I hope we can get enough information from the scene to get this bad guy. After I get a sandwich to go, I'm planning to head to the hospital to check in on Mary Watson. If we're lucky, maybe she can talk and give me something by then."

"Well, I'm sure Doctor Beale over at the emergency room is doing his best with her. We were lucky that he came to our hospital as an intern and decided to stay after he was fully certified. He's good, and he's young, and as I'm sure you've never noticed, I'm getting old and ready to sit and fish, rather than doctor people and be your part-time coroner."

"But, Doc, you've brought many of our fine citizens into this world. You should be real proud of that."

"Oh, I am. I'm just getting older and more tired. But I'm glad that Dr. Beale is in our community so he can take over for me someday. I'll head over to the morgue as soon as I drop Ben off at the house." Unlike television shows about big cities, Dr. Clopper, as a part-time coroner, does not report to the crime scene; he usually responds to the morgue at the hospital to perform his inspections.

"Okay, Berk is handling the scene at the Black Bear with the state police. I'll head over to talk to Dr. Beale. See you over at the morgue later, Doc."

I walked into the diner, and Gert Wilson, the fifty-something, heavyset lady behind the breakfast counter, greeted me with a quick smile and a cup of coffee.

"Hello, Sheriff, here's a coffee. Now what can I get you?"

"Gert, how about a bacon and egg sandwich? And I need it fast. Got to get to the hospital to check on one of the victims from the Black Bear."

"Yeah, we already heard some about that."

"Yes, it's a bad scene out there, I'm afraid. We're working on it hard and fast, though. The state crime lab should be here within the hour. We want to get whoever would do this—and get them quickly."

"Well, Sheriff, you did a great job a few months ago on that cold case. I'm sure you'll get your man this time. I'll put that breakfast to go in now."

"Thanks, Gert."

I sat there on the stool at the counter drinking the hot coffee and thinking about that cold case she had made reference to. It was the Billy Snow case. I had just been sworn in as sheriff, and the prior sheriff, Lance Corey, had told me about it. Seemed this young man had been killed almost ten years earlier and no suspect had been found. I had spent a couple of months working on the case, interviewing people here, in Portland, why even in Greencastle, Pennsylvania, until I was able to figure it out and solve the case. The community had struggled with not knowing who had killed Billy Snow, and it had been a very cold case, which took a lot of time and effort to solve. Especially given the lack of direct physical evidence. Now, I was wondering, *What lies ahead in this case?* I was hoping that since this was not a cold case, we would certainly have a great amount of physical evidence, something that was very lacking in the Snow murder case.

As I continued pondering the prospects of the case, my attention was broken by the television mounted on the wall behind the counter and above the cash register. Suzi was giving a report on the news about the homicides at the Black Bear. For the first second or two that I saw her sitting behind her news desk, all I could think about was how beautiful she is and how her skin glistens in the moonlight when we've finished making love in the early mornings. As my mind began to wander on that topic, I heard her voice shatter the image in my mind as she made her report.

As she told about the incident, she introduced her junior reporter who had a candid interview at the scene with me. Before the reporter started questioning me on the TV report, Gert brought the sandwich out all wrapped up in foil. I paid her and went out to my Tahoe to head over to the hospital. I didn't need to watch myself on TV. Besides, I hadn't released any real information about the scene because it was far too early in the investigative process. That was for rookies, and I've been in this business a long time. I used to see similar reports when I was in the Boston Police Department as a detective. I was often interviewed about hard cases we were working on.

I'd left the Boston Police Department after I shot an unarmed kid exiting a building he had burglarized. He had a metal flashlight in his hand, it was dark, and I took it for a gun barrel. It was ruled a justified homicide, but as John Wayne said in the movie *El Dorado* after shooting a young boy, "It don't help much." I took it very hard and did not return to law enforcement until my friend Dex convinced me to run for sheriff against Lance Corey. So here I am, back at the job again.

When I pulled into the parking lot of the hospital, I had just finished the last of my sandwich. I walked into the emergency room entrance and asked the nurse behind the desk if I could speak to Dr. Beale. She picked up the phone, dialed a number, and then requested, "Dr. Beale to the Emergency Room, please," over the public address system. Then she directed me to a chair in the waiting room.

After about five minutes, Dr. Beale came around the corner and walked over to me. Dr. Richard Beale is about thirty years old but has the face of a teenager, putting you in mind of Doogie Howser. He is tall and well built: he plays on the Sunday afternoon basketball league, and we have sometimes been paired up on the same team. I will say, for a doctor, he plays a mean game of basketball!

"Hi, Dell. I assume you came by for an update on Mary Watson?"

"Not just an update, I hope. Richard, I really need to talk to her and see if she can give me anything."

"Well, you won't get that chance right now. She's in a coma at this time, and I can't even give you any idea when she may be able to talk to you."

"Natural coma or induced one?"

"Oh, it's a natural coma. But the reality is that if she weren't already in a coma, I would probably have induced one anyway based upon her injuries. I'm not sure if there's anything I can do for her. The bullet really tore her up badly, and I've fixed what I can for now. I may have to go back in; as it is, I just don't know."

"So there's no prognosis at all?"

"No. I wish I could sound more optimistic about it, but I haven't seen this amount of damage in a long time. If the bullet had gone in a millimeter either direction, the prognosis would be greatly improved. Just a millimeter!"

"I feel your pain, Richard, I really do. Did my deputy who came in with her get the bullet or fragments?"

"Yeah, the newer one—Wayne, I think—he got what was left. Fragments is right, Dell. I don't know bullets, but it sure looked like the bullet broke into many fragments. That's what seems to have made the damage so extensive."

"Okay, that's Deputy Bill Wayne, and he's new. Good guy, though. Came to us from Augusta PD. Good at evidence collection and working on coroner cases. I expect he's already downstairs with Doc Clopper starting on the other two."

Since all the initial investigation and evidence collection was well underway, my next course of action was to meet with Lieutenant Bell back at the Black Bear. There, we could go over what had been done initially and set up a workflow that would allow him to maintain jurisdiction, while I supplied the local investigation manpower. Lucky for me, I was already a little familiar with Lieutenant Bell and his style. Unlike in politics, we had to work together well to solve crimes.

As I pulled in to the Bear, I noticed the State Police Crime Scene vehicle parked on the west side of the parking area, away from the gas pumps. I walked over to the entrance door of the vehicle and asked if Lieutenant Bell was available. A young trooper, whom I had never before seen, asked me to wait a minute and then called the lieutenant over his radio.

A few minutes later, Lieutenant Bell walked from around the rear of the building and over to greet me at the truck. Frank Bell is slightly shorter than me, about six feet even, and weighs around 165. He's around fifty, but his hair is still jet-black. His outward appearance is all business, but having met him before, I know he actually can be a jovial sort when not faced with work issues. He had come to the lake once on a case and had stayed for lunch at my cabin.

"Hey, Dell. Would have preferred to be here fishing rather than this."

"Yeah, me too. Have you already hooked up with my guys?"

"Yes, Berk has been very helpful. He said he has most of the initial stuff done. I'm sure you know I'll need a few of your guys on this one, Dell."

"No problem, Frank. Since it's my county and people, I want to be there throughout."

"I figured you'd feel that way. Frankly, your guys are as well equipped to handle most of the stuff as we are. Maybe just a few things our lab can do better. More state funding swings my way, that's all."

"Frank, you still thinking robbery?"

"At this point, that's our best guess. I'm sorry to say it looks like old Paul just got in the way. Pity that!"

"A real likable guy, Paul. But boy for a game warden, he sure was a lousy fisherman! Came out to the lake one day last summer to check on licenses. I asked him to stay and fish with me awhile after he was done. Don't you know he told me he had never learned how to cast or anything!"

After we chuckled a bit over that thought, Frank said, "Yes but he knew his trees. I don't think I ever remember someone asking him a question about a type of tree or what a tree's growth cycle was that he couldn't answer on the spot. Never had to look anything up about trees. Just seemed to know it all like an encyclopedia. I remember him from the Police Academy. One smart guy about trees!"

We stood there for a few more minutes reminiscing over Paul Windom, and then I told Frank that if he came by my office the next morning, I would be sure to have all the preliminary reports prepared. I was sure that Berk could get the written ones done that day, and I hoped that Dink Abernathy could get me the initial crime-scene photos by breakfast tomorrow. Lieutenant Bell's people would have their own photos for sure, but Dink's were taken before any initial investigation was conducted, so they might show something different than Bell's. It is far too easy for something to have been moved a bit or in some other way degraded during the initial investigation and the process of securing the crime scene, so those first photos often can prove critical to a case.

After a little more discussion, we agreed to some coffee in the morning in my office, and I left the Bear and returned to my office in town. Irish, my administrative assistant, came in immediately with a cup of coffee and the overnight reports for me to review. Her name is Eileen Ryan, and she has red hair and freckles and an Irish family history, so naturally we all just call her Irish, for short. Irish is about thirty years old, but she runs my office like a well-seasoned drill sergeant.

I sat down behind my desk and took off my CCPD ball cap. As I took a sip of the coffee, I instinctively reached over and plucked a cigar out of the humidor I keep on my desktop. As I rolled the Paul Garmarian cigar lightly between my fingers and thumb, I asked Irish if she minded if I smoked while she was in the office.

"You're the sheriff. I guess if I minded, I could just walk out, now couldn't I?"

"Well, I'm not a bad cigar smoker. I at least always ask before I light up anywhere but at my cabin."

"I know; you're nice that way. By the sounds of your day thus far, I expect you need one!"

"Don't think it'll hurt none, Irish."

I lit the cigar and took a long first puff. Then I reached for the coffee again and took a deep breath. I never liked death cases, and hoped I never would. But this case was pretty harsh, especially for our community. Up here, in the outlying areas of the Maine woodlands, the population was small, and frankly, the crime was fairly minimal. Oh, we had some break-ins now and then, mostly committed by youths, and we had our share of drinking problems and domestic fights. But rarely did our community have a murder, and when it did, it wasn't a multiple murder. This was already a double homicide and might get worse, depending upon how the clerk at the hospital did.

While Irish went out to work on her stuff, I smoked my cigar, had my coffee, read the overnight reports, and tried to relax. I think much better when I'm relaxed.

As I took one last puff on my cigar and laid it in the ashtray to go out, Irish stuck her head in the door and told me that Deputy Linda Wilcott was asking to see me. Linda is one of my deputies assigned to work in the field, but she's also trained in some investigation techniques and in the service of civil papers. That latter training is very important because serving civil papers correctly is actually one of the critical duties of a sheriff's office. Should the sheriff fail to properly serve a civil court document, it can not only create huge problems for the individuals involved in the civil case, but the sheriff can be held accountable for those problems by the initiating court. So I was glad that Deputy Wilcott was properly trained in civil process, since, having been a police officer myself, I had no knowledge whatsoever of the correct processes. The duties of a sheriff or a deputy are often quite different than those of a police officer.

"Good morning, Linda. How's it going out there today?"

"Not too bad, Sheriff. I may have a little problem brewing with an eviction, and I think I may need a little help from someone much higher in the food chain than I am."

Linda is a shorter woman of about forty, who's a little on the heavy side for her height but has a very attractive face. I motioned her toward the chair in front of my desk, and she sat down and pulled out her notebook, flipping a few pages to the desired one.

"Sheriff, I got an eviction notice to serve on a company called Teldon, Inc. yesterday, and I went to their building to serve notice that I'll be conducting the eviction in five days. You know, all the standard stuff."

"Well, I don't really know yet what's standard, Linda, but I'll take your word for it," I said with a smile.

"Well here's the thing, Sheriff. As I looked around in the front entrance of the building, I saw *a lot* of computer stations in the background. So I thought maybe they were some telemarketing company. So when they had their site manager come out to speak to me, I casually asked him about the computers. He seemed very evasive about giving me an answer, so I just read him the eviction notice and handed him his service copy."

"Okay, sounds like you handled that well enough."

"Yes, but his immediate reaction was that he turned white, and I mean *completely white*, and began stammering about this not being possible. Now, at first I just assumed that he thought all the bills were paid and up to date, but he really seemed scared. So I asked him if he understood that I would have to totally remove them from the building in the five days so he needed to start moving out before then to save us a lot of trouble.

"So, after composing himself a bit, he finally leans over a little and whispers in my ear that I really don't know what they do there. So I asked him exactly what the company does, and he tells me that they control many of the satellites our country has placed into orbit around the earth."

"Holy cow! You mean they actually control their movement?" I asked.

"That's what this guy told me. Now, my question is if I go there in five days and evict them, are we going to have a few hundred satellites come crashing to earth?"

"Gosh, Linda, we need to get some clarification on this one. Any idea where we should start?"

"I already contacted a woman in the government who the guy at Teldon told me to call. She actually confirmed the fact that they do control a major number of satellites from that building, but she's a low-level contact, so she can't help us get this problem solved."

"You're right, this is a problem. We have to comply with the court order, but I don't relish being the sheriff who brought satellite Armageddon upon us, that's for sure! Have you identified someone for me to call on this?"

"Yes, Sheriff. I have a number the government lady gave me for some deputy director of science attached to the Department of Defense in Washington, DC. She suggested we call this guy for some help. I figured *that call* was yours, boss. Even a deputy director is way above my pay grade!"

"Okay, give me the number, and I'll give this guy a call right away."

"His name is Peter Wassman, and here's the number. I hope you can get this straightened out before I have to evict those folks at Teldon, Inc."

"I hope so as well."

Linda told me she had a few other cases she was working on, and she was covering all calls this morning while another deputy was in court, so she would check back with me later in the day.

After she left, I dialed the phone number in DC she had given me. As the phone began to ring, all I could think about was Linda evicting the company, shutting down their computers, and us all watching a few hundred satellites begin to fall toward the earth like huge raindrops across the horizon. It could be true Armageddon, for sure!

The phone was answered quickly by a female voice who told me she would see if the director was in to take my call. After a minute, she came back on the line and said she would transfer the call now.

On about the fifth ring, the phone was answered by a voice that sounded like it came from someone about fifty years old.

"Deputy Director Wassman."

Short and to the point, I thought. These federal government guys never seemed to show much humanity when dealing with others, at least in my experience with them.

"Hi, Director Wassman, my name is Dell Hinton. I'm the sheriff of Castaway County, Maine."

"Oh, well, Sheriff Hinton, what can I do for you today?" I took his tone to be rather sarcastic, but who knows, that may have been my disdain for feds that made me hear that.

"Actually, Director, it's more like what can I do for you today."

"Okay, Sheriff, I'm a bit confused. What do you want?"

"Well, Director, are you familiar with a little company up here called Teldon, Inc.?"

"Can't say as I am, Sheriff. What does it have to do with me?"

"My office received an eviction order on Teldon yesterday, and one of my deputies went out to serve the site manager with the notice of intent. We're planning to evict in a couple more days."

"Okay, again, Sheriff, but what do you want from me?"

"Well, the site manager told my deputy that their business is to control a lot of the satellites flying over the earth, and I figured you guys might not want us shutting down their computers and letting those satellites go flying every which way."

"Teldon, Inc., you said? Let me check on that a minute." I could hear some papers rustling in the background, and then I heard a slight sigh escape from the director's mouth. I figured that was the best confirmation I was likely to get from this guy that he might now be interested in my call.

"Okay, Sheriff, I can see why you called me now. Obviously, I can neither confirm nor deny any information at this point about Teldon, Inc. I will, however, make some calls and see if I can help facilitate you in a responsible resolution to this problem. I'm sure someone from your area will contact you further on this issue. If, however, you do not receive a resolution before the appointed eviction date, please do not proceed without calling me first."

Yeah, this guy now has a grip on the potential problems this case brought to the table for both of us. My guess was that he would be making some real quick phone calls as soon as we hung up the phone.

"Okay, Director, thanks for your help on this one."

"Not at all, Sheriff. Glad to be able to help our local law enforcement partners. Good-bye."

Local law enforcement partners, my ass. The only reason that blowhard gave me the time of day was because he's worried about those satellites falling down from the sky just as much as I am, I thought to myself.

Just as I hung up the phone from my conversation with Deputy Director Wassman, Irish stuck her head in my office door and asked, "Did that go well for you, boss?"

"Come on in, Irish, and take a seat. Yeah, I guess it went okay. That guy didn't seem to have a clue what I was talking about, and then he got the idea real quickly and came 'round. What a jerk some of these fed guys are!"

"Well it sounded like you handled him pretty well ... ah ... of course I really only heard a bit of the conversation though."

"I'll bet. I know you by now, Irish. You always have my back, and that means you have to listen carefully. Don't worry. It doesn't bother me. I'm just glad we have a good working relationship, since you were originally hired by Lance Corey."

"Doesn't matter who hired me, boss. Just matters who the current sheriff is, and that's you. By the way, since you mentioned our old sheriff, can I ask you a question?"

"Sure, go ahead."

"Well, when Linda Wilcott came to you with an issue, and she already had begun to make phone calls to solve it, you seemed to be happy about it. I mean, you didn't seem to think she had usurped some of your authority by setting things in motion and waiting to bring you in on the final phone call. Lance would *never* have handled it that way. He wanted to be involved in all the decision making."

"Well, Irish, that's because he and I have two different leadership styles. I want my staff to have the authority to handle things and make decisions on their own. That enables them to grow, to gain more knowledge, and to be prepared to take on more responsibilities. That way, when I retire or get voted out, there's someone here who can easily move into my position because they've prepared, grown, and learned. Now, my guess is that Lance Corey wanted to be in control. He may have felt that since he would be held responsible for any bad decisions, he wanted to be able to make them himself."

"That's probably a fair assessment of Lance. He was a bit of a control freak at times."

"In my experience, a controlling supervisor or administrator does not allow his staff to develop much. I had a supervisor back in Boston who expected to make the decision on almost every issue that came up. Well, he got injured in the line of duty and had to take medical retirement, sixty-six and two-thirds percent of his salary. When command looked at his subordinates, there wasn't one who could even score above 60 percent on the supervisor's exam. It wasn't that there weren't some smart men and women working under him; they had just never been given the chance to make any big decisions. He had always made them."

"I can see your point, boss. They hadn't been able to even try."

"Exactly right. And the truth is that we humans learn best from our mistakes. People have to be given the chance to fail, to make simple mistakes; it's all part of the learning process. And it's one of the big parts as well, so if a leader isn't willing to let his people make decisions, because he fears that they might fail, he's depriving them of the ability to learn and grow. At least, that's the way I view it. My job is to help and allow everyone working here at the sheriff's office to make decisions in their area and to be in a position to develop their abilities to the best they can. Sorry about the cliché, but that's the end game for me."

"Well, it explains a lot about how you work versus how Lance Corey worked."

"But don't feel that I'm saying that he was wrong. His way may have worked best for him. Each of us develops a different leadership style based upon our own needs and our personalities. While his may have fit him, mine fits me better than his would fit me. Neither is wrong or right, just what we each develop over time."

"So, what about the decisions you should make?"

"Don't get me wrong, Irish. There are a lot of decisions that fall directly to me as the sheriff. And I expect to be kept in the loop on what's happening in my office. I just want to give staff the authority to work on things that are in their areas, things commensurate with their positions. I don't micro-manage them, but the final reality is that I am in charge. I will be held responsible. So I back them up, and hopefully they do the same."

After a few more unrelated comments, Irish decided she was going back to her desk to work, and I returned to thinking about our current case. It was now midafternoon, and I thought I would head over to see Doc Clopper and check on his identification of the bullets he had taken from the victims. Hopefully he could give me something more to think about.

·4·

I walked over to Dr. Clopper's office and went in through his large vestibule into his waiting room. His part-time receptionist, Clare Wexton, must have been out to lunch, so there was a little bell on the countertop for anyone wishing to see the doctor. I slapped my hand down on the bell three times just to get the old man's attention. I liked to give him a hard time; even though he was a bit on the crotchety side, he was a nice man with a great sense of humor. He kind of reminded me of Doc Adams on the old *Gunsmoke* television series: mean and gruff at times, but a real softie underneath that outward façade.

Doc Clopper came from one of the rear rooms, wiping his hands on a towel and voice booming, "Okay, who the hell is banging on my bell? It better be a case of life and death!"

"It's just me, Doc. I came over to talk to you about the autopsies."

"Well, do you think you're trying to wake them back up with that bell?"

"No, no, I was just being sure you heard the bell. I thought you might be asleep or something."

"I don't doubt that for a minute, Dell. You're just trying to get my goat this afternoon, that's all!"

"Okay, Doc. So have you been able to tell anything yet?"

"Well, I'm no ballistics expert, but I think the bullets I removed from the deceased were all similar enough to have been fired from one gun. Maybe a .380 or a .38. Again, I'm not an expert. I turned them over to your deputy to go to the state police lab in Augusta."

"Yeah, they have jurisdiction on this one anyway."

"So, will that cause you any trouble, Dell? I mean sometimes the state police don't seem to work well with local sheriffs and police."

"That's true enough. They often seem to take a holier-than-thou approach. But in this case, I already know Lieutenant Bell a little, so I think we'll get along better."

"Yeah, but I'm sure he has someone above him pulling his strings, and *they* may not be as considerate as Lieutenant Bell."

"That's a fact. Hadn't thought about that one, but you're right, and on a case this big, that person might try to seize the moment for the publicity it might gain. I'll just have to play it by ear, I guess. Any other information you've obtained?"

"Not really. I will say that the shots seem to have been pretty good kill shots. No strays anywhere on the bodies—just the shots that accounted for the deaths."

"Well, that suggests either a fine marksman or a pro to me."

"Could be, Dell, could be."

As I walked back to my office, I began thinking about the possibilities related to the information Doc Clopper had given me. Clearly, the manner of the shots implied great marksmanship on the part of the shooter, but that didn't clear up much. Was he or she just a good shot? Were they just lucky in firing the kill shots under stress? Or was the shooter a professional? If they were a professional, were they a professional robber or a professional hit man? *All good questions,* I thought. Well, it didn't matter what I thought. I needed to meet with Lieutenant Bell so I could give him the information and the preliminary investigation material. It was all prepared now, and I had called Frank Bell early in the morning to reschedule our breakfast meeting until lunch. We needed a little more time to get everything together for him.

When I got back to the office, I called Frank and told him I'd like to meet at the Lobsta Grill. We decided to meet at two o'clock for a late lunch.

Since I had a little extra time before the meeting, I decided to walk over to the jail to see how things were going. I find that simply going through all sections of the office fairly frequently allows my staff to know me and to interact with me in times other than being called to my office for some issue. As I see them in their daily work, I often either ask questions to broaden my knowledge or I provide some praise for their continued good work, which tends to bolster their morale. Either instance is a win for me as their sheriff.

As I walked through one of the cellblocks in the jail, I asked the inmates housed there how staff was treating them. I got varied responses, but most of them were positive, as positive as could be expected from men who were secured in a jail in the first place.

In another cellblock, I noticed that the inmates were watching an afternoon base-ball game on the television on the table, so I asked about the score, and we spoke a few minutes about how the Red Sox were playing. I thought it had worked out good for me moving from Beantown to Maine since most of the folks in Castaway County liked the same ball teams as the folks in Beantown. That way, I didn't have to change teams when I moved!

I always like to talk to the inmates as I walk around the jail: it gives me some indic-ation of what's going on in each housing area. For instance, if I ask about the game on TV, and no one answers me, or someone gives me a real surly answer, the likeli-hood that there's some problem fuming between the inmates in that housing block is pretty big. On the other hand, if two or three of the inmates start talking about the game, things in the unit are more than likely going okay. A deputy can get a good feeling about problems within a housing unit just by engaging the inmates in some light conversation during each block check they make. Some of the younger deputies don't understand that concept, and they just want to walk right through, looking at the inmates, counting them, but never speaking to them. I learned early in my career that when you're dealing with people, you have to talk to them and listen to them to learn things about how they're feeling at any given time. Often, even in a fight situ-ation, if you listen carefully to the other person, they will provide you with some warning that they're going to strike out against you. In my experience, very rarely does anyone attack without some warning, either verbal or physical. You just have to be looking and listening to pick up on it.

After making a full sweep of all the housing areas in the jail, I spoke to the duty deputy and signed the post log sheet to show that I had made a round of the facility and found everything to be in good order. These logs are required by the State Depart-ment of Corrections, as the oversight organization for local jails. I then walked back to get my Tahoe and get over to the meeting with Frank at the Lobsta Grill.

As I walked in to the Grill, I saw Frank sitting near the front windows at a booth. I motioned to the young lady behind the counter area for a cup of coffee and sat across from Frank.

"Well, Dell, how are things at the lake?"

"Fish are still bigger than average this year and seem to be biting on orange-bellied lures for some reason. You'll have to come out one weekend and give 'em a try."

"Yeah, I'd like to do just that. We'll see. Now, what are you thinking about this murder?"

"Well, I'm thinking that you're in charge of the investigation, and I'm just in the position of helping you with it," I said. "Does that sound about right?"

"Aw, you know the law, Dell. I've got the lead, but I surely want your help with the local issues."

"You mean, of course, that you want me and my guys to do the legwork, right?"

"Dell, you just aren't going to make this easy, are you? I know that my guys and your guys don't have a real warm and fuzzy relationship, but you and I certainly have a pretty good one, don't we?"

"You're right, Frank, and I'm sorry. I do know the law, and we have to work together on this case. I guess it's just hard to forget the feeling of having a case taken away from you and your agency when you know darn well you can handle it as well as anyone."

"I get that, Dell, I really do. Especially after the great job you did on the cold case—the Billy Snow case, I think it was."

"Well, Frank, we'll help you guys any way we can. What's your working theory of the murder?"

"It's early, but I like the botched robbery scenario the best right now. The one register was missing money. I'm thinking that the robber was either hurried by something or someone, or he just missed the second register and took what he got. Either way, I think that Warden Windom just got in the way of the robber, probably when he was first entering, since Windom's body reflected him getting shot at the front of the building where he landed. Might have more once the forensics are in, but for now, that's my working theory."

"Sounds good for now, Frank. Doc thought the bullets were from a .38, likely. Not too big a gun."

"Probably a cheap, Saturday night special. Could've been a hopped-up kid lookin' for some drug money."

"Maybe, maybe, Frank. None of my guys had any FI notes on anyone around that time, though we're spread pretty far and between on patrol most nights."

By FI notes, I meant the field investigative notes that I had instructed my deputies to file on each traffic stop, citizen interview, or any contact with people, especially over the nightshifts. We used them in Boston, and you would be surprised how many times as an investigator I would be working a case and locate an FI note from one of the scout cars where they had spoken to some suspicious guy on the street near a robbery, for instance, near the time of the robbery, and it gave me a suspect to look at that I would otherwise never have known about. Many agencies use FI notes to try to help them solve crimes. I had Berk institute them a few months after I took office because I felt they were a real good tool, even in an outlying community with a low crime rate. You just never know when they might come in handy!

"Well, Frank," I said, "probably not much more we can do right now. We'll keep trying to locate people who were at the Bear near the time of the murders."

"And I'll let you know when I get anything new from our forensics guys. Are you headed back out to the lake?"

"Yeah, since it's this late in the afternoon, I think I'll run by the town dock and check on the fishing derby preparations for tomorrow and then go home." *I'm sure either Chauncey or Suzi will need some attention,* I thought.

We had a few more brief comments to each other and then said good-bye. I drove my Tahoe back toward the lake and stopped at the town dock. There were a few of the local characters milling around, some cutting weeds along the walkways, and others posting signs about the fishing derby rules and basic lake directions.

I parked the Tahoe and walked over to talk a few minutes. Before I got to the group of men, I saw one of our older residents standing on a slight hill, waving me over to him. Darby Webb was about seventy with white, short hair and wearing the typical dark green pants and shirt that was often associated with local camp caretakers and woodsmen in the late seventies.

"How are ya, Sheriff?"

"Well, I'm fine today, Mr. Webb. Are you doing well?"

"Yeah, I'm doing fine as frog haya. You haven't lived hea long enough to know much about this ole lake, have ya?"

I thought about it a minute and realized that I did not have much knowledge about the lake and its prior inhabitants. I figured the information might be quite useful, one time or another, and besides, I do love history, so I asked Mr. Webb to tell me about the lake's history.

He stood back, looked at the lake, and began the story. "Well, fer stattas ..."

Old Mr. Webb told me that the lake had once been the summer playground for the more wealthy and aristocratic people from the eastern half of the United States. All people "from away," as they were called. Most of the people who owned islands in the lake were writers, cartoonists, doctors, college professors, and captains of big businesses. In the old days, many of the island owners arrived by seaplane or were driven to the lake by their chauffeurs. They brought their cooks to prepare the family meals and had tennis courts and croquette lawns built on their islands for exercise. In the day, the boats owned were large wooden ones, often expensive Chris Craft or Old Town brands, highly sought after by the rich and famous.

Mr. Webb went on to tell of the great parties thrown by the island owners. Often they were "progressive" parties that began on one family island with cocktails and appetizers and ended islands later with dessert and after-dinner drinks. In those days, Webb said, "The lake was busy with boats, drinkin', and playing 'round."

Gradually, as new generations of families bought or inherited the islands, things seemed to quiet down. The names of the islands changed, as often through inheritance by an elder daughter as by outright sale of the properties. "Why, if you was to ask me to name the islands in the lake, they'd be a lot different than the names you know 'em as today, Sheriff," Webb said with a wink of his eye.

"Them days is long gone, yeah, they sure are," he said at last. I think his eyes looked a little misty as he looked up at the lake again. I guessed that Mr. Webb was seeing the lake as it was in the golden years, and I felt a bit sorry for him. Finally, after he heaved a few sighs, he turned to me and told me to come back again and see him, and he'd tell me about a pair of old ladies who owned a property on the main land, not too far from mine. He said they were a real pair of "hoots," and I'd find their story interesting.

As I walked back toward my vehicle, I thought about Mr. Webb, and it seemed to me that he liked having someone to tell his stories of the old days on the lake to, and, well, I was a good listener. I decided then and there that I was going to try to go over and visit him some more; maybe this was a mutually beneficial relationship.

As I walked back past the town dock, I realized that the others had already left for home while I was talking to old Mr. Webb. So I climbed in the Tahoe and headed around the east side of the lake toward my cabin.

5

I drove around the lower portion of the lake from the town dock and up the long, wooded lane to my cabin on the lakeside. As I pulled in, I noticed that Suzi's car wasn't in the drive, so I assumed she was working a bit late due to the case. Her boss, I was sure, wanted her to have all the relevant case materials ready for the nightly broadcast just in case there were any new developments since they had taped the earlier news segments. The night anchor, Bill Wilson, was great looking and ideal for that job, but he hadn't a lick of common sense. Everything had to be ready so he could just read the copy and show segments of pretaped material. If he had to adjust to a change or, God forbid, ad lib, the station was taking a big chance on what might actually come out of his mouth. He was kind of like Ted Baxter on the old *Mary Tyler Moore Show*. He had a lot of bullshit in him, but it was usually totally out of line for the segment or the audience, or both.

I walked in to find my cat, Chauncey, looking at me as if to say, "So where have you been? I need some petting!" He quickly did the kitty-flop at my feet. I petted him and rubbed his belly for a few minutes, and then I got a cold Corona Light out of the fridge and sat down in my easy chair to listen to some music. After what seemed only a few seconds, I heard a car door slam and then the kitchen side door. I quickly realized that I might have dozed off for a few minutes, sitting and listening to that music. *Gosh,* I thought, *I'm turning into my dad, who could fall asleep in a couple of minutes.* Suzi came walking past me and touched me lightly on the shoulder.

"Sleeping a bit, honey?"

"Well, um, not so's you'd notice."

"Well, give me a few minutes to take a quick shower, baby, and we can eat something, okay?"

"Sure, sweetie. I'll just try not to fall asleep again."

As I sat there while she showered, I thought about old Darby Webb again. I really liked talking to him and listening to some of the stories he could tell about the lake as it was in years past. I was definitely going to have to visit him again.

After a few minutes, Suzi came out of the bedroom area with nothing but a smile on her face. She had dried off from the shower, but her fair skin was glowing from some botanical cream she used, post showering. I let my eyes roll down the curves of her body and could not stop the smile from erupting on my face as well. She reached out her hand and escorted me back to the bedroom. My God, she is a beautiful woman, and every time I see her with no clothes on, I just get as excited as a kid on Christmas morning. I hope I never lose that feeling about her!

After we made love, we lay in bed for a while embracing each other and basking in the afterglow of our escapade.

Suzi, who was in my arms with her back to me, looked over her shoulder and said, "Don't you think we ought to get up and fix something for dinner?"

I said yes, but suggested we just find some things to snack on since it was so late and I didn't want either of us to have to cook and clean up. She agreed, so we put on our robes and went to the kitchen to see what we could find.

She asked me how I was doing thus far with the homicides at the Black Bear. I told her that we still had robbery as our working theory and that I had spoken to Lieutenant Bell twice already about the case and how we were going to work it.

"The state has the case by law, but Frank wants us to help him with legwork and stuff."

"So, are you okay with that, baby?"

"Don't have to be okay with it; that's the law up here. But I think I can work with Frank. Maybe not all of the staties, but Frank's good."

"I guess it's rare when state cops don't look down a little on the locals, right?"

"That's true, and we all seem to hate the feds! It's just a little power struggle I guess we all find ourselves playing from time to time."

"Yeah, I guess. Hey, it's after eleven. Turn on the news and let's see how Bill's doing with the copy I set up for him."

I turned on the TV, and there was Bill, slicked back hair and pompous as always.

"And there were no witnesses to the killings. Robbery is the suspected motive at this time." As Bill completed that statement, his eyes widened, and he got a very perplexed look on his face. Although the viewers could not see his hands on screen, you could easily hear some papers being shuffled around just out of camera shot.

"Oh, shit, Dell, here it comes. Watch for it."

"He's lost the page in the copy, hasn't he, sweetie?" I asked as I watched Bill clearly having a brain fart on live TV.

"Yup, watch for it."

Then Bill smiled and began ad libbing. "So I guess those folks were killed for drug money out of a cash register. Guess that's what our drug problems have created in our country. Any kids out there listening to me, you just remember: say no to drugs. And now, to our commercial."

"There it is!" Suzi said. "He just can't help himself. Now the station will have to call the families of the victims to apologize. And what was that 'Say no to drugs' line, anyway? What a buffoon!"

"He surely doesn't do very well when he gets off script!"

"No, he doesn't. But I guess he raises our ratings as a comedy show though."

After a little more discussion about the lack of journalistic virtues Bill Wilson had, we finished our little snack and went back to bed for the night. I guessed that tomorrow, as it normally did, would bring a whole new set of issues, problems, or viewpoints.

★

I got up at about six fifteen the next morning, just as the sun's rays began to hit me in the eyes from the window over the bed. Suzi was dressed for work and having her last cup of coffee and a donut. As I walked into the kitchen to get my coffee, she gave me a peck on the cheek and said she had to run. She was running late for an early meeting with the camera technician and assistant producer for the station. I patted her on the butt as she left for work.

I grabbed a donut for myself and walked out onto the screened porch to relax with my coffee. As I was sitting there eating the donut, I realized that I had developed a really nice daily routine, that is, when I didn't get called into action by some type of criminal activity.

Each morning, I get my coffee and a donut or other available pastry (maybe that's why my pants don't seem to be fitting me as well as they used to), and I grab a book and go sit on the porch. My choice of books is usually a Western, maybe a Louis L'Amour or a William Johnstone novel.

I read Westerns because I enjoy the action, but even more so, I enjoy the presentation these writers make of the code of honor in the Old West. A man might ruthlessly kill some desperado who had been a murderer or rapist without the least thought, but if faced with a young gun hand trying to make a name for himself, they would use restraint, trying to give the young man a way out of a deathly gun battle. Or in other cases, even a bad man in the book might rob banks, steal cattle, and kill other men, but he would not support or condone any hurt or molestation toward a woman. There were lines in these books that men just didn't cross, and once they did, there was usually quick and very decisive retribution and justice had upon them.

So, each morning I find myself sitting on the porch reading my Westerns and listening to the birds, squirrels, and sounds of the lake. I really love living on Spoodicook Lake! The sounds of the water lapping the rocky shore, and the winds blowing the leaves of the beech tree just outside the window are music to my ears. Add to that the occasional loon calling or squirrel chattering, and it brings nature to my door. The longer I live here, the less I seem to watch television. Oh, Suzi and I watch the newscasts and some special events and sports, to be sure, but I most often prefer the sounds and sights of the lake and the abundant wildlife surrounding the lake. I should imagine that the prior owner of my cabin, who used the building as a summer camp, without electricity, phone, and insulation, must have been very satisfied with camp life on the lake.

Obviously, when I bought the place, I was in need of a year-round home, so I put in electricity and phone and insulation, turning a summer camp into an all-year cabin. But I still enjoyed the same sensations that I'm sure possessed the prior owner to build here in the first place.

So there I sat, in the middle of my daily routine, enjoying the early morning on Spoodicook Lake. It was also a time for me to sit and think about cases we were working on at any given time. And now, I was contemplating the murders at the Bear. For some reason, I was having difficulty with the one cash register having been opened but the cash not being removed. While it fell in with the theory that the scene was a botched robbery, the guy getting interrupted and leaving before raiding the other register, the shots the victims received seemed to be pretty accurate for someone who would have conducted an inept robbery. However, stranger things had happened, so I couldn't just assume that was the case, but it did give me pause. It surely did.

As I sat there, I saw one of the little red squirrels come up to the porch screen and lightly tap it. That was the sign for the owner of the house to put out some more peanuts for the squirrels. I regularly bought out the grocery store of their big bags of unsalted peanuts to feed these little varmints. They sure did fight when I took out the peanuts! I tried placing several piles of nuts in different locations to separate them, but they often still tried to come to each other's piles and would squabble a lot at one another. This morning, as I watched the larger peanut feeder for the squirrels, I noticed that a rather large blue jay was flying in periodically to steal peanuts from the squirrels. When he arrived on a branch one time, there was a rather fat, little squirrel in the feeder, and the blue jay swooped down and batted its wings around to try to scare off the squirrel. The squirrel just sat there chastising the blue jay, so he nimbly pecked in the feeder and stole a peanut right from beside the squirrel! I watched these antics for at least another half hour, enjoying the nature at my doorstep.

As I was walking into the kitchen to refill my coffee cup, the phone rang.

"Hey, Dell, it's Frank."

"Hey, Frank. How's the investigation going?"

"Just what I was calling about. Did you notice something about the gunshots on our victims?"

"Well, yeah, like we talked about earlier, the shots seemed to be pretty precise."

"Precise doesn't even say it, Dell. Our ballistic guy told me that in looking at the autopsy information and the size of the projectiles, each shot was placed *exactly where they needed to be for a direct kill shot.* Had any of them been off by a minute amount, we might have more live victims. Seems a bit odd for a botched robbery to me."

"I was thinking the same thing, Frank, and so was Doc Clopper. Also, there were no other shots fired that we were able to find, so the shooter didn't seem to fumble and then get lucky."

"Yup, and I don't know about you, Dell, but I don't believe much in coincidences. I'm thinkin' we're looking at a pro."

"I agree, Frank. Those shots were just too good for some 'Johnny come lately' robber. But what the hell would a pro be doing robbing the Bear? And if he wasn't doing a robbery, then who was he trying to eliminate?"

"Dell, I think you guys need to do some more background on our victims. Maybe we can find something to give us an idea about those things."

"Okay, Frank, as soon as I get in to the office, I'll see if Berk can go with me, and we'll get started. Haven't heard anything from the hospital about our other victim, so I guess no news is good news at this point."

"Okay, I'll call you tomorrow, Dell, unless you guys come up with something and call me first. Happy hunting!"

I hung up the phone. I'm not a hunter, in the Maine woods sense of the word. But working on a criminal case is a lot like hunting; you work hard tracking the criminal, and then hopefully, in the end you bag them. So Frank's exhortation was actually pretty germane to our line of work.

I made my way in to the office around nine o'clock; Irish knows to expect me to be a bit late on nice mornings and when I don't have any big meetings set up in advance. She knows that I enjoy communing with nature if the weather is nice. As I walked in, she handed me a cup of coffee and said good morning. She also handed me the overnights, copies of any reports from the hours between when I left the office the day before and now. There were only two reports, so it must have been a slow night.

"Irish, you know what I need first thing every morning," I said, referring to the coffee she had just handed me. "I think you're a keeper, lady!"

"Now, what kind of an administrative assistant to the sheriff would I be if I let you get your own coffee in the mornings, boss?"

"Good point there, Irish. Hey, can you ask Berk to come see me in the next hour or so, please?"

"Sure, boss, consider it done!"

I started reviewing the reports. One gas drive-away from the station on Route 272 near Rome, and a peeping tom report at Daphine Crossroads. The night deputy caught up with the guy who drove off without paying for his gas and found that he had thought he'd used his credit card correctly in the machine, but it had apparently been rejected. Since the pump was set up to allow for pumping gas and then paying the cashier in the station afterward, he just pumped and left, assuming that the card had worked. The deputy had taken the guy back to the station, and everything was settled there. He had filed a report just to cover the time and energy taken to chase the guy down and clear up the problem.

The second report was about someone peering in the bedroom window of a house at the Crossroads. We had had two other reports of someone leering into windows over the past six months. This time, the Peeping Tom had been apprehended; seemed he made the mistake of peeping into the bedroom window of one of the border patrol agents and got pistol whipped for his trouble! The report indicated that he was in the jail awaiting arraignment on the charge. *I guess he picked the wrong window to peep into this time,* I thought.

After my second cup of coffee at work, Berk came into the office.

"Hey, boss. Irish said you wanted to see me?"

"We need to do some interviews in the Black Bear case. I thought you might like to assist me with them?"

"Sure would. What are we looking at?"

"Well, we started with the botched robbery theory, but with what we're getting about the accuracy of the kill shots and the lack of other shots being fired, Frank and I agree that we may be looking at a professional shooter."

"Wow, but who would want any of the victims dead? And, really, all three?"

"Well, that's exactly why we need to conduct some interviews, Berk. I don't have any of those answers, and that's our business: to get answers about crimes committed."

"Well, who do you want to start with?"

"Let's go out and talk to Mrs. Windom a bit. Give her a call and see if a quick visit is okay, would you?"

Berk went out to call and returned, sticking his head in the doorway to tell me that we were set to interview Mrs. Paula Windom at her home in Weaverton Port just after lunch. So I made a few calls, and around noon, I headed up the street to the Woodburn Diner for a quick lunch.

"Hey, Sheriff, how's it going?" asked Gert.

"Pretty good today, Gert. What's the special?"

"Lobsta Roll and fries, $8.10."

"Is it crammed full of meat?"

"Yours will be, honey. We take good care of our sheriff in these parts."

Boy, did I know that. They always seemed to give me larger portions of whatever I ordered. *Another reason those pants might be getting tight there, Dell,* I thought.

Now, if you have never had a lobster roll, a true Down East one, you're missing a grand culinary treat! First you take hunks of fresh, cooked, cold lobster meat and mix in just enough mayonnaise to hold the chunks of meat together a bit. Then you take a New England hot dog bun, the ones that you grill on each side with a tad of butter.

Then you put a bed of lettuce in the bun and fill it until it's overflowing with lobster meat. They're very rich, and you'd be lucky to be able to eat two in one sitting. Boy, are they great! Some places put some finely cut-up celery in the lobster meat mix, and that also tastes great.

"Okay, Gert, give me a special and a glass of iced tea, please!"

"Coming right up, Sheriff, honey."

After devouring the lobster roll and fries, I finished my tea and walked back toward the office to meet Berk. He drove his vehicle, a police package Chevy Impala, and I got in on the passenger side, and off we went to do our interview of Mrs. Windom.

Weaverton Port is just a bit farther south from Weaverton, resting right along the Passahoney River. Route 17 south has a short spur, 17A that runs into Weaverton Port and makes a half circle around to join 17 again on the other side of town. By town, I mean that there are about twelve to fifteen homes in a cluster on 17A, and it makes up the whole of Weaverton Port.

As we pulled up into the driveway, I noticed that the house, while being a New England style home, had new siding and what appeared to be a relatively new addition on the southern end of the building. *Maybe they added an in-law apartment or something of the like*, I thought.

We walked up the steps and knocked on the door. A woman in her fifties answered the door and told us she was a friend helping Mrs. Windom through these trying times. She escorted us through the house to a small library area at the rear of the house. There were a significant number of books in at least five built-in bookshelves throughout the room, and there was a comfy-looking easy chair, two smaller chairs, and a wide, soft-looking sofa. *Boy, they don't build houses like this anymore!* You might imagine that this was an old sea captain's house once since the library was large, and the windows, also large, looked directly over the Passahoney River as it bent its way around this portion of the town. It was an ideal spot for a captain to read about great adventures and be able to look out at the waters, remembering his earlier exploits at sea.

Mrs. Windom was sitting on the sofa, holding a handkerchief, and appeared to have been crying just before our arrival. Seated beside her was Father Dexter Delaney, my old high school friend and the main reason I was in Castaway County and, in fact, had been elected sheriff in the first place.

Dex and I had grown up in Greencastle, Pennsylvania, a rural farming community. We had been schoolmates, and after that, I got married to Elaine, wife number one, and moved to Boston to work in their police department. Dex moved to Maine and became the pastor of one of the local churches. Dex had the calling after being quite a hell raiser in school. After Elaine and I split, I married Liz, an ex-stripper, and then there was the shooting incident that devastated me to the core, so I left Boston PD, and we came up to Castaway County to see Dex. I liked the area, but it was too native for Liz. We bought a summer camp on Spoodicook Lake, and I made it an all-weather, all-season cabin, the one I'm still living in. After a while, Liz decided that this was not the area for her to live the good life in, and she and I split, making her ex-wife number two.

Dex had convinced me that I should run for sheriff after I had been living in the county for a year, and that's how I became the sheriff of Castaway County. *I guess I really need to thank Dex sometime*, I thought.

As I walked over to them sitting on the sofa, I told Mrs. Windom how sorry I was about her loss and asked if I could have a few minutes of her time to ask a couple of questions. Dex, about my age, five feet ten, 185 pounds, and a great basketball player, stood up to move into another chair so I could sit beside Mrs. Windom. Berk took a chair across from the sofa.

"Hi, Father Dexter. I didn't expect to see you here today."

"Hi, Dell. Berk. Mrs. Windom's daughter, Silvia, is in my congregation, and she called and asked if I might come over to provide some assistance to her mother."

"Oh. Well, Mrs. Windom, Father Delaney is a great guy. I've known him for years, and I'm sure he can provide you with some comfort in your time of grief."

"If I can provide Mrs. Windom with a few minutes of peace and hope, then I will have done my job. May I get you a cup of tea or something while you talk with Dell and his chief deputy, Mrs. Windom?"

"Oh, I'm not sure ... well ... I guess ... yes, Father, that would be good."

As Dex walked into the kitchen to ask the woman who let us in at the door to locate all the necessary items to make her a cup of tea, I decided to ask Mrs. Windom a few quick questions.

"Mrs. Windom, do you know if your husband had any known enemies?"

"Well, I'm not sure, Sheriff. But I thought ... this was a case of robbery, wasn't it?"

"We have to ask questions so that we investigate from every possible angle, Mrs. Windom. We need to be sure we have the correct case scenario, and to be sure of that, we have to try all others until they don't pan out."

"Oh ... in that case, no, I don't know of any enemies that Paul had. Everyone seemed to like him. I'm not sure if he had any from recent cases he was working."

"Did Paul seem strange recently, like he was bothered or worried by something or someone?"

"No, can't say that he was. As far as I can say, everything seemed fine." Mrs. Windom began to tear up again. She pulled out her hanky and blew her nose, loudly.

Dex walked into the room carrying a cup of tea that was hot enough to have steam rolling off the top. He set it down on the coffee table just in front of Paula Windom. She thanked him, and he sat down in the chair.

"Well, I guess that's enough for now, Mrs. Windom. I don't want to upset you any further. If I have any additional questions, I can certainly ask you later. I know this is not the best time to be questioned. And again, please accept my heartfelt condolences about Paul's passing. I know he will be sadly missed by us all."

"Thank you, Sheriff. I really miss him, and I just don't know what I'll do now that he's gone."

Berk and I stood to leave, and we both said good-bye to Father Delaney. I asked Berk as we went out the front door to have a quick look around the outside of the Windom residence. I watched him walk past the front of the house, look in a window of the garage, and take a quick look over the backyard fence. I walked around the opposite side of the house and looked back toward the river.

When we got into the car, I asked Berk if he had seen anything worth noting.

"Well, I'm guessing you saw the year-old Corvette in the driveway, but there was also a Cadillac in the garage, and it looked pretty new as well."

"Hmm. Two fairly expensive vehicles for a guy on state pay, I'd say. And did you see the house?"

"It was a nice home for a guy still working and waiting to retire, wasn't it?"

"You think we might have found something here, Berk?"

"Yeah, but we don't know about his personal life. Might have had a wealthy family or inherited a whole passel of money, or hit a small lottery ticket. Who knows?"

"That's right, Berk! You make a good cop because you don't jump to conclusions. You let the evidence drive your thought process. While these are things we need to check out, they're not necessarily indicative of a true problem. Very good!"

"When we get back, boss, I'll start checking on Windom's background and financials. Maybe we can clear up these questions."

7

When Berk and I returned to the office, Irish said I had an important call from Washington, DC. She handed me a phone message slip with Deputy Director Peter Wassman's name and number on it.

"Glad he's getting back with me on that. I'll call him, and if he handled the problem, I'll give Linda Wilcott a call. Thanks, Irish. Any chance you have a fresh coffee ready?"

"On the way, boss!"

I sat down at my desk and called the number on the message slip. After three or four rings, Mr. Wassman's secretary answered and then sent my call to the deputy director himself.

"Oh, hi, Sheriff Hinton. Thanks for returning my call." *Now he sounds quite friendly. Seems to be a clear change of attitude. He must have decided my original call was important after all,* I thought to myself.

"Well, I guess you found a solution to our mutual problem, Director Wassman?"

"Yes, I did. I made some phone calls. And mind you, I can neither confirm nor deny the existence of Teldon, Inc. or its application to our network of utility satellites, but I believe that your office will be receiving notification from your local court that the eviction has been recalled."

"Well, I'll have my civil process deputy check on that with the court. Thanks for helping our office out with this issue, Director."

"Think nothing of it, Sheriff. Always glad to help the locals out, you know. Call anytime."

45

After I hung up with Deputy Director Wassman, I thought about his "locals" comment. In this particular case, this local probably helped him prevent a calamity of large proportions. *But that's the way the feds operate; most times they treat us like school-boys, and when circumstances happen, and they need our help, they take it gladly along with any credit to be had.* It always amazes me how things get done between the various law enforcement agencies—federal, state, and local—when we continue to have all the little turf battles and credit grabbing between each. But I will say that since 9/11, there has been improvement in the base communication between all law enforcement agencies. *Maybe I need to give Director Wassman a break.*

I then placed a quick call to Linda Wilcott.

"Hey, Linda. I just got off the phone with Deputy Director Wassman in DC. He claims that the court will be sending you a repeal of that eviction on Teldon."

"Whew, I'm glad of that. We're getting closer and closer to the date of eviction that was set. Wonder how they got it settled."

"I couldn't say. Just glad they did. Probably better that we don't know anyway. Wassman was still spouting that standard line about neither confirming nor denying existence."

"Hey, as long as it's handled, boss, I surely don't care how it gets done. I'll check on my court paperwork right after lunch. Thanks for the assist."

"Thank you for coming to me in the first place. Good job! This is a team effort, you know."

"Thanks, boss."

Once off the phone, Irish came in with my cup of coffee, and I decided to relax a few minutes, so I pulled a small Paul Garmarian cigar from the humidor on my desk and began to puff. I really enjoy the texture of a fine cigar and the aroma of the burning leaf. In this case, the P.G. had a wonderful earthy, spicy aroma and flavor and complemented my fresh coffee perfectly. So I sat back in my chair and enjoyed a brief pause in my otherwise busy day.

While Berk was working in the office on Paul Windom's general background and finances, I decided to look up next of kin for the other victim who had died at the scene out at the Bear, Mrs. Dillon.

Betty Dillon had been working at the Bear for only a few months. She had apparently moved to Castaway County from Portland last fall. To my knowledge, she was a widow; at least that was what I had heard at one of the church socials I had attended with Dexter and Suzi. She was very well liked by everyone, especially given that she had lived in the area for so short a time.

I called our day dispatcher, Tom Murray, and asked him to run Betty Dillon's name and see where she lived in Portland and where she came from prior to that, if Portland wasn't her place of birth. Tom said he would call back in a while if he could find any information on her. I figured it was the only way for me to begin trying to locate any family members. I didn't think Frank had mentioned any next of kin when they were trying to call about the initial murder notifications. But I decided to call him and check.

"Hey, Frank, it's Dell."

"Does this mean you came up with something?"

"No, not yet. We interviewed Mrs. Windom but didn't get much from her. We're still checking on her husband's background: they have two nice cars and a good-looking house that don't exactly reflect a game warden's salary, but you never know what their family might have until we check."

I always feel a bit like a voyeur looking so hard into other people's business, I thought, *but I know that it's part of the proper investigative techniques.*

"Well, then, what did you call about, Dell?"

"I just wanted to ask if you guys ever located any relatives of the one victim, Mrs. Dillon?"

"Yeah, we finally found a sister living in Portland to make the notifications to. You know, her husband died a few years back. He died in a fire in Portland. I guess it was after that she moved up here."

"That's odd, Frank. You know how everyone knows everyone else's background, especially in the church groups, but I've never heard any talk about her husband having died in a fire. Just that he *had* died and left her a widow."

"Well, maybe she just hadn't wanted to share that fact with the others who attend the socials. Who knows?"

"Sure could be, Frank, just seems a little odd. That type of information is not usually missed in the social discussions. Oh, well, probably nothing anyway. I'll check some more and see if I need to go to Portland to interview anyone. Say, if I do, Frank, you want to join me?"

"Love to, Dell. Just give me a call so we can meet. Maybe around Waterville?"

"That would work for me. I'll let you know once I decide. See ya later!"

As soon as I hung up on Frank, Tom called me back to say he'd found a couple of potential relatives. Betty Dillon's apartment in Portland had been owned by a couple by the name of O'Malley, which was Betty Dillon's middle name as listed in the Maine Department of Vehicles. Tom suspected they might be relatives, and I agreed. I thanked him for checking so quickly for me and took a phone number he had found for the O'Malleys in Portland.

I called the phone number, and a woman answered the phone.

"Hello, Mrs. O'Malley?"

"Yes, this is Becky."

"My name is Dell Hinton. I'm the sheriff of Castaway County, up north of your location. I'm trying to speak to relatives of Mrs. Betty Dillon. Are you her sister?"

"Sister-in-law. My husband is her ... I mean was her brother. Well, he still is, she's gone. Anyway, Sean and Betty were brother and sister."

"I'm sorry for your family's loss, Mrs. O'Malley. I'm working with the state police on trying to determine who committed this horrible crime. May I ask you some questions? I mean, is this a good time?"

"As good as any, Sheriff."

"I understand that Betty was a widow?"

"Yes, happened a year or so ago. Her husband was a real shit; in my mind, he got what was coming to him."

"Oh, what makes you say that, Mrs. O'Malley?"

"Oscar was a violent guy in a violent business. He let that violence loose on Betty from time to time."

"Oh, she was an abused wife?"

"Yeah, he sent her to the hospital quite a few times. He was a real bastard, that one! If his family hadn't of come from the Emerald Isle, there wouldn'ta been any reason to like him at all. He hadn't a bit of the milk of human kindness in him."

"His family was from Ireland, then?"

"They were, originally. From Limerick, I think. Once they got into Portland and his mum got in the family way, they decided to give him a non-Irish name. Why they picked Oscar, I'll not be knowing, but he was nasty even when he was young. Don't know why Betty fell for his bullshit, bless her memory."

"What does your husband—Sean, was it? What does he do for a living?"

"He's a brick layer. A damn good one, too! Puts food on the table every day for me and our little ones."

"May I ask how he and his sister Betty got along?"

"Pretty well, especially after old Oscar left this world. I think it was pretty hard for Sean to watch his sister get hurt by the bastard and then just stay with him, waiting for the next time he hurt her."

"When the state police notified next of kin the other day, they talked to a sister of Betty's. Was that you, and they had the names mixed up?"

"No, she and Sean do have a sister, Grace Tildon, but she's a bit eccentric, I guess you'd say. She lives here in Portland. Makes pottery to sell at local stores. She doesn't associate with other people much, just stays to herself. She did call us to tell us about Betty when the officer called her. That was nice of her. She's an odd one, that girl!"

"Well, I've taken enough of your time today, Mrs. O'Malley. I may try to schedule a trip down to Portland with the lieutenant from the state police so we can talk to your husband and you at a later date. I'll call you once I set something up, okay?"

"Sure, that's grand, Sheriff. I'm sure Sean will be glad to tell you anything you want about his poor sister."

"Thanks again, and please pass on my sympathy to Sean."

After hanging up, I called through my door to ask Irish for another cup of Joe, but she was already walking in with one.

"That's what I like about you, Irish; you read my mind."

"Sorry, boss, but in case you never noticed, men are rather singularly minded, so most of us ladies can tell what you guys want." We both laughed at that one, until I realized that she was pointing out the male one-track mind, and I began to feign offense.

"Oh, don't get too upset, boss. It's just the way men and women are different. You break the case yet with any of your calls?"

"No, got some more background is all. But the woman I spoke to was clearly of Irish descent and spoke of other family in Ireland. Made me think of my trips to Ireland."

"One of your favorite places?"

"Oh yeah. I love Ireland! Actually, she mentioned family members who came from Limerick. I often go through that city on the way south, toward Kenmare. Traveling through, though, I seem to hit the bad parts of the city. Looks kind of dark and cold, less color than lots of the small towns in Ireland. Most have brightly painted houses in many colors."

"Sounds beautiful there!"

"It really is. Especially the town of Kenmare, where I usually go. About every other storefront in town is a pub, some with excellent restaurant food. And everyone is so nice and friendly. It's nestled in between a couple of mountains and the Kenmare Bay. Real cute little town!"

"Planning any trips there soon? I mean, if you are, the least you could do is take your *excellent administrative assistant*. It's the least you could do, you know?" Irish had a huge smile on her face.

"Well, I won't be going anywhere for a while. I doubt the citizens of the county would like their sheriff running off to Ireland for a month when there's law enforcement work here to do."

"I don't know about a month, but they know you get vacations, so I would think a week or two couldn't hurt."

"Well, right now I have to get working to solve this homicide at the Bear. Vacation will have to come later. And besides, I would want to stay at least a month. Hell, I might get there and just decide not to ever come back!"

"You can't do that, boss. We need you here in Castaway."

"Hey, I can still dream of moving to Ireland, can't I?"

"Sure, boss, sure. Keeps you happy, it's good with us."

Just as I was getting ready to leave the office for the day, I got a call from the jail that they had a very violent prisoner who had been brought in earlier. So I decided to head down the street to the jail to see what was going on there.

As I walked in, I could already hear the screams of someone coming from back in a holding cell. I walked back there with Allen Smith, my chief deputy's brother, to see what was going on.

As we watched the inmate through the window in the door at the end of the holding cellblock, I saw a totally naked guy run directly at the iron door, head first! He just ran right into it and then collapsed back on the floor from the collision and seemed to be temporarily knocked out. After a couple of minutes, he regained consciousness and stood up, looked at the door again, and took another run at it. Bang! Head first again into the iron and fell back again.

"Holy, jumpin' Jesus, Sheriff! He's been doing that for a while now. You'd think he'd just give up trying, or knock himself out cold for a long while."

"Okay, Allen, what's this guy's story?"

"Well, one of the Weaverton Town cops found him walking around in the street, blocking traffic downtown a couple of hours ago, and when he approached him, the guy tried to cold-cock him. It was a hell of a fight before they got him here."

"Well, he's certainly screwed up on something. Or he's just some nut job. Either way, we need to get him moved safely to a combined medical and mental observation facility."

"Can we get Doc Clopper to come in and give him something to calm him down?"

51

"I'll call him, Allen, while you get a vehicle ready to transport him. First you guys can take him by the ER, then see where after that, based upon what they find."

"Okay, I'll get one of the field guys to swing by to assist me with this one."

In a little while, Doc Clopper arrived and decided he could give the guy a shot of something to temporarily calm him so he wouldn't be so violent, and Allen had a vehicle ready and a fellow deputy to assist. So the three of us walked back to the holding cell area while Doc Clopper waited by the vehicle in the sally port area to give the guy the shot.

As we arrived back at the cellblock, I told Allen to go get us one of the inmate blankets. He looked at me strangely but went to get the blanket. When he came back with it, I told both deputies that we would wait until this guy ran at the door again, and once he had knocked himself backward, we would run in the door and wrap him up in the blanket.

"If he happens to recover and stand up, we'll be behind the blanket, so he can't see us to be able to get a good punch in on us, and we can just wrap him up like a hot dog in a bun and carry him safely to the vehicle. We'll put cuffs and irons on him while he's still in wraps for safety. He's already naked, so Doc Clopper can give him a shot in the ass, and away you guys can go."

"Shit, now I know why you're the sheriff, boss! I'd a never thought of that!"

So we did exactly as I had suggested. We rolled up the inmate in the blanket and carried him out to the vehicle, put on the restraints, and the doc gave him a shot. Within a few minutes, he was lying in the back of a vehicle headed for the hospital. And none of our guys ever got a scratch! It worked like a charm.

Doc Clopper looked over at me and said, "I only gave him a very mild sedative, Dell. Since I don't know what he may already have in his system, I don't want to take any chances with his life."

"Good work, Doc. At least we got him in the restraints, and no one got hurt."

"Yes, but the drug may wear off soon, so you better hope your guys drive fast." Then Doc winked at me and left.

Allen Smith called me about half an hour later and said that by the time they got to the ER, the effects of whatever Doc Clopper had shot him with had begun to wear off. I told him that both deputies needed to be ready in case the guy got violent again, but hopefully the hospital could keep him sedated until they found out what his problem was to begin with. I suggested that he call the hospital security guard to come down to the ER to stand by to help in case the inmate got rowdy again. Since they were already at the hospital, I decided it was probably safe to head on out to my cabin.

When I arrived home, I saw Suzi's Rav 4 in the drive and realized she had beaten me home for the day. Sometimes I made it home first, but more often she did since her workday normally began earlier than mine.

As I walked in the kitchen door, I smelled the most magnificent aroma coming from the oven. Suzi was standing over the stove cooking something on the cooktop, so I came up behind her and hugged her. As I did, I gently kissed her neck. She sighed and told me that I needed to "stop that immediately" or our dinner was going to be ruined because she would not be able to contain herself. *Hey, I'm okay with bologna and cheese sandwiches,* I thought.

"Well, baby, dinner could be put on hold for a bit, couldn't it?"

"Oh, you silly man! I'm not going to let this perfect meal I've cooked go bad just to have a little roll in the hay with you." Then she kissed me deeply and whispered in my ear, "That will be our dessert, honey."

"Well, okay, then! What's on the menu?"

"We're having salmon braised with honey and my homemade macaroni and cheese with bits of ham and cracker dust on top and pan-grilled asparagus spears. Any of that get you excited?"

"It all gets me excited, but not near as much as you do, sweetie!"

"Well, you go freshen up, and I'll put on the finishing touches, Dell."

I went into the bedroom, changed my shirt, and then wiped my face and washed my hands in the bathroom. I came back to find that the table was beautifully set and dinner was on the table. Suzi even had candles on the table; it was a beautiful setting.

As we ate our dinner, we could hear a couple of loons out on the lake calling to each other. It was their mournful, long cry, the one that sounds more like a wail than their more classic laughing call. I had always been told that cry indicated bad weather approaching, but I was never sure the people who said stuff like that really had any knowledge of what the animal was saying. Like a lot of things people say, I guess it just sounds good when they seem to know what they're talking about.

Suzi told me during dinner that Bill Wilson had been chewed out by the station manager for his little impromptu rant about drugs being a factor in the Black Bear shootings. I told her that he was just bad at ad libbing, and I knew he meant no harm. Sometimes he's comical, other times just weird. *Besides,* I thought, *it could turn out he's right about drugs. Who knows!*

After dinner, I told Suzi about old Darby Webb and how interesting a character I found him to be. I asked her if she wanted to go along with me that night to talk with him about the history of Spoodicook Lake. Suzi said she would definitely be interested; she thought it would help her reporting to have a better background about the lake. So we agreed to drive over to see him.

Darby's place was four doors down from the Spoodicook town dock. Darby met us at the front door, and after I introduced Suzi, he had us come in and sit down on his screened porch. It was on the backside of his home, which faced the lake. He turned off the television in the far corner; he'd been watching *Wheel of Fortune* as we had walked in. He sat down in an overstuffed easy chair, lit a cigarette, and took a sip of a glass of iced tea sitting beside the chair on an end table. He offered us a glass, but we both passed since we had just finished dinner not too long before.

"So, Darby, you were telling me about some of the older lake people, stuff that happened a long time ago."

"Eya, I was. Told you I'd tell you about some of the old ladies on the lake, so I did."

Darby began by describing the old summer camps located on many of the properties around the lake.

"They was them big, old log camps. You know, the ones made of big, round cedar logs with the bark still on 'em. They was laid horizontally on top of each other. Even with the chinking between the logs, they always had bats. Hate them damn things!"

"So the old camps were full of bats?"

"Many of them were. Sometimes in the evening you could hea' someone on the lake shooting small-bore shotguns, trying to kill the bats as they left the camps for their nightly rounds."

"Well, I wouldn't stand for bats in my camp, I can tell you that!" Suzi commented.

"Surprisin' to seem, but some of the old ladies on the lake seemed to not be bothered by 'em. They'd sing songs while out canoeing in the evening like, 'Bat, bat, come under my hat, and I shall give you a piece of bacon,' stuff like that. One old lady I worked for, she actually named her bats. Sometimes she'd make remarks about how they had flown through the room just to see who'd come callin' that night."

"Sounds like these ladies were a bit eccentric," I said.

"Well, in a way, yes, but these women was just a different brand of person than we have today. They were tough ... but it isn't just that. They was just a different breed, you might say."

"Well, I don't know any ladies in my circles who like bats, let alone who would sing to them or even name them!" Suzi was clearly not impressed with this story line.

"But these ladies were tough. The ones I'm speaking about would come up to their camps early, when the black flies were still hanging 'round, and they would stay up late into October when it was cold enough to freeze your butt right off! And, mind you, this was when they were probably in their seventies and had no menfolk to take care of them, except me coming by to see them every day and tend to the fire wood and such."

"So you saw these ladies every day?"

"Oh, yes. I took real good care of them. They were real nice to me. I'd fetch wood for them and check on the gas for the camp and the boats. And I'd just generally sit and chat a bit to be sure they were doin' okay."

"It sounds like you enjoyed being a caretaker, Darby." I could see it in his eyes as he spoke of the old days.

"Oh, I did, most of the time. There was almost always some egghead who wasn't nice and just saw me as another of their domestic servants, but most of the folks treated me pretty good. They was all 'from away,' but they was mostly pretty nice.

"One of my favorite old ladies, Mrs. Riker, she was real nice to me. I remember one time she had ordered her a new wooden boat out of the Old Town Canoe Company catalogue. She just looked through it and found one she liked the looks of. Dandy boat too, in-board out-board motor, real high sides on her; she was meant to be on the ocean, not a lake. She was a bit big. Anyway, it got delivered one day at the town dock, and I proudly drove it over to Mrs. Riker, see. I tooted the horn as I rounded the point headed toward her dock. Well, she came down on the dock and took one look at that boat, and she says, 'Where in the world did you get that *white elephant*, Darby?' So I said, 'Well you ordered this one from the catalogue, Mrs. Riker.' So she laughed, then I laughed. Then I took her out for a ride in her new boat."

"Sounds like an interesting lady," I ventured.

"Eya, they all was. The other two were sisters to one another and related to Mrs. Riker somehow. I think she was their aunt, but they were all about the same age. The sisters had a place on the mainland, same old style camp. I'm not sure anymore, but I think the sisters were on the lake first. Then Mrs. Riker and her husband, L.C., bought their island and camp. L.C. was a good bit older than his wife, so he passed on long before she did."

Darby told a few more stories about the old ladies on the lake canoeing and playing croquet. After a while, Suzi and I noticed that he was looking tired and had slowed down his thought process, so we told him we had to get home because we had a lot of meetings the next day. Darby got up and walked us to his door.

"Well, I hope you'll come back and see me again. I enjoy telling stories about the old days on the lake, and you be sure to bring this lovely lady of yours back with you. I might be old, but I still like to see a beautiful woman."

Suzi said, "Oh Dell will be back, and so will I. Maybe I can think of some specific questions about the lake I could ask you?"

"I'll be glad to do my best, young lady! Although, I must admit that sometimes these days I have more trouble remembering things than I used to."

We all said our good-byes, and Suzi and I drove back to my cabin. As we walked in the kitchen door, I patted her on the behind and said, "Now, how about that dessert, beautiful?"

"Oh, Dell, I thought you might have forgotten."

As she walked toward the bedroom, she casually let her dress fall off of her body and wisp away to the floor. Her beautiful skin shown in the hallway light, and she was only wearing bikini panties, nothing else.

"No, I think I'm quite ready for dessert."

I followed her into the bedroom and closed the door so Chauncey wouldn't disturb us, wanting to be petted. I decided he could wait until later.

9

Suzi and I had barely finished our "dessert" when my phone rang. Even though I just wanted to lie there with her, I knew that late-night calls were often of the important variety, so I was compelled to answer the phone.

"Hi, Sheriff, Debbie Allen here." Debbie is my nightshift dispatcher. If someone calls to awaken me, it's usually her or the state police dispatcher. I always try to be extra civil to them since I suspect it would be easy for them to get a complex if I was gruff when they wake me up. At least this time I wasn't already asleep.

"Hi, Debbie, what have you got for me this time?"

"Deputy Billy Teal just took some kid in for possession, and he says the kid may have some information on the Bear homicides. Billy thought you might like to come down to talk to him."

"Okay, tell Billy I'm on the way. Be there in about a half hour. Thanks, Debbie."

After I hung up on Debbie Allen, I rolled over and kissed Suzi on the shoulder and neck.

"You want to go again, baby?" she asked in a hushed tone.

"Sorry, I have to decline, sweetie. I have to go in and talk to a kid they just arrested. Might have some information on the Bear case, who knows. Keep my side warm?"

"Absolutely!"

I got up and dressed in some casual clothes, left the cabin, and headed for the jail. As I was driving, I wondered, *What do you suppose some druggie has in the way of information on the case?*

I met Deputy Teal in the front office area of the jail. He said that the kid he arrested, Brent Jennings, was a local kid who used and sold various drugs. He'd been in trouble since middle school. He was now twenty-two and had no job or career of any kind, except his small-time drug business. He'd been arrested a few times before for possession and had never been holding enough for selling, but he was a known "shit-bird."

I went to the holding cell and found that Brent had a slight build, dirty blond hair, about five feet nine with a very poor complexion. I introduced myself and asked if he wanted to talk to me. He indicated he did, and I read him the Miranda rights, just to cover our discussion. Contrary to popular belief, you don't have to give everyone the Miranda rights; they're used when you are accusing someone of a crime. If you're not at the accusatory stage, they're not necessary. However, in this case, since Brent was already charged with possession, I figured I wanted to be sure that anything he said was usable in court. I'm sure Deputy Teal had already read them to him, but it pays to be sure, so I read them again.

"Okay, having these rights in mind, Brent, what do you want to tell me?"

"First, Sheriff, I want to make a deal."

"What kind of deal?"

"If I give you information about the killings, I want inoculated from this possession charge."

"You mean you want *immunity* from this specific charge?"

"Yeah, that's it. I want immunity!"

"Well, it doesn't work like that, kid. You tell me what information you have, I'll check it out, and if it's good, then I'll talk to the prosecuting attorney. We don't just drop charges because you have some information for us."

"Well ... I don't know now."

"Fine with me. I've got some sleep to catch. I'll tell Deputy Teal to finish getting you booked in."

"Now, wait a minute ... okay, I guess I'll tell you."

"Then do it, kid. I haven't got all night."

"Well, you know that game warden, Windom? He wasn't no stand-up guy like you think."

"What do you mean?"

"He was involved in some big stuff, you know. I mean, where do you think I got some of my stuff sometimes?"

"Are you trying to tell me that Warden Windom was selling you drugs?"

"Well ... yeah. Yeah, that's it. I once seen him pull a whole baggie of pills outa his pockets. And he was even in uniform then!"

"Come on, kid. What are you doing? You just trying to get your crime reduced with a bunch of stories?"

"No ... well, yes ... I mean I want to get free of these charges. But I did see a baggie one time."

"Okay, thanks for the bedtime story. I'll check it out. But if you're lying to me and trying to defame a dead warden, we'll be talking again."

I walked away from the holding cell and into the adjoining office area. Deputy Teal asked me if the kid gave me any good information. I thought about it for a minute before answering. *The Windoms seemed to have a higher than expected life style, but this kid's information seemed too easily fabricated and far too opportunistic to get him out of a jamb to be believed.* I knew I'd have to do a little more investigation before I believed anything that kid told me.

"I'm not sure anything he said was true, Billy. Won't know until I do some checking. I'm thinking he's just trying to trade bogus information in an attempt to reduce his charges. You know, the usual story."

"Sure do, Sheriff. Run into it every few arrests, especially the shitbirds!"

"Yeah, but I still need to check it out. Once in a while, even a shitbird gives you something good. Thanks for the call, Billy."

I left the jail and headed back to my cabin and hoped that Suzi was still keeping my side warm.

★

The next morning as I was arriving at the office, Irish told me she had a call for me from Deputy Teal. I walked into my office and picked up my phone.

"Deputy Teal, I thought you would be sleeping soundly right now. Why the early call?"

"Well, Sheriff, I just wanted to let you know that when I was running that Jennings kid's full background, I noticed something I thought you might like to know. In among his multiple arrests for possession and minor assaults, he was busted twice for spotlighting deer with a weapon in the vehicle. And guess who the Game Warden was who charged him both times?"

"Paul Windom!"

"You got it, Sheriff. Maybe that's why he wanted to implicate him so bad?"

"Yeah, sounds like I need to go back down and talk to him again. Thanks for the call, Billy. Happy dreams."

I sat there for a couple minutes thinking about this new information. The Windoms clearly had more assets than were normal for a person on a state job, but there were any number of reasonable explanations for that. I had never heard anyone imply before that Paul Windom was anything but straight up. And now I could see a reason the Jennings kid would implicate Paul in drugs; he felt he had a beef with him over some prior charges. And, for that matter, Jennings had been a little too quick to try to get immunity on his charge for giving information in the Bear murders. And, if I remembered correctly, Jennings had danced around the idea that Windom was into drugs, *without making a clear statement that we could use to charge him with*. He had simply *implied* that Windom was into the drug scene, not made an overt claim about it. *Maybe this kid had already learned the prisoner routines to get out of jail pretty well during his past incarcerations,* I thought.

When Irish poked her head in the office door to ask if I wanted a cup of coffee, I was still deep in thought. I told her I could use one about now, and she brought a fresh cup in and set in on my desk.

"I heard you were up late interviewing some shitbird, boss, so I thought you might need a pick-me-up."

"I was, and I did. Thanks, Irish. I think this kid was just lying to save his ass. I doubt his information is any good."

After we talked a few minutes and I finished the coffee, I decided to go over to the jail and talk to Brent Jennings again. Allen Smith was on duty, so I asked him to roust Jennings out of his rack and bring him to the office holding cell.

"Okay, kid, you still maintain that Game Warden Windom was selling drugs?"

"Well ... I never said that, I er ... I just ... I stand behind what I said last night when you talked to me."

"Well, what you didn't say was that Warden Windom had charged you for spot-lighting violations, not once, but twice!"

"Yeah, well, so what if he did?"

"That makes me think that you were just trying to get back at the Game Warden, kid."

"Getting back at him was just a perk in the deal!" Jennings blurted out.

"Oh, so what was the whole deal then?"

"Aw, I just figured you'd let me go on this possession charge if I gave you some information on the big murder case you guys are workin'."

"So, ruining the name of a dead game warden, one who had a very good career, was just a 'perk' as you say?"

"Yeah, it would have been a perk. He was a bastard to me."

"Well, he was a good officer. He didn't need some shithead walking on his grave and trying to make him look bad just to save his skin! Now, you can count on me to do everything I can to see to it that you get the maximum time on this charge."

"Hey, what do ya mean?"

"I mean I don't like your attitude and the way you're willing to screw a good officer to get yourself out of trouble. So, I'm going to do what I can to keep you locked up for as long as we can!" With that, I turned from the cell and began walking away.

"Hey, where are you going? What are you gonna do?"

As I continued walking away, I called back to Jennings in his cell, "I'm headed over to see the prosecuting attorney and talk to him about your case. I'm pretty sure he'll be interested in how 'helpful' you have been."

Then I turned to Deputy Smith and in a loud voice said, "Take that shithead back to his cell and make him comfortable. He'll be here a long time!"

Deputy Smith winked at me as I passed him, and Brent Jennings was still hollering as I went out the door of the jail. His attitude and actions had made me pretty much discard his potential information. I still wanted to locate the source of the Windoms' finances just to close out that train of thought entirely. While I had only met Paul a few times, I saw nothing that would indicate that there was any sinister reason the Windoms had extra money. But, in the long run, one never knows what lies in the hearts and minds of other men.

As I was walking back to my office, my cell phone rang. Irish said I had a visitor waiting for me.

10

A s I walked into my office door, my old friend Father Dexter stood up and threw out his hand.

"Hi, Dell. I just came by to see if my powers of detection were still as good as in the old days at school with you."

"Oh, and how's that, Dex?"

"Well, I noticed as you guys were leaving the Windoms' home yesterday, your chief deputy was checking out the garage, home, and even looked in the backyard. I figured you were evaluating the cars and work done to improve their home. Am I right?"

"You're as quick as you always were, Dex. Yes, we were noticing all the money the Windoms had spent recently. We have to check all issues."

"I know, Dell. That's why I asked Mrs. Windom to come in to see you so she can give you the reason for the improvements to dispel your possible questions of corruption on Mr. Windom's part."

As he spoke, Dex moved slightly to his right, exposing Mrs. Windom sitting on the chair just in front of my desk. I immediately walked past Dex and greeted Mrs. Windom.

"Oh, Mrs. Windom, I had no idea you were sitting here in the office. I hope you understand—I'm not trying to impugn your late husband's reputation. I just have to check out all possibilities."

"Yes, Sheriff, I do understand. That's why I wanted to speak to you as soon as Father Dexter made the observation of your chief deputy and suggested that you might have questions."

I asked if either of them wanted some coffee or other drink. Mrs. Windom asked for hot tea, and Dex just wanted some water. I called out to Irish and asked if she could get the beverages.

"Okay, Mrs. Windom. Obviously, my chief deputy and I noticed that you and your husband had spent some money on improvements to your home as well as purchasing two rather expensive vehicles. What was it you wanted to tell me about those things?"

"Paul's uncle Harry, Harry Tressman, passed away about a year ago from cancer. Harry had practically raised Paul after his mother died and his father took to drinking. Well, to make the story short, Harry had left some money to Paul in his will. Harry hadn't any kids of his own, so he left most of his estate to Paul, with a small amount to Silvia and Danny, if they ever locate him."

"Danny? Who's Danny, Mrs. Windom?"

"Why, Danny is our son."

"I'm sorry, Mrs. Windom. I didn't know you two had a son."

"Well, we don't talk overly much about Danny. We adopted Danny when he was a baby, and by the time he was a teenager, he became estranged from us. One day, he just took off, and we haven't heard a word from him since. That's why I said they would have to find him first before they could give him his inheritance from Uncle Harry."

"So, the money you put into the house and cars was from the inheritance?"

"Yes. There's still some left, but Paul wanted to give me the home and cars he thought I wanted for all these years, but that he couldn't afford on a state salary. It was nice, but it was intended to be shared with him." At this point, Mrs. Windom began to cry. I handed her some tissue, and Dex tried to comfort her.

Irish walked into the room and carried a tray with the tea, water, a coffee for me, and some biscuits on a paper plate. *Hey, just because we're cops doesn't mean we can't put out a proper afternoon tea,* I thought, *even with paper plates and Styrofoam cups!*

After Mrs. Windom regained her composure, I decided to ask a little more about the estranged adopted son I was now just learning about. I was adopted myself, at the ripe age of five days, so I've always been both supportive and interested in others who have been adopted.

"So, tell me a bit more about Danny, Mrs. Windom. "

"You know, Mrs. Windom, the sheriff here is also an adopted child," Dex said to her.

"No, I didn't know that. Maybe it will give you a better understanding then. Well, Danny was a good child early on, but Paul and I made a terrible mistake as we raised him. Since we had adopted him so young, a few months old, we decided to raise him as our own child and didn't tell him that he was adopted. Did your parents tell you, Sheriff?"

"Yes, ma'am, they did. I always knew I was adopted."

"Well, Danny didn't. And then one day, I think he had just turned fifteen a week or so before, he was helping his dad clean out the attic. Oh, they were going through old file boxes of papers, mostly old stuff from Paul's work. But one box had some personal, household papers, and Paul had set that box aside to be kept. Well, naturally, Danny being an inquisitive kid, later that day he snuck back up in the attic and started to rummage through that file box. Apparently he found some of the original adoption papers and confronted us at dinner that evening.

"Danny was very upset, yelling at us both, and I could see the hurt in his eyes. We both tried to explain to him that since he was adopted so young, we had just decided to let him think of us as his only parents. But our relationship was never the same and seemed to deteriorate almost daily from there on. Oh, I'm sure part of it was attributable to his being a teenager and having the hormonal changes and all, but there was also the lost trust and feeling that we had betrayed him in some way. We thought we were doing the right thing, you know, but it just blew up in our faces." Mrs. Windom's head went low, and her shoulders dipped down and began to quake. She began crying again, and I could tell that she was reliving those awful feelings of the loss of her son. Again, Dex leaned over to give her some words of comfort, and I handed her another tissue.

Once she regained her composure, I continued, hopefully on a less emotional line.

"So, you have no idea where Danny is today?"

"The last we heard about him was actually from Uncle Harry, about four years ago. Danny and Harry had always gotten along well, so I guess Danny kept in contact with Harry for a while after he took off. Harry told us Danny was living in South Carolina, near one of the beach areas."

"Do you think Uncle Harry kept contact up right until his passing?"

"They might have continued to talk; as I said, Danny always liked Harry real well."

"Did Harry leave a wife or anyone else he was close to?"

"Yes, Harry's wife, Elizabeth, is still around. As I said before, they had no children."

"Where is Elizabeth?"

"She's in a home down near Portland. Piney Woods or Woods View, something like that. She has Alzheimer's, but if you catch her on a good day, she's mostly lucid. She just drifts sometimes. I'm sure you've dealt with Alzheimer's patients before."

"Yes, I have. Terrible disease."

"It is, indeed. She was just starting to get a little foggy before Harry passed, so he found the home for her and had just moved her in. Guess that all worked out at least. It probably would have been much harder for any of us relatives to convince her to move, especially after Harry was gone."

"Well, thank you, Mrs. Windom, for dropping in to help me with these facts. You have been able to clear up issues and have raised some new ones I can look into. I'm sorry for your losses, and I hope between your daughter, Silvia, and Father Dexter, you can gain some strength."

"Well, you can thank Father Dexter for my coming by to talk since I hadn't noticed you and your deputy looking around. Nor did I have any idea that the cars and renovations would give you any question about Paul."

"Well, Dex and I go way back to high school days, so I guess he knows me pretty well. Thanks, Dex—I mean Father Dexter—for bringing Mrs. Windom by today. It was a big help."

"Dell, I always try to be helpful, unless we're playing against each other in basketball. Then it's every man for himself!"

"Thanks again, Mrs. Windom, and don't hesitate to call me if you think of anything else or hear from any of your relatives about Danny. If I locate him, I'll provide his address to you right away."

"No, Sheriff, if Danny wants me to know where he is, he'll contact me. I suppose I owe him the right to be as independent as he wants to be from me. But if you do locate him, please pass the address on to the attorney's office so they can get his inheritance to him. He shouldn't be kept from getting it; he may be in need of it. Who knows?"

"Yes, ma'am, I will gladly do that. Which attorneys?"

"Samuel Dagget of Dagget, Cooly, and Smith. They're over in Bangor. They handled Harry's estate."

"Okay, thanks, Mrs. Windom."

"If you do find Danny, just tell him I'm sorry and I hope he's doing well. We always had his best interests in mind, even if we didn't handle it so well. And we, I, do love him."

"I'll be glad to tell him for you, if I do find him."

After they left the building, I called Irish in and asked her if she had seen Berk that afternoon. She had not, so I asked her to call him and see if he could drop by the office before he got off duty for the day. After the call, she came back in the office and sat down.

"You know, Irish, talking to Mrs. Windom about her adopted son makes me wonder how I would have felt had my parents not told me about my being adopted and then I found out about it from reading some old court paper."

"I'd guess that would be pretty hard to deal with, boss."

"Yes, I believe it would be. To find out that the two most important members of your family were not only not your real family, but were also hiding that fact from you, I'm guessing that would make you pretty mad at them."

"Yes, and how old was he when he found out, boss?"

"She said about fifteen. A bad age to have to deal with that kind of news. I wonder if it could drive a kid to seek revenge on the adoptive parents."

"I don't know, boss, but I guess stranger things have happened."

"Well, it certainly was unfortunate timing. Finding out would be bad enough, but then to have all the normal influences of adolescence on top of that—whew, the kid must have been f'd up!"

"That term fits most teenagers, boss," Irish said with a wink.

"You're right about that. Well, as soon as Berk comes by, I'll update him, and we can switch gears and try to locate Danny. Hey, I need to call Mrs. Windom back as soon as she gets home. I forgot to ask her something."

"What did you forget?"

"I need to know what Danny's birth name was. My guess is that if he was as mad at the Windoms as we think, he didn't use their last name when he took off. Probably used his birth name or a made-up one. Hopefully, the birth name will help locate him."

The police band radio monitor sitting on the file cabinet in the corner of my office chirped out some radio traffic, and Irish said, "Oh, looks like Berk just marked out at your office. Should be in to see you any minute now."

In a few short minutes, Berk walked into my office and sat down. I told him about the information I had received from my interview with Mrs. Windom. I said that we should still look at the Windoms' finances, but that we now had a pretty good idea about the home improvements and cars, assuming that we could verify the inheritance. I gave him the law firm's name in Bangor so he could follow up with them.

I also told him about Danny, who neither of us were aware even existed until that day. I told him I would call Mrs. Windom to get the birth name, and we could start trying to track him down. I also said that we might have to interview Elizabeth Tressman at the home in Portland in the hopes of locating the missing son.

After Berk was fully updated on the case and left, I called the Windom home and left a message with Silvia for her mother to call me when she returned home. I spoke to Silvia briefly about Danny, but she was not aware of his birth name. She indicated that the family *always* considered Danny a true Windom in spirit.

As I sat there behind my desk thinking about my own adoption and the parents who raised me, I wondered exactly how I would have felt if they had hidden my past from me. I think it would have been very upsetting to find out at an older age that I was adopted. As it was for me, since I knew all my life about the adoption, I always felt that I was truly wanted as a child, and that was a great feeling. It seemed to me that in Danny's case, that revelation at the age of fifteen must have shattered his world. I suspected that it created feelings of resentment and betrayal in Danny's adolescent mind. *Of course,* I thought, *I'm no shrink. Maybe I was a good candidate for one, but it isn't my bailiwick.*

At about five fifteen, Mrs. Windom returned my call. When I asked her about Danny's birth name, she had to think a few moments but was able to give it to me.

Danny had been born Clinton Alexander.

Before I left the office for the day, I called Lieutenant Bell at State Police Investigations headquarters in Augusta.

"Hey, Frank. I think it's time for you and me to make a small trip down to Portland to talk to some of the people we need to either interview or just locate."

"Okay, Dell, does that mean you have some good leads?"

"Not exactly leads, but certainly people of interest. I want to talk to the O'Malleys a bit more about the family background of one of the victims, Betty Dillon. I also need to try to locate Danny Windom, the Windoms' estranged son. He found out he was adopted and then took off for parts unknown. He has an elderly aunt though, Elizabeth Tressman, who lives in a nursing home and may be able to help."

"Sounds like we'll be getting two or more birds with one stone, huh?"

"Well, it can't hurt to check these out, and it may save me some time searching for Danny in other states. Last was known of him, he was in South Carolina, but maybe Mrs. Tressman has heard from him."

"Didn't want to just call these folks, Dell?"

"Well, I've spoken to Mrs. O'Malley, but not her husband, Sean. And in Mrs. Tressman's case, she has Alzheimer's, so my guess is if I'm to get anything useful from her, it'll have to be face to face. Look, do you want to join me or should I just take Berk?"

"Don't get your panties in a bunch, Dell. I'm in. I just wanted to be sure if I was going to miss a big part of a day that it was worth it."

"I can't make any guarantees, Frank, but I do think we need to see these people."

"Okay, Dell. Pick me up at the Waterville exit on I-95?"

"That works for me. Say around seven thirty?"

"I'll be there."

After I hung up with Frank Bell, I double-checked that there were no problems brewing at the jail through our dispatcher and then headed home for the evening. I also checked my phone for messages before I left and found one from Suzi. She said she had some type of production meeting that was expected to run late and asked if I could start something for dinner. So I decided to make a quick stop at the grocery store in town on the way home. I figured I'd pick up some pork chops, Shake 'n Bake, some fresh veggies, and a couple of baking potatoes. I also noticed some small flower arrangements in sleeves, so I picked up a colorful bouquet. Then, with bags in hand, I headed for the lake.

By 6:50 p.m., I had all of my dinner ingredients cooking or baking. The chops were baking in the oven with a generous coating of Shake 'n Bake. The potatoes were cut up into wedges and were in a pot on the stove, boiling in water. I planned to mash them, skin on, and add some milk, butter, and garlic just prior to serving. I had cut up the veggies and had them in a wok with some oil, awaiting my sweetie to arrive.

In the meantime, I had set the table and placed the flowers and two candles in the center of the table. I wanted to have a romantic ambiance and the meal prepared by the time Suzi arrived. I figured she usually does the lion's share of the cooking, so when I jump in, I want to make it worth the effort. Besides, what better way to show her how much I truly love her than wanting the meal to be special?

Suzi came in at 7:05 p.m., clearly dragging from her day. As soon as she saw the flowers and candles, her face brightened.

"Oh, baby, the table looks great! Have you been planning something romantic?"

Damn, she's a mind reader!

"Well, I just thought you could use a nice meal after your hard day, sweetie."

"Well, you sure know how to melt a girl's heart, baby. Maybe I'll melt yours later!"

One thing about Suzi, she can always get me excited, just by being there in the room and by her subtle conversation. She's all woman! *Or, maybe* I thought, *I'm just a typical horny guy.* Either way, I can accept myself and her for what we are: a couple in love with each other, with separate careers.

During dinner, I told Suzi that I was planning to meet Frank early in the morning, so I had to get up at "oh dark thirty." I expected to be down in Portland for a good bit of the day, and she should not expect me home the next evening until pretty late. I said that Frank and I might well stop for dinner on the road, but that I would call her and let her know for sure.

After dinner, Suzi and I sat on the cabin porch and watched the waves on the lake subside, as they often do after sundown. In the distance, we could here a couple of loons calling to each other farther up lake. As we sat talking and drinking a little after-dinner sweet wine, the moon came up, peering around the trees along the lakeside and spilling its golden path across the top of the shimmering water.

"Sure is beautiful here on the lake, isn't it, sweetie?" I asked.

"Yes. I wouldn't want to live anywhere else, baby."

"How about I show you how much I love you and am going to miss you tomorrow?"

"Oh, Dell, you silly man!"

We went inside, turned out the lights, closed the bedroom door so Chauncey wouldn't interrupt us, and retired for the evening.

★

When I got up to take my morning shower, it was really early. There weren't even any little specks of light on the horizon yet that would suggest a new day was dawning. I finished my shower, got dressed, kissed Suzi on the cheek, and headed out the door. I figured I would stop along the way to have a cup of coffee and something to eat. I headed out of our access road to the lake, and within twenty minutes I was rolling down Route 9, often referred to as the Airline Road. It stretches across counties to link up at Bangor and provides easy access to I-95, North and South. The road is about ninety miles long and travels through a good portion of Maine wilderness. There seem to be lots of small logging roads running off of the Airline into the deeper woods, as well as some hunting lodges. About halfway down the Airline toward Bangor, there's a snack bar, motel, gas station, convenience store combo on the right side of the highway. While it may not look like much, they serve great food, especially breakfast.

I went to the counter and placed my order for a bacon and egg on toast sandwich and a large coffee, to go. After paying, I went into the little one-stall bathroom in the corner to wash up. My cell phone notified me I had a text, and I checked it. It was from Frank saying he was still on and for me to pick him up at the exit on I-95 South. After fixing up my coffee with creamer (I have to use nondairy powdered creamer to avoid stomach problems), I waited another five minutes or so and was given a brown paper sack with my sandwich in it.

As I continued along the Airline, eating my breakfast as I drove, I thought about our case. It seemed to me that the ballistics and physical evidence pointed toward a professional shooter, and if that was the case, I knew they're often never located. Being professionals, they have a real tendency not to leave incriminating evidence. They're often simply voices on a phone who move about the world from job to job, never making much of an impression on anyone, much less drawing attention to themselves. Even if you could identify the voice on the phone, there's often a third party who makes the contact for the job and arranges the payment process. That's not to say that some hit men aren't found and prosecuted, but the percentage is smaller than we, in law enforcement, would like to admit.

But sometimes it's easier to locate the person who contracted the hit. Often, that's a person you can locate, and you can identify their desire or need to have someone eliminated and then hopefully build a reasonable case against them. While the professional hit man is normally cold, methodical and detached from his victim, the person who hired them is most likely close to the victim in some way and benefits from their death in a personal way. That makes them easier to identify and prosecute.

While I was thinking about the case as a professional hit, I also realized that we could be entirely wrong. The shooter could just be a very good or well-trained shot. The physical evidence makes a suggestion as to a potential killer, but there was much more information needed to form any real objective opinions, and far more to form the basis for a successful prosecution. *Nobody said this was an easy job,* I thought to myself.

About an hour later, I saw Lieutenant Bell's cruiser sitting along the exit ramp, just off I-95. I pulled up beside him, and he said that he wanted to leave his car at the gas station at the exit, so I followed him there so he could secure his car and ride with me. He carried a small briefcase and his cup of coffee from McDonald's.

We pulled back onto I-95 South and headed toward I-295 and Portland. As we pulled into the north end of town, we located our first stop: Greene's Pineywoods Assisted Living Unit. Before getting out of the Tahoe, we both secured our weapons in a gun locker I keep in the rear cargo area.

"I don't like going into a secure Alzheimer's Unit, Frank, with any weapons on us. Let's be sure we maintain everyone's safety. You never know if someone there may get a bit close or seem to be acting irrationally. They might try to grab one of our weapons."

We walked into the unit after identifying ourselves and being buzzed in through the secure door. We met with a staff member and asked to have a private meeting with Mrs. Elizabeth Tressman. The staff member directed us to a small room on the right side of the hallway with a wooden table and a few wooden chairs. The young lady then told us she would bring "Beth" out to sit with us in a few minutes.

About ten minutes later, the same young lady wheeled an older woman out to the room in a wheelchair. She introduced Elizabeth Tressman to both of us and told her that we had come down from Castaway County to talk with her for a while. The young lady asked Mrs. Tressman if she wanted her to stay with her, and Mrs. Tressman said she would. So we closed the door to the room and sat down to interview this woman who we hoped could give us some information about Danny Windom, the estranged son of the Windoms.

"Mrs. Tressman, we're trying to locate Danny Windom. Do you know Danny?"

"Oh, I know Danny. He's a nice boy. Always liked him."

"Do you know where he is today, ma'am?"

"Oh, he's the cigar man."

"What do you mean, Elizabeth?"

"He sells them, you know. Best cigar salesman ever. I know he is. Best one ever!"

"Do you know where he sells cigars?"

"Down at that big cigar store. You know, the one in South Carolina, near the beaches. The one everyone goes to buy cigars."

"Do you remember the name of the store?"

"No ... don't remember names much these days. I just know it's big. I have a photo of Danny in the store ... somewhere." Mrs. Tressman began looking through the large handbag she had tucked beside her on the seat of the wheelchair. As she was rummaging through the contents of the bag, she began muttering to herself.

"Should be here ... can't find anything these days ... maybe those other ladies took it ... oh drat! ... maybe I left it in my room ..." Then finally, as if she had just found a lost treasure, she exclaimed, "Here it is!"

She handed the photo to me: it was of a young man, standing in front of a cigar store counter with hundreds of cigars and boxes of cigars surrounding the room and the countertops. The man's face looked a bit younger than I expected Danny to be now, but he might just have had a youthful appearance. I asked Mrs. Tressman if I could have the young lady staff member make a photocopy of the picture to assist me in finding Danny, and she agreed.

"Have you heard from Danny recently?" I asked.

"No one comes to see me in here."

As she said that, the young lady shook her head slightly at us and told Mrs. Tressman, "Now, Beth, one of your relatives came by to see you just the other day, a niece of yours I think. Don't you remember?"

"No, I don't remember anyone coming in to see me, Dominique. Was it my mother? Where is she?"

"No, dear, your mother can't drive here to see you. The trip is too far for her."

At that point, Mrs. Tressman just started mumbling again. She was talking about her mother and then changed to talking about some missing children.

She turned to Frank and asked him if he had found her missing children. Before Frank could think of any answer, the young lady redirected Elizabeth, telling her that she needed to take her back to her room to get ready for the musical guests who were to arrive before lunch. She winked at me and put up a finger to tell us to wait a minute and she would return.

As she turned Mrs. Tressman to leave the room, I patted her on the shoulder and thanked her for seeing us. She told me that we could come visit her anytime, and Dominique wheeled her back to her room.

"Well, Frank, that's about the best I think we're gonna get from her. She started well but seemed to get confused pretty quickly."

"Gosh, Dell, Alzheimer's is really an insidious disease, isn't it?"

"It sure is. Wouldn't wish that on anyone, even if I didn't like them."

In a few minutes, the young lady, Dominique, returned with our copy of the photo. She told us that Mrs. Tressman did get visitors from time to time, most often a niece, and sometimes she brought her boyfriend. It was just that Elizabeth didn't have any memory of the visits once they left. She also told us that the "missing children" was one of the normal manifestations of her disease.

I asked about her mother, and the young lady told us that Elizabeth's mother had died many years before, but she often asked staff and visitors alike where she was because she had no understanding that the mother passed.

"Why don't you just tell her that?" I asked.

"Well, you have to put yourself into her reality when you talk to her. Otherwise, you just get her upset, and she won't believe you anyway. The doctors tell us to just agree with their reality and try to redirect them to another, more happy issue."

"I must admit, I've been a cop most of my life, but I could never do your job. I have a lot of admiration for you and the job you do here."

She thanked us and escorted us out of the secure area of the facility. Frank and I stood outside in the sunshine and breathed deeply. It certainly is hard to see our older people in that condition and to know that there are really no better alternatives in caring for them. *It kind of makes you not want to grow old*, I thought. *There but for the grace of God ...*

12

Our next interview was with Becky and Sean O'Malley, the late Betty Dillon's brother and sister-in-law. As we approached their house, I noticed that it was a neat row house with an emerald green door. The doorknocker was a gold-colored Celtic trinity symbol, all of which made the Irish effect the better. In this part of town, with its high level of Irish ancestry, many of the houses were bright colored, resembling "the old country."

When we knocked, a slightly plump, redheaded woman of about forty came to the door.

"Ah, and you'd be Sheriff Hinton, I'm supposin'. And who is this other fine gentleman then?"

"Mrs. O'Malley, this is Lieutenant Frank Bell of the Maine State Police Criminal Investigations Bureau. As I said on the phone, we wanted to talk to you and Sean about our case and your sister-in-law."

"Come in, come in. Sean will be here in a moment. He left work a little while ago. Pity that, about Betty. Sean is taking it pretty hard, but they really needed him at work."

"Well, we're very sorry for your family's loss," Frank said.

"Sit yourselves down right there and be comfortable. Can I get you either a coffee or a tea?"

"Mrs. O'Malley, I would love a coffee. How about you, Frank?"

"Oh, a coffee would be just fine, ma'am."

"Now the both of you call me Becky. Mrs. O'Malley was me mother-in-law, God rest her soul, not me!"

"Okay, Becky it is then," I said as we sat down in two easy chairs she had pointed out for us.

As she was puttering around the kitchen making us some coffee, I looked around the room and saw several photographs of what appeared to be family members in Ireland, as well as some famous Irish prints framed and hanging in appropriate places on the walls. The table between the chairs we sat in was covered with a piece of beautiful Irish lace, and beside the lamp was one of those small harps made out of Irish peat. *You can't escape this family's heritage for a moment*, I thought.

Presently, I heard a door open in the kitchen and heard a man's voice greeting his wife. He apparently kissed her, and she directed him into the front room where we were waiting to talk to him. As he came in the room, I saw he had broad shoulders, was about five feet ten, and had sandy hair. He walked over and thrust out his hand to Frank first, then me.

"Mr. O'Malley. Lieutenant Bell and I wanted to speak to you while we were in town. I've spoken to Becky before, but wanted to ask you a few additional questions, if you don't mind. We're truly sorry for your loss and want you to know we're working hard to try to find out who did this terrible thing."

"I miss Betty, to be sure. She and I were the closest of our parents' kids. Grace, unfortunately, was kind of the odd duck out in the family. But Betty and I were close."

I noticed right away that Sean, although having an Irish name, didn't seem to have the brogue his wife had, and I mentioned that fact. He responded that while he was first-generation American, she had actually been born and raised in Ireland. She had attended school at Kylemore Abbey, in the west of Ireland.

The Abbey was a famous boarding school for girls, run by Benedictine nuns, serving generations of people throughout the world until the school closed in 2010, but the nuns remained and kept the building open as a tourist attraction and convent for the order. I was familiar with the Abby since one of my mothers-in-law had also attended school there. On one of my visits to Ireland, I had toured Kylemore and had seen firsthand the beautiful lake, the mountainside, and their historic gardens. *What a beautiful place to have gone to school*, I thought.

"So, Becky gave me some of the background information on Betty's husband, Oscar, I believe it was?"

"Yes, he was a real shit, that man. I found out he was knocking her about, and we had it out!"

"So you told him to stop?" Frank asked.

"Well, you could say that. I kicked his ever-lovin' arse is what I did."

"How long ago was that?"

"About six months before he died. But he never hit her again, so far as I know."

"Becky said that Oscar was in a tough business?"

"He worked for one of the bookies in town."

"Any idea what he did for the bookie?" Frank interjected.

"Yeah, he was an enforcer. He would be sure that the person who owed the money paid up."

"My guess is that meant use of violence as necessary?" I asked.

"Pretty much. He was a violent guy at heart. Never used a gun on someone, but he sure could take to them with a bat or brass knuckles. He could be a terror, that one. No milk of human kindness, as Becky would say."

"And he died a year ago, right?"

"Yup, and good riddance to the bastard, I say!"

"How did Oscar die, may I ask?"

"Died in a suspicious fire, just down in the Old Port. A little shack beside one of the buildings on the pier caught fire, and old Oscar burned up in it."

"So what made the fire suspicious?" Frank asked.

"Well, I hear that they never found what started the fire in the first place. And besides, the little shack was just for storing tools and the like, so there was only a little in there that was flammable. You know, just some bags of rags, maybe some old boat sails, not much more than that, I hear."

"But they evidently identified Oscar's remains?"

"I think they identified them because they had a witness see him go in the shack but not come back out. I'm not sure what testing was done; you'd have to ask the police that one."

"So, Sean, had you talked to Betty since she moved to Castaway County?"

"We talked on the phone a few times. She seemed to be happy and enjoyed her job at the truck stop. She said working the nightshift gave her down time so she could sometimes work on her book."

"What book is that?"

"She was writing a kind of a memoir about having been married to Oscar and him being in the enforcer business. She was hoping the book might make her some money for retirement."

"Do you know if anyone else knew about the book she was writing?"

"I doubt it. She was very closed mouthed about her writing. She didn't think she was any good at writing in the first place, and she wouldn't likely mention the project to anyone else until she was finished and had decided she could, after all, write a book."

Frank and I looked at each other as if asking if there were any other questions we might have, and it was clear from our mutual expressions that we couldn't think of any more to ask Sean. We continued talking to Sean and Becky about Betty's funeral plans and other more pleasant issues like Sean's work and how beautifully Becky kept house. After we finished our coffee and took our empty cups to her kitchen and put them in the sink, we said our good-byes and got back in my Tahoe.

"You know, Frank, we were going to try to see Sean's other sister, Grace Tilden, but I think we got enough family history from Sean and Becky. Why don't we just run by Portland PD and see about Oscar's death?"

"Sounds good to me, Dell. You got some idea brewing?"

"Well, I want to know just how they determined Oscar was the body in the shack by the pier. What if, for the sake of argument, Oscar wasn't dead?"

"You thinking he might have wanted his wife killed?"

"Well, he got a good thrashing because of her from Sean. And maybe he knew about her planned book. Who knows?"

"Okay, Dell, the police department it is!"

About twenty minutes later, we were entering the Portland Police Department headquarters. We located a Sergeant Bill Reilly on the second floor and began asking him about the Oscar Dillon case.

"Aw, we don't have much in the way of material on that one," Reilly told us after searching through a bunch of old files in boxes. He pulled out a very thin file and handed it to us to look through. "I remember that call though. A burning shack down in the Old Port. Not much damage before they put it out, just a body inside."

"Do you know how they identified the body as that of Oscar Dillon?" I asked while Frank continued to look over the two-page report form he'd found in the file folder.

"Don't think it was necessary. I mean we had a witness to him going in the building and not having left. And did you guys know this Oscar was a local enforcer?"

"Yes, we did."

"Well, to tell the truth, I think we just figured he'd gotten what he deserved, so there wasn't too much extra time taken on his case. You know what I mean?"

About then, Frank broke in. "According to the report, the witness was Harry Grimes. Who's he?"

"Oh, just another employee of the bookie/ loan shark, Big Eddy Whalen. Big wheel in the old days, but not much these days. Big Eddy, I mean."

"So Oscar and this Harry Grimes both worked for Big Eddy?"

"Yup. But like I said, Big Eddy isn't a big fish these days. Portland's grown out of that old stuff. Years ago, now."

"Oh, I believe you. Portland's a beautiful city, and the Old Port section is a great area. My girlfriend and I travel down sometimes to go to the Comedy Club in the Old Port. We like to see Bob Marley, the comedian. Funniest guy I ever heard, and that Maine humor!"

"Yeah, I like that guy too," Frank said, "and I understand he's a great fellow to boot!"

"We see him around town a lot, and he does some charity work in town," the sergeant said. "And you're right; he's a peach of a guy!"

After we talked a few more minutes to the sergeant, Frank asked him for a copy of the report on the Oscar Dillon case, and we left the station.

"Frank, it makes you wonder about the body and just who it may have been."

"I agree, Dell, but it's late, and we need to get back. How about if you call the local coroner tomorrow and check on that end of it?"

"Yeah, that works for me. How about I buy you some dinner on the way back home?"

"Sounds good. Where are we going?"

"Ever been to the Harraseeket Lunch and Lobster, Frank?"

"Nope. Good?"

"Best you'll ever have. They have a plate: small lobster, steamer clams, potatoes, and an ear of corn. And they're all just great. Then we can top that off with their wild, Maine blueberry crumble!"

"Sounds great to me, Dell."

"It's just up the road a bit in South Freeport."

"Great. Then we can stop at L. L. Bean after supper?"

"Sure, Frank. They're open 24/7. What are you looking for?"

"I need a new pair of their hunting boots. The pair I have are at least twenty years old, and I'm afraid they're finally starting to show some age. Besides, I'd like to look around at their camping gear."

"I didn't know you camp, Frank!"

"I do."

"Well, I can always look through their kayaks and gear. I enjoy going out on the lake in a kayak. Just gliding over the surface, low to the water, with no sounds but nature!"

"Well, Bean's is the place. If you can't find it there, you just don't need it. Nowadays, they have multiple buildings just full of good stuff."

"Damn, Frank, you sound like a commercial!"

"No way, just a good fan of the company and their products. I mean, really, Dell, L. L. Bean *is* Maine!"

"Yup, I guess you're right about that. Good news for us is, since it's open all the time, we don't have to hurry through our dinner at the Lunch and Lobster."

"What about Suzi, Dell?"

"Gosh, I almost forgot. I need to give her a call and remind her I won't be home for dinner. She knew it was a possibility."

"Well, go ahead and make your call. I'll just sit here thinking about the additional information we gathered for our case. Seems we got even more questions than we did answers."

"Yeah, that's what makes the job fun, Frank, following the leads in all kinds of different directions."

"Okay, Dell, you call. I'll contemplate."

Then both of us said at the same time, "Then we eat!"

We really are incorrigible. We really are!

13

After Frank and I enjoyed a nice lobster and steamer dinner at the Lunch and Lobster in South Freeport, we drove the two miles up to the L. L. Bean stores in the center of Freeport. Frank shopped for some camping equipment, while I went to the building that had the kayaks and other water sports equipment. We spent the best part of an hour looking around the various departments at Bean's and picked up a few small things here and there. I met Frank back near the main entrance of the flagship building, and we headed to my Tahoe and back up toward Waterville.

"Frank, I've been mulling it over. I think we now have a couple of good potential suspects in the case."

"Yes, there are more questions than answers in my mind."

"We need to locate Danny Windom or Clinton Alexander, whichever name he goes by these days. I really want to talk to him and see if he held a grudge against the Windoms."

"What do you think, Dell? Could he be that upset at his adoptive parents?"

"Yes, I think he could. Between finding out about being adopted the way he did and the fact that he was a teenager at the time ... yes, I think that could push him over the edge. Especially if he wasn't that well balanced in the first place. Who knows?"

"What about Oscar? You think he might still be around? I mean it seems to me that Portland PD may have made some assumptions and let it go at that."

"Well, I don't want to be critical, but it sounds like more questions could have been asked. I don't want to second guess another agency though. Maybe they had their reasons."

"I'll see if I can get hold of the coroner's office tomorrow. Maybe they made positive ID and it just didn't make it into the PD's report or file. I've seen that happen before. Pages of reports do get lost or misplaced."

"Okay, and I'll spend some time tomorrow trying to track down the whereabouts of Danny Windom."

"Where did the old lady say he was, Dell? A big cigar store in South Carolina near a beach?"

"Well, the first place I'll start is in the Myrtle Beach area. It's one of the biggest and best-known areas and, as I recall from traveling there when I was younger, and there are a few really good cigar stores along the Grand Strand."

"Well, we can both work on our investigating, and how about I call you tomorrow evening around five? That work for you, Dell?"

"Sounds good. I'll get home in time to catch a few hours of sleep."

I dropped Frank off at his cruiser in the gas station parking lot and headed back to Castaway County. The ride out the Airline Road seemed twice as long since the snack bar halfway down was long closed by the time I got there, so there was no coffee break for me.

I arrived home just after midnight, went in quietly, washed off a bit, and crawled into bed beside Suzi. It was late, and she was already sleeping, so I tried not to wake her. I lay there beside her for a second and just looked at her beautiful, creamy skin in the moonlight coming through the partially open window. *She's really a beautiful woman, and I'm lucky to have found her,* I thought. I reached over and put my arm around her, and she just murmured and slid her warm body back against mine so that I was cradling her entire body. It was all I could do not to start something, but I knew it was late and she had to get up early for work, so I was satisfied with holding her close. In a few minutes, I fell right off into a pleasant dream.

★

Suzi's alarm rang at about four-thirty, and she got up to shower and head into work. My alarm rang at seven o'clock. Normally, I would have probably gotten up when Suzi was out of the shower and had some coffee and crumb cake with her, but I was tired from the trip to Portland, so I stayed in bed until the alarm went off. Just before Suzi left, she came in and gave me a peck on the cheek and told me she was planning to cook dinner tonight.

After my shower, Chauncey came into the kitchen to get some petting while I tried to enjoy my coffee. He walked over to me and did the kitty-flop right near my feet, but just far enough away that I needed to take a step and reach down to pet him. I've always thought that was Chauncey's way of showing me who was the king of our house. He almost never makes it easy for me to pet him, like sitting on my lap or something. He just wants to be petted and makes me move to go to him. *Guess I know who's in charge here, don't I?* I thought to myself as I took a step and bent down to pet him. *He's still my little boy!*

After my coffee and crumb cake, I decided to head into the office a bit early. I wanted to start looking up information to try to locate Danny Windom. I also wanted to get with Berk so I could brief him on yesterday's interviews.

When I arrived at the office, Irish gave me a cup of coffee and sent Berk a message to stop by my office to see me. I began looking through the overnights to see what was going on in the county. Since I had been out of the office all day yesterday, Irish had also provided copies of the day reports to get me caught up. Most of the reports were of the normal activities expected: a gas drive off, a couple of false alarms at businesses, a petty larceny from a store, two property damage accidents, and the like. One report was about a small trash fire at the jail. The report listed a small amount of smoke damage in one corner of the cellblock, but no injuries. It sounded small, but I wanted to be sure, so I walked over to the jail. Berk's brother, Allen, was on duty, so I chatted with him.

"Hey, Allen, how's it going today?"

"Fine, Sheriff, fine. Had a small fire yesterday in one of the blocks. Figured I might see you this morning."

"You are."

"Guess you want to see the area?"

"I do."

So we walked back into the cellblock area. I noticed the aroma of burnt paper and noticed that in the far corner of the deputy's walkway there were some blackened places on the paint of the wall. The metal trashcan that normally sat in that corner of the walkway had been removed, but there was a clear mark where it had been sitting when the fire was burning.

"Apparently some of the inmates who we had in this block were upset or just bored. They kept throwing paper and toilet paper into the trashcan until it had overflowed. Then some wise apple managed to get a match in here and threw it right into the pile. Up she went. Set off a smoke detector, and you could see the flames in the security camera."

"So where are the inmates now?"

"Moved 'em out and split them up so we can investigate. Once we know exactly what happened, we'll place in-house charges on them. We're just finishing up the cleanup, and I'll get one of the trusty inmates right on a painting detail. It will be back to normal shortly, boss."

"Good."

"Once we get the inmate or inmates identified, I'll see if they have any money on their books, and if so, we can make the in-house charges include some restitution for the painting and cleanup."

"Even better."

"I can check with the prosecutor's office about criminal charges."

"Well, let's finish the investigation first. If it was a dumb prank, in-house charges will get their attention, especially if we take some of their money for restitution. If it was more than that, we can initiate criminal charges."

"Sounds good to me, Sheriff."

"I just don't like taking up the court's time and energy for things we can handle. They have enough on their plate, just like us. Especially these days."

"Right, Sheriff."

"Oh, and don't forget, Allen, we need to forward a copy of the damage report to the State Department of Corrections. They need to be advised of any damage done, however slight, to the building for their records. That way they have it for our next jail certification review."

"Okay, boss, I'll take care of that if you like."

"I would. And thanks, Allen."

Just as I walked back toward my office, I saw Berk pulling into the parking lot. I waited for him, and we walked into my office together.

I spent the next twenty minutes or so briefing him on the interviews Frank and I had conducted in Portland the day before. I told him that Frank was looking into Oscar Dillon's death case and that we needed to try to locate Danny Windom. I asked Berk to give me a listing of the cigar stores in the Myrtle Beach area. He said he would go to the deputy's room and get on the computer. About ten minutes later, he came back and handed me a list of stores and their phone numbers. I asked him to stay, and we began making calls, with the phone set to speaker function so Berk could hear the conversations too.

The first one on the list was East End Cigars in Myrtle Beach. A man answered who had a clear New York accent. When I identified myself as the sheriff in Castaway County, Maine, he responded, "Well, it's great to talk to a fellow officer. I worked the PD in New York. I'm John. I own the place. What can I do for you, Sheriff?"

"I'm trying to locate a guy who we were told worked at a big cigar store, possibly in your area. I'm not sure when he would have been down there but sometime in the last ten years."

"Okay, I've been open here for about eight years. What's the name you got?"

"Well, I have two potential names. Danny Windom or Clinton Alexander are the two we know about."

"Sounds like your guy is a name changer. But I've never had anyone with either of those names work here. Actually, my store is fairly small, so I just employ one or two other people who I know pretty well. But most of the time, it's just me here."

"Actually the kid was adopted. That's why I have two names right now. But who knows?"

"Well you started off saying the cigar store was big?"

"That's the information we got, but we got it from an elderly lady who has Alzheimer's, so there is no telling. She did show us a photo, and it showed the kid standing in a pretty big store with lots of display cases and cigars stacked on shelves."

"Well, that could be Nick's. Nick's Cigar World is pretty big like that. He has multiple locations, even a nice cigar bar. But his main store in North Myrtle is pretty big. You might try there. Here, I'll give you Nick's number."

After John gave us the number, we talked about the area another few moments and bid each other good-bye. He seemed like a real nice fellow, and as another cop, he was very helpful. I then called the number he had given me for Nick's Cigar World. When the phone was answered, I asked if the manager was in and was told that the owner, Nick, was there. In a minute, Nick came to the phone.

"Nick, this is Dell Hinton. I'm the sheriff in Castaway County, Maine. I'm trying to locate a kid who may have been working at your cigar store sometime in the last ten years."

"Well, that narrows it down, Sheriff. What's his name?"

"Well, he could have been Danny Windom or Clinton Alexander; we're not sure which name."

"Was he changing his name to protect the innocent, Sheriff?" Nick asked with a snicker.

"Actually, he was adopted, and we aren't sure which name he might have used."

"I don't remember anyone by either of those names. Let me check my files a minute."

After a couple of minutes, Nick returned to the phone and confirmed that he had never had anyone by either of those names working for him. I described the photo we had been shown by Elizabeth Tressman and her general description of the area Danny had been working in.

"You know," Nick said, "it isn't in South Carolina at the beaches, but the description sounds more like Carolina Sticks Cigars up in North Carolina. It's right along the interstate, 95, and it's one of the largest cigar stores in the east, maybe the country."

"No beaches around it?"

"No, but it's the cigar store a lot of folks stop at on their way to the Myrtle Beach area or traveling the I-95 corridor. Might be worth a call to you."

"Thanks, Nick. John at East End Cigars gave me your name, and he told me you have a nice cigar bar!"

"Opened it last year. It's right beside my main store here, and you can walk right in from the cigar shop side. We serve beer and wine, nice atmosphere to meet and greet. If you ever get down here, Sheriff, come by, and I'll treat you to a fine cigar!"

"Thanks, Nick, I really appreciate you taking time to talk, and I may just take you up on that cigar."

"Sounds good. In the meantime, you can check our website to order anything we have. I expect you don't have too many good cigar shops out there in the backwoods of Maine, do you?"

"Nope, closest to me is in Bangor."

We talked a few minutes more and then hung up. *Another real nice guy!* I then called information to get a phone number for Carolina Sticks Cigars in North Carolina.

When I was connected to a business manager at Carolina Sticks, I gave him the names for Danny and asked about past employment, if any.

"Well, we never had either of those names working here, but we did have a Danny Alexander who worked here. Could that be him?"

"It very well could be. When did he work there?"

"This was about eight years ago, now. He worked here in April of 2004. Seems he lasted for about a year and a half. Got good marks in his file for knowing a lot about cigars."

"Say why he left or where he went?"

"Says here that he was moving out west somewhere. We don't follow ex-employees though."

"No, I'd expect not. Was he close to anyone still there, maybe a good friend?"

"File shows he had Clifford Delse listed as his emergency contact. Cliff's still here."

"Is he in now?"

"No, he'll be in this evening starting around four."

"Okay, how about if I call back then and see if he knows anything about Danny?"

"Okay with me. Maybe Cliff can help you out."

After the call, Berk and I discussed the information we had now, and I wrote the third name of Danny Alexander on the file I was maintaining for the case. Berk was going back out on patrol, so I decided it was time for some lunch and headed down to the Diner to see if I could relax a bit and have a bite. *Hope they have a nice soup or chowder today,* I thought. *Think I ate too much last night in South Freeport, but it sure was great!*

14

I walked into the Woodburn Diner and was greeted by some of our local citizens. As usual, some asked about how the job was going, and others asked about the status of the Black Bear case. I told them we were working with the State Police Investigations Section and that we were still following up on various leads. I also said we were getting great cooperation from everyone in the community and elsewhere, which makes our job easier. I've learned over time that most members of the community understand that the police can't give them much information about an ongoing case. And, frankly, they're okay with that so long as they can see that the police are *actively* investigating and trying to solve the crime. And, in these times when our federal government seems to be showing a great lack of communication and compromise, the citizens of our smaller communities like to know that communication and cooperation are not dirty words. So, as sheriff, I want to give the citizens a sense that we're fulfilling the mandates of our jobs.

I sat at the counter and ordered a bowl of soup and a grilled cheese sandwich. In a few minutes, just as the waitress sat my food down in front of me, Father Dexter walked into the diner.

"Hey, Dex! What brings you in here today?"

"Same as you, Dell, lunchtime."

"How about I move over to that booth and we can sit and chat a while?"

So I picked up my soup and sandwich, and Dex and I sat at a booth toward the rear of the diner. After the usual small talk about basketball, Dex asked about the Bear case.

"Well, we've been following up on a lot of leads, Dex. Traveled to Portland with Frank yesterday to conduct some interviews."

"Anything good come up there?"

"As usual, just more unanswered questions. By the way, thanks for all your help with Mrs. Windom."

"Not at all, Dell. Good family, very supportive of my church."

"Did you know their son, Danny?"

"Only when he was young. He was a good boy in those days. I've heard bits of rumor here and there over the years about him, but not much was good."

"What kind of rumors, Dex?"

"Well, the Grahams went on a vacation out west a few years ago and said they thought they saw Danny walking down the street. When they walked up to him and started to speak to him, he muttered something about 'old life' and walked off. He never even acknowledged them!"

"No kidding."

"No. Then they began to question whether it was really him. But they had both known him since he was a kid, so they figured it was him. He had a short, military style haircut, but they thought for sure it was him."

"Any other rumors?"

"Another of my flock said he thought he'd seen Danny at a big cigar store once when he was traveling down to Florida. He never said where it was, and I don't think he even tried to talk to Danny."

"I know where that was. I tracked him to a cigar store in North Carolina, along I-95. I'm waiting to talk to a coworker of his for more information, but I understand he went west from there."

"That's about it, Dell. No one else has seen or even heard about him that I know of. Seems he just wanted to leave this area behind him and disappear."

"Yeah, it sounds like he was avoiding something or running away from something."

"I always kind of suspected that it had to do with the troubles he had with his father. They were a lot alike, and yet ... well his father was kind of strict and kept at him about stuff, you know?"

"How's that, Dex?"

"Well, I don't think Danny ever lived up to Paul's expectations. Many kids don't. But in Paul's and Danny's case, Paul seemed to push him a lot, like he was trying to get him to 'man up' about life in general."

"I guess that could set the stage for some parental rage."

"You thinking he might be involved in the Bear murders, Dell?"

"Oh, I don't know at this point. Let's just say he's certainly a person of interest. There are other persons of interest as well, so I'm not putting my eggs all in one basket. But I want to find out more about Danny and to locate him so we can talk."

"Well, good luck with that and may the good Lord be with you on this case."

"Thanks, Dex. I'm sure I'll need all the help I can get!"

We spent the rest of our lunch talking about the prospects for the Boston Celtics for the next season and when the next bean supper was scheduled, so that I would be sure to attend. Dex always wants me to attend the church socials: he says it's good for my political career and community support, but I think it's because I usually bring Suzi with me. Dex knows a beautiful woman when he sees one.

After we said our good-byes, I went back to my office. Before I got fully through the door, Irish told me that I needed to respond to the courthouse. Apparently they had some problem over there and wanted some help.

When I arrived at the courthouse, I saw Deputy Robert Burns in front of the District Court courtroom. He had not yet opened the door for the afternoon session.

"Hey, boss, glad you could come over."

"What do you have, Bob?"

"You remember that vehicular accident where the kid, Davies, was killed out by Dauphine Crossroads?"

"Yes, the other guy was OUI and caused the accident."

"That's the one. Well, we have a preliminary hearing today in that case. The prosecutor finally placed charges on the OUI driver, his name is Malecy Smith, and we have both families here for the case."

"What's the issue with them?"

"When I say all the family members, I mean all of them." Bob pointed across the hallway, and I could see about forty people, some sitting, some standing for lack of chairs and benches. And the people were clearly formed into two groups, each one staring at the other, and some beginning to make loud comments. *This could get ugly, real quick,* I thought.

I decided that simply walking over between the groups might actually serve to create more of a problem if they began pitching their opposing views of each other to me while I was just trying to keep them calm. I'd seen that happen before where an officer walked in trying to keep things calm and actually became the catalyst for starting a big uproar. So I told Bob to stay there, and I went out by the front doors and called our dispatcher. I asked them to send Deputy Billy Teal in with King.

Shortly after I had taken office as sheriff, I had dealt with some rowdy inmates at the jail by using Dr. Clopper's dog, Ben, to get the inmates to lock down in their cells. Knowing from my experience in Boston PD what a great asset K-9 units are, I had worked with Berk to get a unit in the budget process. Although the dog itself is often donated to the sheriff's office, there has to be funds budgeted for the training, medical care, food, and specialized equipment necessary to support a K-9 unit. Once that had been approved, the budget process being rather lengthy, I had selected Deputy Teal, and we had received the dog. Then I sent Billy and his dog, King, to a K-9 training school near Worcester, Massachusetts, where both received training. The whole process had taken almost a year to complete, but we now had an excellent K-9 unit for Castaway County.

Billy Teal and King arrived in about fifteen minutes. I met them at the door and told Billy what we had. I suggested that we both walk casually into the waiting area and simply take a position between the two groups and continue having a normal discussion with each other.

Billy and I walked into the area, and as we began a casual discussion, King sat down beside Billy's leg and just stared at the people in both groups. As I looked around, I realized that all of the people were looking right back at King and paying no attention to one another. Finally, two individuals from one of the families stood and walked over toward the public restrooms. As they walked past us, one spoke.

"Man, that dog looks mean!"

"Well, he doesn't like problems. That's why he's here. Hopefully no one will start any, and King can just relax on the cool floor for a while."

"Hope he's well trained. I don't wanna get bit!"

"If you don't start any problems, he'll never bother you at all. He only gets upset when people start acting foolish."

I told Bob he could open court when his judge was ready, and Billy and I stayed out in the hallway for the entire hearing. When it was about to end, Bob called me on the cell phone, and I walked into the courtroom to assess the mood of the crowd. Although there were clearly some heightened emotions raised by the preliminary hearing process, there were no indications of any pending violence. To be sure, I had Billy and King edge closer to the doors of the courtroom, and we actually walked the families out of the building in a fairly orderly manner. Once everyone had left the building, I thanked Billy and King and walked back toward my office. *I'm sure glad we put that K-9 unit in the budget!*

When I got back into the office, Irish handed me a cup of coffee, and I grabbed a cigar out of my humidor. I leaned back in my chair and puffed, quite content with thoughts swirling around in my head.

I thought about how being a sheriff was so much different than being a detective or beat cop. When I was a detective and I had a big case or two, I would work those cases all day, every day until I solved them or they became cold. The point being, I could essentially concentrate on doing only those specific investigations. But here, in a smaller community and in a sheriff's office, I had many areas to supervise, all the while trying to solve a big case. There was just no way I could concentrate on one big case, because as soon as I did, something happened at the jail or the courts or civil process or just personnel matters, all of which required my time and attention. I just had to continue giving as much attention to the big cases as I could, while running the day-to-day functions of my office. *This isn't an easy job, here, Dell, but it is very satisfying. Guess I expected a challenge, and I got one,* I thought.

It was almost four fifteen, and I remembered it was a good time to try to catch Clifford Delse at work in the Carolina Sticks Smoke Shop in North Carolina. He was a friend of Danny Windom's, or at least we thought, so I wanted to get up with him.

I called the store and asked for Clifford. Pretty soon a guy came on the phone and identified himself as Cliff.

"Cliff, I'm Sheriff Dell Hinton from Castaway County, Maine. I called to ask you a few questions about one of your coworkers."

"Oh, hi, Sheriff. They told me you were going to call today. It's about Danny Alexander, right?"

"Yes, that's the name he went by when he worked at your store, we think."

"That's him. I do know he mentioned once he was from Maine."

"So did you two talk often?"

"Sure. We roomed together most of the time he worked here."

"Did he ever mention any family here in Maine?"

"No, never mentioned any family at all. Now that you ask, I just always assumed that any family he had was dead."

"When he talked to you about Maine, was he speaking negatively about living here?"

"Not so's I noticed. I think he only mentioned Maine the one time when we had just seen an ad on TV about some ski resort up there. And then he just said he knew of it because he was from Maine."

"Well, Cliff, what was Danny like when you knew him?"

"Pretty good guy. Fairly quiet though. Always did a good job at the store and seemed to like cigars a lot."

"Any odd things about him you ever noticed? You know, things that made you question him or just wonder about him?"

"Well, when he first arrived at the store, I don't think he had any interest in hunting. I mean we, the rest of the employees, would talk about hunting trips and the like, and Danny never seemed to get involved in the discussions."

"So that changed?"

"Well it seemed to. I started to notice some new *Guns and Ammo* magazines and other hunting and gun books lying around our apartment that I knew I had never bought. I just thought he was trying to fit in or something, you know?"

"And I'm guessing something happened to make you question that assumption?"

"Yeah, when he told me he was leaving and moving west, he said he was planning to take a job with a sporting goods store in their gun department."

"Hmmm, did Danny ever tell you where he was moving in the west or what store he was planning to work at?"

"I think it was a place called Plunkett's. The only reason I remember is because I thought it was a strange name. I'm not sure, but I kind of think it was somewhere in Arizona. Don't remember if he mentioned a town though."

"So do you ever hear from Danny?"

"Last time I heard from him was a postcard he sent me from Montana. Billings, I think. But I don't know if he was living there or just passing through. Other than that, I had almost forgotten about him."

"How long ago did you get that postcard, Cliff?"

"Oh, it was probably two years ago now, I'd guess."

"Okay, Cliff. You've been very helpful. Thanks for taking time to talk with me. If you remember anything else, just give me a call." I gave him my office number.

"So now that I've answered your questions, what did Danny do?"

"Well, we're not sure he did anything. His name has just come up in a case we have as a person of interest. Could be nothing or maybe he has some information about the case we need. Thanks again for talking to me."

After I hung up with Clifford Delse, Irish waved at me that I had another call. It was Frank.

"Hey, Frank. How's it going on your end today?"

"Well, I told you I'd call and we could touch base. I checked with the coroner's office in Portland, and they said they made the ID on Oscar Dillon through the police report and partial dental records."

"What do you mean partial?"

"Glad you asked, Dell. By partial, I mean that a lot of his teeth had been knocked out prior to the fire, so they used the few left and got a match from them."

"So with a lot of the teeth missing, the match can't be too significant, can it Frank?"

"Well, not in my opinion. It would be like calling a fingerprint match on just three points, instead of ten or twelve. At least it gives room for doubt in my mind."

"Yeah, me too, Frank. Me too."

"So where did you get today, Dell?"

"Besides handling my office, you mean? Well, I did confirm that Clifford Delse knew Danny for a while. He lived with him in Carolina for about a year."

"Give us anything to go on?"

"Not too much. He said that Danny didn't speak of any parents, did say he was raised in Maine, and initially didn't seem interested in hunting or guns."

"Information is coming slow."

"Well apparently Danny got interested in guns, maybe hunting, and moved out west to work in a store selling guns."

"Well, that's interesting, isn't it?"

"It is. And Clifford said the sporting goods store was named Plunkett's, and he thought it was in Arizona. So I guess I have more to investigate."

"I guess you do, Dell."

"Okay, Frank, I'm going home to get a home-cooked meal and some rest. I'll call you tomorrow if I get any new information."

"Sounds good, Dell. Give Suzi my best."

As I picked up my desk and file folders and prepared to turn off the lights to leave the office, I could only think, *Never mind, Frank. I'm going home and giving Suzi* my *best!*

· 15 ·

By the time I got home to the cabin, it was about five thirty, and to my surprise, Suzi was already home. As soon as I walked in, I realized she had not yet started dinner, so I made a suggestion.

"Sweetie, since it's early yet, why don't we go out and kayak a while before we make dinner?"

"Well, it is a beautiful afternoon, and we've plenty of sunlight left ... okay, let's!"

So we both changed into our bathing suits, and I went out to the shed and pulled out our kayaks. Suzi likes one of the Old Town brand Loon kayaks that's a standard shape and size. She's agile; I'm not so agile. So my kayak of choice is a Sea Kayak. Mine is longer and flat. I ride on the top of mine, and she sits down inside hers. For me, the main difference being, now that I'm getting older, I seem to be less balanced. When I try to get into her kayak, I just flip it, and me, over in the water. But on my kayak, I can keep it upright and still paddle across the lake. It could be a guy thing or just a getting older thing, but either way, I'm only safe on my style of kayak.

Once I put them in the water beside the dock, we both got in, or on, our respective kayaks, and off we went. It was a beautiful and calm time on the lake, and there were few other boats around, to our surprise. As we kayaked around the shoreline and headed up the lake, we saw a few loons taking leisurely swims, and there was a bald eagle sitting in a tall pine tree on one of the points of land jutting into the lake. I suspected he was watching for fish or to see if we were fishing.

As we continued around, we came to Grant's Island. From the rear as we approached, we could see their boathouse and noticed that they were "in camp." The Grants were a very nice couple with whom Suzi and I had shared a glass of wine on several occasions in the past. So we continued around their island until we came to the side where their camp was located. There was a very large, flat rock cropping to which they attached their dock and that separated the dock from the camp. When you pulled into the dock, you walked at least twenty feet across this rock cropping, and then you stepped directly up into the camp porch. It really was beautiful and a great use of the natural rock formations!

As we came toward their dock, the Grants came to the camp screen door and asked if we would like to come in and have a glass of wine with them. So Suzi and I docked our kayaks and went up to their camp.

Being on an island, their camp was a seasonal-use building. It had less insulation than would be necessary for winter use, if any. The Grants were considered "summer folk" by the locals, normally arriving after black fly season, often in July, and rarely staying any later than late September, due to the cold. During any given summer, they might spend three or four weeks total at camp, spread between multiple trips. Some of the other island owners, who lived farther away, might come up only once during the summer but would stay at least two months. Each family on the lake had different times for using their camps, but they frequently overlapped, so they formed a nice little community atmosphere with one another.

"Hey, Bill, Linda. Thanks so much for inviting us in."

"Oh, Dell, you know you and Suzi are always welcome when we're in camp!" Bill replied. "Linda will get you a glass of wine. Red or white?"

"I like red, myself. How about you, sweetie?"

"I'd like white, thanks."

After Linda came back with the glasses of wine, we sat on their porch and looked out over the lake. Each island owner originally built their camps in locations on their property to provide the view they were most interested in. Some wanted a view of the largest expanse of the lake, so their camps faced up lake. Others wanted the best sunset view, so their camps would be more westerly situated. Still others preferred a great sunrise, so their camps faced east. And sometimes the camp was situated to allow necessary deep-water access for their docks. Quite a few of the islands opted for the scenic view. You could tell because on a few of the islands, the main camp was quite a long walk away from their dock or boathouse. In the Grants' case, their camp faced the setting sun, almost due west.

"So, Dell. How's your murder investigation going?" Linda asked.

"It's been moving along. I'm working with Frank Bell of State Police Investigations, and some of the time, Berk, my chief deputy, also helps with interviews and calls."

"Do you already have a suspect?" Bill asked.

"Not exactly a suspect yet—more like a couple of persons of interest. I need some more questions answered before I can really call either one of them, or anyone else for that matter, a suspect."

"Is the one clerk still alive, Dell?"

"Yes, Mary Watson is still alive, but she's in a coma. We're hoping she'll come out of it and can give us some information about the people who did this."

"Well, best of luck in your investigation. Everyone around here is pulling for you to be able to solve it soon."

"Well, at least we have leads and people to interview. It's easier than the cold case I worked last year. With this case, there's more physical evidence, which should help."

After talking to Bill and Linda for a while longer, Suzi and I put our life vests back on and kayaked back out on the lake. Just as we came around the point of Grant's Island, our view opened up to an expanse of lake with the sun setting. It was a beautiful sight to behold! The clouds in the sky gave the setting sun bountiful slivers of red and orange dashing through the lavender background underlining the clouds. And the lake was so calm that the striking colors were mirrored on the water's surface. It was breathtaking, to say the least!

"Suzi, we'd better head on back to our cabin. I don't want to be out here with no lights on our kayaks, and that sun is setting fast."

"Oh, I know, Dell. But isn't it just beautiful!"

"It sure is, sweetie. But then, so are you."

"Oh, you silly man!"

So we turned around and headed back toward our place by the straightest route, without going through any heavily trafficked boat channels. When we arrived at our dock, you could barely tell where the land began and the lake stopped. I hadn't planned on being out so late on the lake, but it was a beautiful sunset. One not to be missed!

Since it was getting so late, Suzi and I shared the meal preparation and had our dinner ready in no time. Sometime between the salad and the salmon, the phone rang. I reached over to answer it, hoping the call wasn't going to have me up all night.

"Dell, it's Berk. Got some bad news. Mary Watson didn't make it."

"Aw, Berk, I was pulling for her. Did she ever wake up from the coma?"

"No, Dr. Beale said she didn't, and I kept track real close in case she did, but she just went right from the coma."

"Okay, Berk. Thanks for calling and keeping good track of her condition. We can talk strategy tomorrow after I get in. Hey, did someone call Frank yet?"

"I'd expect they had from the hospital, but I can call him to be sure."

"Please do. We need to be sure he's kept in the loop."

"Okay, boss, I'll take care of it. See you tomorrow."

As I hung up the phone, I was thinking about Mary Watson. Poor lady had no relatives that we knew of, anywhere. Her husband, a local guy, had been killed years ago in the local paper mill. They had no children yet, and she never remarried. There really wasn't anyone for us to even follow up with now that she was gone. I felt sad for her passing without any loved one by her side. But then, I guessed that meant that no one's heart was breaking, as it otherwise may have been. I guess only God knew she was leaving this earth. So in that moment, I said a silent prayer for Mary Watson and then sat back down at the table.

"Trouble, Dell?"

"Mary Watson passed on. Guess the bullet just did too much damage. What a shame."

"Oh, I'm sorry. Did she have any relatives in the area?"

"No, we don't know of any relatives at all. Poor lady."

"Aw, poor woman. I didn't know."

We both ate, but it was a pretty quiet dinner. When we were finished, I helped Suzi clean up, and she decided to go on to bed and read a while. I told her I was going to stay in the living room and go over my files a bit longer. There was something nagging at my mind about this case, but I wasn't sure what it was. I told Suzi I'd be going to bed in a little while, and she retired with Chauncey following right along behind her.

I sat down by the fireplace in my easy chair and began going over the case paperwork and walking through possible ideas in my mind. At about nine thirty, I couldn't stand it any longer, so I picked up the phone and dialed Frank's home number.

"Hey, Frank, it's Dell. You weren't in bed yet, were you?"

"No, I've just been sitting here going over the case in my mind."

"Me too. I guess you got the call about Mrs. Watson?"

"Yes. Twice. First the hospital, then your man, Berk."

"Sorry, just wanted to be sure you were kept in the loop."

"No, I appreciate it, Dell. A real shame about Mrs. Watson, though."

"Yes, it is. Now we have three murder victims."

"So, what were you calling about tonight, Dell?"

"Well, I think I'm concerned about old Oscar Dillon's death."

"There could be some questions, I guess. Not the best identification I ever saw."

"That's the way I see it too, Frank. You think we could get the body exhumed so we can make a certain ID with DNA?"

"I don't know, Dell. We really have nothing but a hunch. I doubt any judge would sign an order based on such little evidence. Especially if any family members contested the action. It would be pretty thin."

"Well ... maybe ... we ... ah ... could ..."

"Look, Dell, I agree it would help our case, maybe at least to exclude someone who's already supposed to be dead. Another issue to consider besides convincing a judge is that if we do get the body exhumed, the Portland PD isn't gonna take it too well. I suspect we would be making some enemies there."

"Yes, you're right, Frank. And while I don't often have to work with that agency, you may have to. We don't want to make your working relationship with them bad. That's not fair to anyone."

"All right, Dell. Let's just keep the idea in our hip pocket for now. If push comes to shove and we run out of other leads later, then we'll revisit the idea of trying to get an order to exhume the body."

"I agree, Frank. We'll use it as a last option, if needed."

"One thing we can do, though, is try to develop some information we *could* use to go before a judge."

"Okay, my guess is that means another trip to Portland to see if we can interview Oscar's friend who identified him and maybe his old boss."

"Well, that would be as good a place to start as any. How about tomorrow after the press conference? You didn't forget about that, did you?"

"Almost, Frank. When and where was it again?"

"Our main headquarters in Augusta. The press conference is scheduled for one o'clock. Hopefully you can get here a little before so we can go over our presentation?"

"Yeah, I think I can make that happen, Frank. I'll call you in the morning with my best time estimate."

"Sounds good to me, Dell. By the way, call me anytime you can't sleep, my friend. Hey, is Suzi home?"

"Yeah, why?"

"Because if I were in your shoes, Dell, I'd hang up and walk right in the bedroom and *get busy!*"

"Thanks for the great idea, Frank. Goodnight."

After I hung up with Frank, I sat there for a few more minutes thinking about the case, the press conference tomorrow, and replacing all the materials back in the files from my review. The crime-scene photos were on top of the file, so I looked over them again. While I didn't see anything new or useful, it brought memories of walking through the scene just a few nights ago.

I finished packing all the files away in my briefcase and shut off the lights. I walked into the bedroom and started taking off my clothes for bed. After I brushed and flossed my teeth and turned out the bathroom light, Suzi called over to me.

"All done with your review and work, honey?"

"Still have lots of questions, sweetie."

"Frank wasn't able to help?"

"Not much. He just told me to go to bed with you."

"Well, let's give him the credit due him. Come over here in my arms, honey. I'll hug those blues away!"

We cuddled in the moonlight shining through the window. Afterward, Suzi fell asleep fairly quickly, and I dozed off myself about ten minutes after she did.

It looked like tomorrow was going to be a busy day for me and Frank!

· 16 ·

When our alarm clock sounded, I rolled over and gave Suzi a kiss on her bare shoulder and woke her up. Slivers of the sunrise were breaking over the lake at that time of the morning, suggesting that it might be a beautiful day.

"Sweetie, I may be gone until really late tonight. I have to go to the Major Crimes Unit headquarters in Augusta to do a press conference with Frank."

"Aw, he can't handle that on his own?" Suzi quipped.

"Yeah, he needs me to give it some polish! After the press thing, we're going back down to Portland to do a couple more interviews. Might be pretty late."

"Well, just promise me that if you run late and are tired, you guys will just stay somewhere down that way tonight. I don't want you half asleep, dodging moose on the highway. Baby, by the way, our station is sending a remote truck and reporter. You might pass them on the road."

"Okay. Maybe we'll stay overnight. I haven't asked Frank what he thinks. Besides, we need to see where these interviews go. Anyway, with your remote, you'll get to see me save the presentation if Frank falters," I said with a smile.

After we got up, had some coffee and a pastry, got our showers, and I called the office to leave Irish a voicemail about the trip and my plans. After leaving her a message, I called Berk on his cell.

"Hey, Berk. I'm heading down to Augusta for a press conference, and then Frank and I are going to Portland again. Want to talk to a couple more people. You got the county covered for the day?"

"Sure, I got it. Not much from the overnights to report. Pretty quiet night, and hopefully today will be the same."

"Hey, if we run late, we might stay somewhere between here and there. I might not be in to the office until around noon tomorrow."

"No problem, boss. Have a safe trip, and I hope you get more answers this time than you do questions."

"Thanks, Berk. I'm hoping we do too!"

After kissing Suzi good-bye a few times, I got in my Tahoe and headed toward Bangor. I made my usual stop at the Airline Snack Bar for some breakfast and coffee and then resumed my trip. I was in no hurry this morning since I had plenty of time before the press conference, so I didn't arrive in Augusta until about eleven o'clock. I walked into the Major Crimes Unit and located Frank's office.

"Made it safe and sound, I see, Dell."

"Nice not to have to hurry for a change."

"So are you ready for the press conference?"

"Sure. How many ways are there to say 'no comment'?" I quipped.

"We have to give them something, Dell. Besides, Mrs. Watson has changed this case from a double to a triple homicide."

"You're right, Frank. I'll just follow your lead."

"Hey, as long as we present a professional, unified face to the press, I'm happy."

"Me too."

After more small talk about how we were going to go fishing on the lake when this case was over, we went out to grab a small lunch and get back for the press conference. I say small lunch because anyone who has ever done any public speaking knows you don't want to try it on a full stomach. It's hard to present a professional demeanor if you're belching throughout the presentation. Or breaking wind for that matter!

We returned to headquarters and went into the conference room, which was set up for the press conference. There was a nice podium for Frank and me to use and a bank of microphones from various news services throughout the state. Some of them had the logos for national news companies like NBC, but I assumed that they were affiliates of those larger organizations. But being affiliates meant that any local story could easily be carried nationwide. So I guessed Frank and I needed to be on the ball.

Frank began the press conference.

"While the Maine State Major Crimes Unit is working on various cases throughout the state, we are here today to provide an update on the murders in Castaway County. With me is Sheriff Wendell Hinton of Castaway County.

"Now as you already know, this case involved three victims at the Black Bear Truck Stop. Our initial briefings listed two deceased and one in critical condition. Unfortunately, since that time, the other victim, one of the clerks at the truck stop, has passed away from her injuries. We offer our condolences to all of these victims' families for their loss.

"Our agency is conducting a thorough investigation into this crime. Our crime lab continues to explore the physical evidence collected at the scene, and we are conducting interviews of persons daily. We have developed a couple of persons of interest in this case, none of which can yet be classified as suspects. We will need additional interviews and evidence review before any such classification can be made.

"Sheriff Hinton and members of his agency are assisting us with many of the interviews and assisted at the crime scene during the initial hours of the investigation. It is our hope that by working together we can locate the individual or individuals who committed this crime against the citizens of Castaway County and the State of Maine.

"Now I will open the floor for any questions."

A young woman from an Augusta TV station asked the first question. "So at the present time, you have no suspects, just persons of interest, is that right?"

"Yes, ma'am. Although individuals are of interest to our investigation, none can be called a suspect at this time."

The next question came from a male reporter from the *Bangor Daily Newspaper*. "What's the difference between a 'person of interest' and a 'suspect' in your mind, Lieutenant?"

"Persons of interest are those people we seek for the purpose of interviewing. They may or may not even be connected to the case being investigated at the time. We won't know whether they're involved in the case until we're able to speak to them.

"A suspect, on the other hand, is someone upon whom we have developed reason to believe they may be the person or one of a group of people who most likely committed the crime. Do those definitions help your understanding of the differences?"

"Why, yes, thank you."

"Any more questions?" Frank asked.

The girl from Suzi's station raised her hand. "Yes. Sheriff Hinton, we have received information that the murders may have been a professional hit: a contract killing. Can you confirm that?"

I stepped up closer to the podium microphones. "No, I am not at liberty to provide such information. We are following all logical leads, and any speculative analysis at this point would not be proper, nor enhance our efforts to solve the case."

She had a follow-up. "But can't you tell us what your working theory of the case is?"

"No, ma'am, I can't."

"Then, Sheriff, you don't have a working theory?"

"We do. But it is just that, a *working* theory. As we progress with the investigation, we may find it is not correct. A working theory just gives us a place to start from."

Another hand went up. "When will you have a suspect or suspects, Lieutenant Bell?"

"When our investigation is nearer completion, we expect to have a suspect or suspects identified and enough evidence for an arrest and prosecution."

"So you expect to have this murder solved quickly?"

"I didn't say that. We hope that through a thorough investigation we will be able to identify the perpetrators and make an arrest and prosecution. I cannot determine how soon that will happen. We have to see where the investigation leads us. Okay, we'll take just one more question."

Another young male reporter, this time from a Portland newspaper, asked the final question. "Does this case have any ties to some type of organized crime or crime syndication?"

"I cannot answer that question as of this time. We have an ongoing investigation, and we have to follow all possible leads. Thank you all for coming, and that concludes this press conference."

Frank and I walked out of the room and went into his office. I could tell that some of the reporters wanted to ask more questions, but we had given them all we were about to at this point. Unfortunately, reporters often will continue asking the same basic question, in different variations, trying to get you to slip up and commit to something you otherwise would not. *I know it's their job to push until we say something we didn't want to say, but it still annoys me how the press tries to badger you,* I thought.

Once in Frank's office, he turned to me and said, "Well, that went pretty well in there. At least we didn't give them too much to chew on."

"Yeah, but they sure tried. And how do you suppose they came up with the professional hit idea?"

"Oh, I don't know, Dell. Maybe someone at the hospital talked?"

"I'm sure the doctor didn't. Know him pretty well from basketball. Don't think he'd do it."

"Oh well. No harm done anyway. The press having their own ideas won't make or break our investigation."

"Good point, Frank. But just the same, I'll talk to the doctor and suggest he let his staff know that they need to watch what they say to reporters."

"Well, now. Shall we drive down to Portland and see some fellows about a murder case?"

"Yes, and let's see if we can get more answers than new questions this time!"

Before we could leave the office, Frank's secretary came in and said she had a phone call waiting for him. I went over and took a chair near the window and pulled out my iPhone so I could see if Irish or Berk had sent me any e-mails or texts.

"Go ahead and take the call, Frank. I'll just sit here and check on stuff."

I tried not to listen to Frank's conversation, but from the look on his face, it was, at times, fairly animated. At one point, he told the other party to check and call him right back. Frank only had to wait about three minutes, and the return call came in.

After a bit more discussion, Frank thanked the caller and stood up to get his coat.

"Okay, we got an appointment to see Big Eddy at seven o'clock at the Dock Side Bar."

"An appointment?"

"Well, let's just say we have a meeting with him. Okay?"

"Sure, Frank, sure. And that call was about scheduling the meeting?"

"Yeah. I know a guy who knows a guy. Know what I mean?"

"Yeah, you've got some informant from the old days who still has some juice, and he got us in, right?"

"Well ... you might put it in those terms. I guess."

"Okay, Frank. Let's go to Portland! Before we get to the 'appointment,' how about we try to look up Oscar's buddy who was the witness to him being in that shed when it burned?"

"Might be easier just to ask Big Eddy. The guy is probably still on his payroll."

"Okay, we start there. Sounds like you and I are going to be bunking together tonight."

"Yeah, I expect this may be a long evening, Dell. Can you make it without Suzi?"

"I expect so. Already told her we might stay over somewhere. In fact, it was her suggestion in the first place."

"Maybe she's trying to get rid of you, Dell. You know, trade you in for a new model."

"I hope not. She's just about got me broken in!"

"Well, let's see what tonight brings us, shall we?"

"Hopefully one step closer to a suspect, Frank!"

17

This time we decided to use Frank's unmarked state police cruiser for the trip. We pulled into Portland, drove down to the Old Port section, and located the Dock Side Bar with a few minutes to spare. We sat in the car talking about our best questions for Big Eddy Whalen. We wanted to suggest that Oscar might still be around, without actually committing to that thought. So we decided to try to finesse the information out of Big Eddy, if we could.

At the "appointment" time, we walked into the bar and noticed a large man sitting in a booth with several other men. Before we had time to approach that table, another man dressed in a bomber-style jacket and wearing a knit hat came over and asked us to join Mr. Whalen at his table, the last booth near the end of the bar. As we neared the table, we saw two other men dressed in similar longshoreman clothing and a fairly short, heavyset man with a balding head. This man was dressed in a cheap suit and had a tie hanging loosely around his neck. His gaze never left the plate of ribs he was eating as the first man who had met us at the door introduced us to him.

"Ah, Mr. Whalen, here are the two officers down to ask you questions." Then he turned to us and said, "Give him your names, men."

"Mr. Whalen, I'm Frank Bell from the state police, and this is Dell Hinton, sheriff of Castaway County."

"You're the guy who broke that cold case last year. Kid got killed. Found by a hunter, right?"

"Yes, sir," I said. "That was my first case as sheriff."

"Dell did a great job on that one," Frank chimed in.

"Yes, yes, now what can I do for you cops?"

"Well, we wanted to ask you some questions about two of your employees. Harry Grimes and Oscar Dillon."

"Oscar's dead. Harry still works for me. Ask your questions."

"Well, okay if we sit down?"

"Yeah, go ahead. Boys, move out so's these guys can sit down!" Big Eddy was talking to the two men sitting opposite him in the booth. As soon as they moved out, we sat down, and then they pulled a couple of chairs from the freestanding table nearest the booth and turned them around to sit on. They kept at least six feet or more away from our table, but clearly they wanted to be close and observing. *I can't believe they might think we're here to assault their boss,* I thought.

"Okay, you're sitting down. Now what are your questions?"

Frank began, "Well, Mr. Whalen, we wanted to know more about Oscar. What was he doing for you just before his death?"

"Worked as a bill collector for me. Someone owed me a payment, he went by and picked up the check or cash and brought it back to me."

"And how did he die?"

"Burnt to a crisp in a fire."

"So you had to get a new collector?"

"Yes."

"Was Oscar a valuable employee until his death?"

"Very."

"Do you miss his expertise?"

"Naw, the new guy is just as good as Oscar was."

"What if Oscar hadn't died in the fire?"

"Waddya mean by that?" As he responded, I looked very carefully at his face for any tell that might give me an indication that Frank had struck a nerve with that question. I saw a small twinkle in his eye, but nothing that would be considered a good sign.

Frank pressed on. "Well, just for grins since I know it isn't true, what would Oscar be worth now if he were still alive? I mean, a guy who's a good collector, and now everyone, including the police, thinks he's dead?"

The twinkle in his eye was now brighter, but I interpreted it as Big Eddy realizing that this was a great idea.

"Well, a guy like that would be very useful and worth a lot. But, unfortunately for me, Oscar *is* dead. Can't bring him back from the grave. Good idea though. Maybe you should write crime novels."

"Oh, I was just thinking out loud. It just seemed like a good idea at the time."

"It was. I could really use a guy like that—back from the dead and all."

"Well, let me ask you about Harry Grimes then. What does Harry do for you?'

"A bit of this and a bit of that. Whatever I ask him to do."

"So he's the kind of guy who fixes stuff for you?"

"Yeah, sometimes."

"Does he fix problems for you as well?"

"He's been known to."

"He wouldn't lie to protect you, would he?"

"None of my people tell lies. They're all honest. Have to be in the business world. Why would you ask me a dumb question like that?"

"Sorry, Mr. Whalen. I won't presume to ask such questions, okay?"

"Damn right, or this meeting is over."

"Okay, can you tell me where Harry Grimes is so we can talk to him ourselves?"

"Yeah. William, will you call Harry and tell him to come to the bar?" One of the guys sitting at the other table facing us stood up and walked toward the front door, dialing a cell phone as he walked. *This guy has some very obedient guys working for him. I can see that.*

While we waited for Harry to arrive, we continued questions for Big Eddy. This time, I started the ball rolling.

"So, Mr. Whalen, were you notified about Oscar right away? I mean, did you see the fire or remnants of it or just the body of Oscar later?"

"I had a meeting with him about ten minutes before the fire. I got a call after he left. Said the shed was on fire and Oscar was in it."

"Did you go to the shed to see the fire?"

"Nope, seen a fire before. Know what they look like."

"Did you see the body when it was pulled from the fire?"

"Nope. Just heard that the police had identified it as Oscar."

"Obviously, that didn't surprise you then?"

"Nope. Harry said he saw him go in, never saw him come out. No reason to question it."

Frank and I were running out of questions about Oscar and his fiery death, so we talked to Big Eddy about the Old Port area and how it had become a place for visitors and tourists. He didn't seem to be too appreciative of how the area had grown and changed over the years. And this guy wasn't a chatterbox; he clearly believed that the best answers to give any cop were the shortest ones.

Shortly, another man walked in and came over to our table, also wearing clothing associated with a longshoreman. He was introduced to us as Harry Grimes, and we were told by Mr. Whalen that Harry was there to answer any of our questions. Harry looked at Mr. Whalen first, as if agreeing with him, and then at us, awaiting questions.

Frank began again. "Mr. Grimes, I understand you were the person to identify Oscar Dillon. Is that correct?"

"I saw Oscar go into that shed if that's what you're asking me."

"Yes. Now, did you see him come out?"

"Not until the cops brought out the body."

"Did the shed have any other door than the one you saw Oscar go in?"

"No, that old shed only had one door."

"Any windows?"

"Nope, just a door."

"Were you watching the door from the time Oscar went in all the time until the fire broke out?"

Harry Grimes gave a quick glance over at his boss, Big Eddy, who gave him a small nod to go ahead. "The fire started pretty quickly after he went in, almost immediately. So yeah, I was still looking in that direction."

"How did the fire start? I mean, was there an explosion?"

"Not an explosion, I guess. Just the fire started real quickly, and the shed was all afire real quick like."

"And Oscar never came out alive?"

"No, Oscar never did. Just got carried out by the cops or coroner or someone."

"Didn't anyone try to save Oscar from the fire? Maybe you?"

"Couldn't. Fire was taking the whole shed. Figured he was already a goner."

"No explosion, just a fire?"

Harry looked again at Big Eddy before responding. "Nope, just a hot, quick fire is all I saw."

"Sounds pretty cut and dry to me, as you boys say," Big Eddy ventured. And from the look on Harry Grimes's face, I suspected that was the signal to stop talking.

With no more questions, we thanked Harry Grimes for his time, and his boss sent him away.

"Will that do it, boys?" Mr. Whalen asked.

"That's about it, Mr. Whalen. Thanks for your time this evening," Frank replied.

"Always available for the law."

As we turned to leave, I asked, "Mr. Whalen, why do they call you Big Eddy?"

"Well it ain't my stature, is it? It's because I'm the boss."

"Quite so, Mr. Whalen, quite so. Thanks."

With that, we walked out into the Old Port and got into Frank's cruiser. We sat there for a minute thinking about our interviews, and then I told Frank it was late and we needed to find a room, rather than drive all the way back to his place. We agreed on Freeport. I think we both wanted to get out of Big Eddy's area.

As we headed up I-295 toward Freeport, I decided to ask Frank about the interviews.

"So, what did you think, Frank?"

"Well, I don't think we got much in the way of a lead, but I thought I saw a glimmer in Big Eddy's eyes when we talked about the possibility of Oscar still being around to do work for him."

"Yeah, me too. I just wasn't sure if it was an idea he hadn't already thought of beforehand, and he was just now realizing its value, or if we caught him on something."

"I wasn't sure either. Hey, did you see the way Harry Grimes waited to get the go-ahead from Big Eddy before he answered the question about the fire and how it started?"

"Yup, sure did. Wonder what that was about. Reckon maybe there's more to how the fire started than what we already know?"

"Not sure, Dell. But I do know one thing for sure; Big Eddy rules all those longshoremen with a tight fist."

"Yeah, I know where the Big Eddy name came from. He might be small, but I'll bet he carries a real big stick."

As we neared Freeport, I told Frank we ought to stay at the Harraseeket Inn. It's a beautiful hotel on Main Street with a nice bar and outside seating area. Knowing exactly where I was suggesting, Frank reminded me that he was on a state salary budget, and I agreed that a sheriff's office budget was also not that flexible. So we decided upon the Hampton Inn at the Desert Road exit. We just needed a good night's sleep so we could get an early start back to our respective offices in the morning. And Hampton Inns are pretty much the same everywhere—clean, friendly, and not too pricey. After all, we had just been to a bar for the evening!

18

After Frank returned me to my Tahoe outside his office in Augusta, I began the lonely ride home to Castaway County. A man and his thoughts.

I began going over in my mind the interview with Big Eddy at the bar. One thing that stuck out to me was the control he seemed to have over the guys working for him. I suspected that in the day, he was not a man to be trifled with by any means. Today, he may not have the power he had in the past, but he still seemed to have the respect that power had created. It made me wonder if Oscar's death had been staged to allow him to become more useful to Big Eddy. Seemed to be a logical idea. And one that an old criminal mind might conjure up. And if that were the case, how would we find him? Even if we did locate Oscar, we weren't sure if he was involved in the Black Bear murders. After all, why would he risk identification to kill his ex-wife? Maybe we needed to look into her background a bit further.

As I was pulling into the county, a light rain began falling from the dark storm clouds over the western skyline. I arrived at my office around ten o'clock in the morning. Since we had planned to have to stay in the Portland area overnight, I had brought some clean clothes. And since Suzi was already halfway through her workday, there was no need for me to go home first.

As I walked in, Irish said hello and offered me a cup of coffee, which, as always, I eagerly took. *I really do drink way too much coffee, but with the job, I've grown to like it a lot!*

Shortly thereafter, Berk came in to touch base with me.

"So, how did your meeting with Big Eddy go, boss?"

"Oh, it was slightly fruitful. I found out he still wields a good bit of power over his employees, of which the witness is one."

"You think that guy would lie about seeing Oscar go in the building and not come out?"

"Oh, yeah. In a heartbeat. I think he'd say anything Big Eddy told him to say, and swear to it on a stack of Bibles at that!"

"What about the idea that Oscar is still around?"

"Big Eddy had a gleam in his eyes as we talked about that. I'm not sure if he had already thought of it himself or if he was just pleased with the idea as he was listening to it."

"So, I guess we're back to square one on Oscar?"

"Pretty much. We did find out that the fire began almost immediately after Oscar went in the building."

"How's that a clue?"

"Not sure it is, but it may fit with the idea that the fire was a setup. Kind of unlikely that a fire would start as soon as someone entered a building, don't you think?"

"Yeah, I agree. Well, maybe we'll get something useful soon so we can petition the court to exhume Oscar's body for testing."

"That would be nice."

Berk continued to talk with me for a while. He updated me on all the reports from yesterday after I had left, until now. Just some small matters, thankfully; no big crimes. Then Berk went back out on patrol.

Since I was still thinking about the case and getting nowhere, I decided to think about something entirely different to help clear my mind. My old friend from the Boston PD, Brendan Murphy, had sent me a postcard the other day, and I thought I would give him a quick call and see how he was doing. It had been far too long since we had chatted.

Brendan, one of two Brendans I had known and worked with on the Boston force, was a fine Irish lad from County Claire. The other Brendan, Brendan O'Gorman, was from County Kerry. These two officers were as nice a matched pair as you might find, both quick of mind, hand, and body, and loyal to the end. They'd make any Irish mother proud!

I called the detective bureau and asked for Brendan. After a few moments, I heard an Irish brogue come on the line.

"Aw, and if it isn't me boy Dell. And how you be doing up there in the woods?"

"Oh, I'm fine, Brendan. How about you?"

"Me work keeps me busy. Hey, I was planning on calling you anyway, me boy."

"Oh? What about?"

"I'll be askin' if you know any good lads on the Portland PD?"

"Sure. You could call Sergeant Jeff Dodger, I guess. I worked with him on a case a while back. Seemed like a good enough guy. We're not friends or anything."

"I'll give him a call."

"You got something tied into Maine there, Brendan?"

"Not sure, me lad. We had a break-in at a pawnshop. Few guns, some jewelry taken. We got a partial palm print, although quite smudged. Thing is, the closest match we could find in the system was to a guy who was already dead."

"What was the name of the dead guy, Brendan?"

"Aw, let me look at the file again, lad. Here it is. Oscar Dillon."

"Are you shitting me, Brendan? That's a guy I'm looking for in a case here."

"Well, it was the closest match, I said. Not a confirmed match. And besides, lad, he's listed in the computer as being dead."

"Yeah, I know. He's a person of interest in our case. But we interviewed his boss yesterday, as well as the guy who placed him in the shed that burnt down, and there's certainly some room to believe it was a setup."

"Oh, so you've already spoken to Portland authorities about this guy then, me boy?"

"Yes. It seems that no one really got a good ID on the guy after he burned up. Their ID came from partial dental comparisons. He had quite a few of his teeth knocked out before the coroner's office made the ID. So, like your print, it was more of a near-hit than a hit."

"Well, me boy, seems like there are a lot of near-hits on this guy with no actual identifications. You think he might still be out there in the realm of the living?"

"He might be, Brendan. But maybe your partial hit on the palm print is enough for us to get the body exhumed and get a real, conclusive ID."

"What can I do to help? And it might just help my case as well."

"Just fax me a copy of your reports and the partial print and a printout from the computer showing Oscar Dillon as the closest hit you came up with. I'll get the information to Frank Bell at the state police. I'm working with him on the murders here. Actually, he has the lead; I'm just helping him. Maine is different from Boston, my friend."

"I should imagine it is, lad. I'll get right on the fax. By the way, are the fish biting at the lake good this year?"

"Why, yes they are! Maybe if you get some time off, you and the other Brendan could come up for a weekend or more?"

"Love to do it, lad. I'll have to see how it goes, God willing, we might make it up there later on. It would be good to take a couple nice, fat bass from that little lake of yours!" I could see the wink and twinkle in his eyes, even over the phone, as he said that.

After finishing the call with Brendan Murphy, I quickly dialed Frank up on the phone. I told him about the call with Brendan and how he had come up with Oscar's name in his case. I said that as soon as I received the faxed material, I would review it, see if there needed to be any additional background material, and then send it along to Frank.

"Good, Dell. If it looks as good as we think, I'll get working on a request for the Superior Court in Cumberland County to see if we can get an order to exhume the body."

"Okay, while you're handling that, Frank, I'll keep working on our other person of interest."

When I got off the phone, I eagerly awaited Brendan's fax submission. This might at least be the break we needed to get Oscar's body exhumed. If it was ID'd as Oscar, well, it would close him out as a person of interest. If it was not Oscar's body in that grave, then it opened up more investigation for us, as well as for Brendan and the Boston PD.

But in the meantime, I had learned that you should consider all possible options, so we still needed to locate Danny Windom. I started planning my next move in his direction while I awaited the fax.

After about a half hour, which seemed to take an hour or more to go by, the fax machine began to make noises of connecting with another source and printing out quite a few pages. As soon as it finished, I picked up all the sheets of paper and went in and sat at my desk to review them.

The first document was a report form completed by the initial patrol officer who responded to the call at the pawnshop in Boston. It outlined what he found when he arrived, what evidence was observed initially, and what items had been removed from the premises. The second report was a follow-up report from the crime-scene technician with a copy of the partial print they had taken as evidence at the scene. The next was an investigative report written by Brendan that outlined his investigation thus far.

Brendan's report indicated that he had run the partial palm print through the computer system and that the closest print to a match was that of one Oscar Dillon. His report indicated that he had run Oscar's name and found that he had been arrested several times in Portland, Maine, and that he was now deceased. The report did not go into any further discussion about the deceased Oscar since Brendan had been planning to call me for a good contact at Portland PD.

All the material Brendan had sent looked to be in order, and I knew that Frank would fill in the portions of our investigation that were applicable to requesting an order for exhumation. I put all the reports together again and placed a cover sheet on the stack for Frank. Within about twenty minutes, I had the materials sent on to Frank via fax. On the cover sheet, I had noted for him to call me if there were any other pieces of information he felt might be necessary to obtain that court order.

I sat down at my desk again and picked up my cold coffee. I called out to Irish and asked for a fresh cup since I had only taken a few sips from that one before I let it get cold. She brought a nice fresh cup, and I pulled out a Romeo y Jullietta figuardo from my desk humidor. I clipped both ends and lit it up.

"Got a break in your case, boss?"

"Not necessarily a break, but at least we might be able to get that body exhumed for a positive ID."

Now that we were rolling on the Oscar ID thing, I decided to turn my attention to Danny Windom. I pulled out my file with my investigation notes in it and began searching through it.

Now, let's see. Where was it Clifford Delse said Danny had gone to work? Ah, yes, Plunkett's Sporting Goods somewhere in Arizona.

I began with a computer search for a sporting goods store named Plunkett's in Arizona. Two came up in the search. One was in Tucson, and the other in Flagstaff. So I wrote down both phone numbers and dialed the one in Tucson first.

I asked for the store manager and identified myself. I asked about Danny Windom and also gave the woman the name Danny Alexander. She didn't recognize either name and put me on hold to check her employee files. When she returned, she said that her files showed that he had worked at their store about five years ago, before she had come to that store. Her review of the file indicated that he had only worked there for a month before he was moved to their sister store in Flagstaff. She gave me the name of the manager at that store, and I already had the phone number. I thanked her for her assistance and tried the other store.

When I got the manager on the phone for the Flagstaff store, the man knew Danny Alexander's name immediately.

"Oh, yes, Danny Alexander. He was a fine young man. Good employee."

"Did you ever have any problems with him or any concerns raised about his behavior or how he got along with coworkers, Mr. Dean?" I asked.

"No. He seemed to get along well with the other employees. In fact, he became quite close to our firearms expert, David Wimbley. They hung around each other all the time, even when they were off the clock."

"How do you know that, Mr. Dean?"

"Well, they often talked about going out into the desert to shoot guns on their days off."

"Any idea how good Danny became with a gun?"

"Oh, my, yes, Danny became an excellent marksman. He and David actually entered some shooting contests together, and they won them all!" I detected a real sense of pride emanating from Mr. Dean as he told me that.

"Do you know if they were firing handguns or long arms?"

"They used both. But to my recollection, Danny favored a handgun. He was a crack shot, that boy!"

"Did he buy any handguns while working at your store?"

"Yes. He bought a nice rifle with a large scope for hunting. And he bought a pair of nice stainless .38 caliber handguns. One had a snub nose, I assumed for personal protection, and the other had a six-inch, ventilated barrel of the sort you would use for competition shooting."

"Have you the serial numbers and make and model of those guns in your registry?"

"Certainly. I comply with all federal firearms selling regulations." His tone seemed to have changed to a more defensive one when asked that question.

"Oh, I'm not suggesting that you didn't, Mr. Dean. I just need to be sure I have that information. Can you please fax me a copy of the firearms sales form for each of those handguns?"

"Sure can, Sheriff. The boy get into some kind of trouble up your way?"

"Oh, probably not. We're just tracking a few .38s and were told he might have one of them. I just want to be able to check the numbers and be sure."

"Well, okay. I'll fax those copies right away."

"One last thing, Mr. Dean. Well, maybe two. Do you know where Danny went after he left your employ?"

"Told me he was headed up to Montana to do some hunting. Told me to forward any mail to a spread up in Billings—Patriot's Progressive Ranch, that was it."

"Why would he ask you to forward his mail? Did he get it at work?"

"Not really. He lived upstairs in a one-room apartment we have above the building. Like I said, he was a nice kid and seemed to need some help, so I helped him out."

"Oh. So when is David Wimbley working next?"

"He'll be here tomorrow, open to close."

"And what hours is that, Mr. Dean?"

"Oh, I'm sorry, Sheriff, ten to six."

"No problem, Mr. Dean. I'll call back to speak to David tomorrow sometime. Thanks for all the information."

After I hung up with Mr. Dean, I made the usual notes on our conversation in my investigation file, closed it, and leaned back to think a bit.

It seemed to me that Danny was becoming a better potential suspect all the time. With the firearms training he had acquired working at the sporting goods store, he would surely be capable of making the shots look like they were made by a pro. At least under competition situations. But I really had no indication that he could make those same shots under pressure and with the potential of being fired upon himself. *Maybe that's where that Patriot's Progressive Ranch came in. After all, there are lots of small survivalist groups in America, and many seem to be located in Montana and other western and northwestern states.*

Well, I couldn't hang my hat on guesses, so I still needed to make more phone calls. But, before I could, my phone rang.

It was Billy Teal on the phone. He was calling about an accident involving a sheriff's vehicle.

"Sheriff, you need to come out here on Route 272 at the sharp curve. Chief Berkley Smith was involved in an accident. He seems to be fine. Rolled his cruiser though."

"Okay, Billy, on my way."

I told Irish I was headed out to the scene of the accident on Route 272, just north of Culbert's Corner. I also told her that, depending on how long I was at the scene, I might just go home afterward. She should just take any calls and hold them for me, unless, of course, they were an emergency.

I climbed into my Tahoe and started out of town on Route 7, then to 17 West, across to 20, and turned north on 272 after Culbert's Corner. Unfortunately, in a community where the roads were initially set up from town to town, and sometimes following logging trails, it's almost never a straight line from one part of the county to another. When I first arrived in Castaway County and was talking to a deputy sheriff one day on the street, he remarked that it was normal to have to run lights and sirens for over an hour in the county getting from one call to another. Lots of back roads and woods to navigate between clusters of homes and small towns. But I fell in love with Castaway County!

I was fairly sure what had happened to Berk: it had been raining lightly all day, on and off, so the grease, pine needles, and other dirt on the roadways had not been completely washed off like they would have been by a hard rain. That makes the road surface much slicker than you might expect. And it sounded like Berk had rolled his cruiser on the sharp turn about halfway down Route 272 toward Rome.

Billy Teal called me again to say that the emergency crew at the scene had confirmed that Berk was fine. He put Berk on the phone to speak to me.

"Geez, boss, I'm sorry. I was responding to an alarm at Millie's Bar in Rome, and I guess I hit that turn a little faster than I should have."

"Don't worry about it, Berk. I'm just glad you didn't get hurt. We can always get the cruiser fixed."

"Yeah, I guess." Berk didn't seem to say that with much confidence, but I think his pride was hurt by having the accident in the first place. "Rookie mistake, boss. I'm sorry."

"Never mind that, Berk. Just glad you're okay."

In a few more minutes, I pulled up to the scene. As I suspected, Berk's cruiser was partially upside down with the top resting on the grassy bank just past the apex of the turn on the right shoulder of the road. Actually, the damage looked to be very minimal. Basically, it looked like his emergency light bar had been torn off, and there might have been a dent or two on the roof of the vehicle. But I didn't see much more damage than that. It just looked like he'd lost control going through the turn and rolled over and slid along the embankment with the top of the vehicle as he was coming to a stop.

Berk appeared to be fine—slightly embarrassed, but fine. Deputy Teal was completing a standard state accident form. I walked over to Berk and told him I would give him a ride back to town. The tow truck would reset the cruiser upright and then tow it to the station for repairs. Deputy Teal said he would complete all the required paperwork.

"I'm just glad you were okay, Chief," Billy said.

Berk asked Teal, "What did they find at Millie's?" Apparently, Linda Wilcott had diverted to cover the alarm Berk was originally responding to, and a game warden had backed her up on the call.

"It was a false alarm."

"Figured it would be. I shouldn't have been in such a hurry."

"Well, Chief, you never know. It could've been a hot call."

"Billy's right, Berk. No need to sell yourself short. Shit happens. But just the same, I might send you back to the academy for some high-speed driving classes," I said with a wink.

Both Berk and Billy laughed.

I had Berk get his briefcase and other stuff out of the cruiser, once the towing company had righted it. Then we put his stuff in my Tahoe and headed back toward town. We keep a spare cruiser in a garage behind the jail, so I told Berk I'd drop him off so he could pick it up to drive until his was fixed. I didn't expect the repairs to take too long anyway.

After I dropped him off at the jail, I took a quick look at my watch and decided to go back to my office to make a call or two before I went home. It was already a little after five o'clock, but I was planning to call a police department in Montana, so the time difference worked in my favor. I figured it was only a little after three o'clock there.

As I walked in, Irish was just leaving. She asked about Berk, and I told her he was fine, just a little embarrassed. She said she had just turned off the coffee pot about ten minutes ago, so it was still hot. Not fresh, but hot. I thanked her and told her I was just going to make a call or two and then head home myself.

I poured myself a half-cup of coffee and sat down at my desk. I looked at a resource book we keep that lists all the other sheriff's offices in the US and their contact information. I think Irish ordered the book from the National Sheriff's Association.

I looked up Yellowstone County, Montana. That is the county where the city of Billings is located, and I figured that although the information we had on Danny Windom placed him in Billings, any ranch would be in the outlying county, not the city.

When someone answered the phone in Yellowstone County Sheriff's Office, I asked to speak to the sheriff or his chief deputy. They transferred me to Chief Deputy Arnold Swanson.

"Chief, this is Dell Hinton. I'm the sheriff of Castaway County, Maine."

"Oh, hi, Sheriff. You're a ways east and north. What can I do for you today?"

"Well, Chief, I'm tracking a kid wanted here as a person of interest in a triple homicide case. Last I heard, he was maybe in your neck of the woods."

"We have lots of folks out here, some hiding from people in other states as well. What information have you got?"

"Well, a past employer in Arizona told us he had asked for his mail to be forwarded to a ranch near Billings. His last known name used was Danny Alexander. The employer said he was going to a place called Patriot's Progressive Ranch."

"Oh, oh. That's a place owned by one of those survivalist groups. They haven't caused any problems yet, but we have them on a short list, if you know what I mean."

"Yup, I do. So what can you tell me about these guys?"

"Well, a lot of them dress in the standard camouflage uniforms, and of course, they all have various knives and guns secured in holsters practically everywhere on them. They're well armed, at least when we see 'em."

"Do they seem to be well organized?"

"It would appear so. They have some sort of pseudo-military hierarchy. Some have specific rank designations on their uniforms. And there's one guy who's clearly the leader of the group: Wade Langley Peterson."

I thought about it for a minute and then asked, "What about training? I mean, do they seem to have some internal training program that you know of?"

"Well, we don't have any spies in the organization to be sure about it. But judging from the gunfire from the property and the interactions some of the members have had in town, I'd say they have a pretty active training program for new recruits."

"What type of interactions in town, Chief?"

"One of our local gun shops seems to get a lot of business from the group. Not just some gun sales, but more work on weapons. That shop has a gunsmith in house, so they're able to make repairs on lots of different brands. While they may buy some weapons and ammo through the Internet and other outlets, I think this guy at the gun shop does most of the work on their arsenal."

"Hmmm," I said, as I thought a bit more. "What's the name of the gun shop?"

"Bannaker's Guns. It's over in Lockwood off Old Hardin Road."

"And do you know the gunsmith's name as well?"

"Sure, it's Elliott Bannaker. He's the son of one of the brothers who opened the shop about twenty years ago."

"Easy to talk to?"

"Most of the time, he's just a bit on the surly side. He can get pretty contrary when he drinks, though. He's a helluva good gunsmith!"

"Okay, Chief. If you will, please keep an eye out for our guy, Danny Alexander. We aren't sure where he is now, or frankly how he may fit into our case at all. We're listing him as a person of interest until we locate him or get more on him."

"No problem, Sheriff. I'll give you a call myself if we happen upon him out here."

"Thanks, Chief. I'll follow up with the gunsmith myself."

After wishing each other our best, we concluded the call. I wasn't too surprised by the information I had received from the chief deputy about the survivalist group at the ranch. I had been aware that because of the remoteness of the Montana territories, it has been one of the areas where a number of similar survivalist groups have built their compounds. By the sounds of this particular group, their ranch must have been situated closer to the city of Billings than I might have expected, but with my limited knowledge of the area, it might have been that the wilderness backed right up to the city. Either way, I needed to try to talk to this Elliott Bannaker. I wanted to see if he would talk about the group, or maybe at least confirm their training program for those people just arriving.

I located a phone number for Bannaker's Guns in Lockwood. When I called, a young woman answered the phone.

"Ma'am, this is Dell Hinton. I'm the sheriff in Castaway County, Maine. I was wondering if Elliott Bannaker was available to speak to me."

"Why, sure, I guess he can talk to you. You ain't gonna jail him for anything, are ya?"

"No, ma'am, I'm not. I just want to ask him about a kid I'm looking for, that's all."

"Well, okay, then. Elliott!" she shouted. "Pick up the damn phone, Elliott. Some cop wants to ask you a few questions."

I really wish she hadn't shouted so loud and exposed the phone call for anyone in the store. It didn't seem to be the most professionally run gun shop, at least thus far it didn't.

"Yeah, waddya want?" Obviously, this was Elliott.

"As I told the young lady, Elliott, I'm a sheriff in Maine. I just wanted to ask you a few questions. I'm trying to locate a kid who may have been in your area and come to your store."

"Well, what's his name?"

"Danny Alexander. Do you know or have you seen him?"

"Yeah, a while back."

"About how long ago do you remember seeing him?"

"Last time was about six months ago, maybe."

"Had you seen him more than just the once?"

"Yup."

"Do you remember when you first saw him in your store?"

"Maybe six months before that."

"Okay, so maybe a year ago, he first came into your store, then about six months ago was the last time you saw him?"

"That's about right, I guess."

"How did he happen to come into your gun shop?"

"Brought some guns in for repairs."

"Were they his guns?"

"Didn't ask."

"How many guns did he bring in for repair?"

"'Bout thirty."

"Guess some of those might not have been his, you think?"

"Don't think, Mister, not my business. I just fix the guns and mind my own business. Good idea."

"What's that?" I asked.

"Mindin' yer own business!"

"Okay, Elliott, I get the point. One more question?"

"What?"

"Did Danny Alexander appear to know a lot about firearms?"

"Yup, a lot."

"Well, thanks for your help, Elliott. I may call again if I come up with any other questions."

"If you do, you might ask for my partner."

"Oh, who's that?"

"Someone who cares!" Then the phone line went dead. I guessed Elliott wasn't much of a talker, especially to the police. For all I knew, he might have been a member of the same survivalist group. I really wanted to ask about the group's training to see if they gave tactical training or even assassination training, but frankly, I figured old Elliott had stayed with the conversation about as long as he was going to. I guess he really wanted to hang up on me right from the beginning. *Oh, well,* I thought, *not everyone likes the police or wants to answer questions. Besides, I'm sure I can find someone to answer my questions about the Ranch's training programs.* At least I hoped I could.

· 20 ·

It was time for me to head home for the day. I hadn't seen Suzi for more than twenty-four hours, and I wanted to get home to make her a nice dinner. Well, it was going to be fish, potatoes, and greens, but I wanted to set the ambiance for her at the very least.

As I was going home, I decided to go by the town dock just to be sure everything was quiet before I got home. Before I got there, the radio broke squelch, and I heard the dispatcher telling a field unit to go by the Spoodicook town dock to speak to a Mr. Webb. I knew that was old Darby, so I called in that I was also responding to the town dock.

When I arrived, I saw Darby standing near the end of the town dock yelling and shaking his fist toward the head of the lake. I could just make out a small boat going up through some narrows between two of the islands.

"Here, Darby, what's all the yelling about?" I asked.

"Those damn kids, Dell. Why, they just come down here and use anyone's boat, just anyone at all. Don't mind if it's theirs. They just take one for fun."

"Whose boat did they take?"

"Why, mine, damn it!"

"You mean that old clunker you keep tied up here? Why, Darby, that thing needs to be bailed out every other day or so."

"Yup, it's a clunker, all right. But damn it, it's my clunker, Dell!"

"So it is, Darby, so it is. As soon as my deputy arrives, I'll go to my place and get my boat and go up lake to see if I can find the idiots. Any idea who they were?"

"Eya, some of the kids from town. Billy, Wayne, Dub, and Eldon. Couple of others. They was playing around the dock, then Wayne and Eldon decided to go up to that sandy beach area across from Wesley's Island for a skinny dip. Another kid jumped in, and they took off while the rest just drove away. Guess they didn't want to risk it."

Before we finished talking, Deputy Alec Wardlow arrived on the call. I told Alec to wait with Darby and get all the information for the report. I said I was going to get my boat and head up lake to see if I could get them.

I went by the house and realized that Suzi was already home. Her Rav 4 was in the driveway. So I walked up to the kitchen door, and she met me with a kiss.

"I'm so glad you're back, honey! I missed you."

"I missed you too, Suzi. But, unfortunately, work calls. I've got to get my boat and head up lake to see if I can catch the kids who took Darby Webb's boat for a joy ride."

"That old clunker?"

"Yup, that's the one. I'm actually doing the kids a favor. The way it takes in water, I might be preventing a drowning!"

So I got my boat started and backed out from the floating dock. I put her up to almost full throttle and headed up lake, through the channel between islands en route to the sandy beach. It really wasn't much, just an area of sand about twenty feet square with big boulders on each side. It was just enough for the kids on the lake to call it a beach and to party on.

At least if they built campfires on the beach, there wasn't anything to catch fire for about another thirty yards back from the sand. It was one of the only places where it was actually fairly safe to have a campfire. Anywhere else on the lake, the ground was covered in years of layering pine needles, and they could catch fire in an instant. When you're living or vacationing around one of these lakes up here in Maine, one of the worst hazards is fire. If a fire gets started in this area, there's no telling how much would be burnt before it could be put out! And even when you think the fire has been put out, it may well have gone underground. There are so many layers of pine needles from over the years that fire can actually burn underground for days or weeks before igniting something above ground where it can easily be seen. That makes firefighting a real hazard in the Maine woods!

As I was approaching the beach, I noticed that Darby's boat was partially submerged near the shore, and the three kids were just swimming in to the shore. They must have been getting pretty wet in the boat and decided to get out and swim for shore.

"All right, boys. Stay where you are. You're already in enough trouble."

"Aw, Sheriff Hinton, we just wanted to come up here and skinny dip. We didn't think Old Man Webb would miss this clunker for long."

"Well, you know better than to take another man's boat. And just because it looks like a clunker to you doesn't mean that it isn't worth a lot to Mr. Webb.

"Now suppose you boys get over there and start bailing out Mr. Webb's boat for him." I reached around in my boat and found a pail and one of those hand siphon pumps to pump out the boat with and handed them to the boys. I told the other boy to use his hands.

"Hell, it'll take all evening to bail this boat out," one of the kids remarked.

"That's okay, I've got all evening. And I will be glad to explain to your parents why you were out late. No problems here!"

"Does that mean you're going to throw the book at us, Sheriff?"

"You're all juveniles, aren't you?"

"Yeah, Eldon's the oldest, and he's only sixteen."

"Sixteen and a half!" Eldon said proudly.

"Well, seeing as you're all juveniles, you and your parents will have to come to court and explain your behavior. My guess is that some of your parents aren't going to be too happy about that. Now keep bailing so we can all go home."

After about an hour, the boys had the boat almost bailed out, so I hooked up a towline to it from my boat and got the boys into my boat. We headed down lake toward the town dock at a slow pace since I was towing another boat.

As we neared the dock, I could see that Darby's face was ruddy red and he was mumbling. I unhooked his boat from mine and then pulled it by hand into the shallow ramp area designed for taking boats out or putting them in by trailer. It had already taken in some more water on the tow down lake, so I told the boys to get in the water and finish bailing out Darby's boat. While they did that, I walked over to Darby and Alec.

"Okay, Alec. When these clowns get Darby's boat bailed out, and I *mean all bailed out,* then write them up on a juvenile summons and give them a court date. After that, please take them to their homes and give their parents a briefing and their copy of the summons and court date."

"Will do, boss!"

"Darby, they'll get your boat back in shape before they leave, and I'll stop by your place to talk some more. Hopefully tomorrow."

Then I turned to the boys and told them, "You boys better apologize to Mr. Webb for taking his boat out for a joy ride. My guess is if you had taken time to just ask him to use it, he may have let you."

I didn't give the boys any time to come up with bad answers, and I didn't wait for any more discussion with Darby or Alec. I decided I was done for the day, and I wanted to go home to Suzi.

By the time I had left Alec Wardlow to handle the "captured" boat hijackers and finally pulled into my own driveway, the sun was beginning to set toward the head of the lake. The crimson and gold colors shooting across the sky were beautiful. As I walked into the kitchen, I found Suzi busily heating up some pots and pans with dinner.

"I'm sorry, sweetie. I really wanted to fix dinner for you tonight."

"I know, but I knew you would be late, so I just whipped up something for us."

"Well, I did have to go after those dumb-ass kids. Part of the job, I guess. Anyway, I'm really glad to be home with you."

"I figured you'd be missing me last night. Lieutenant Bell not quite as good to be around as me?"

I knew she was angling for a sexy comment, so I decided to have a little fun with her.

"Oh, Frank's okay, but he's not much of a conversationalist. Doesn't know a thing about interior decorating or how to put a news show together. Kind of boring."

Suzi winked at me and said, "Oh, Dell, you silly man, you know you missed me!"

"Well, I guess I did."

"You guess you did? Why, there goes the fun dessert you were getting tonight!"

"I was planning on giving you a nice dessert, my love, not the other way around."

"Okay, we'll split dessert. Dinner will be ready in about ten minutes or so."

"Let's put it on hold a minute and have a drink on the porch so we can watch the last of the sunset, baby."

"Okay, I'm game."

I had a beer, and Suzi poured a glass of her favorite red wine, and we went out on the porch and sat in our Adirondack chairs. We sipped our drinks and watched as the last portion of the sun set behind the hills and the sky continued to change from yellows to reds to purples, all mixed with the clouds. Sunset on the lake is always one of my favorite times.

After our drinks, Suzi went in to finish dinner, and I sat on the porch for a few extra minutes. *I do some of my best thinking in these chairs on the porch!*

I still figured we had a couple of potentially good suspects in the Black Bear case. Now that we had a suspicion that old Oscar Dillon might have survived the fire in the shed, maybe Frank could get the body exhumed so we could be sure. At least that would either lift him to a possible suspect or just remove him totally from consideration.

On the other hand, we had Danny Windom—Alexander now, or at least we thought. He was another story. I'd tracked him from a North Carolina cigar store to a sporting goods shop in Arizona. Now I had him in Montana at a ranch operated by a suspected survivalist group. The kid had definitely gotten around in the past few years. Anyway, I still wanted to get some more information about the group on that ranch. So I decided the best source was the group itself. Now I knew they would never give me, Sheriff Hinton, any information. If they were a typical group, they detested any governmental entity, and so they wouldn't give me the time of day. *Much like that Elliott Bannaker. I still wonder if he isn't a member of that group.* Well, I needed to call them tomorrow and use a rouse. Maybe I'd try to be a potential guest at their ranch and see if they would provide me with more information. In my experience with radical people, they often seemed to be very proud of their political and governmental ideas, so it shouldn't be too hard to get them boasting about their training and facilities. At least it was worth the try. So I decided to try to make the call tomorrow, just after lunch, which should be midmorning their time.

Then we'll see what pops up!

Suzi came out on the porch to say that dinner was ready, so I picked up my beer glass and put away my thoughts about the case.

After a nice, quiet dinner, Suzi curled up beside me on the couch, and we watched a little TV. As normal, Chauncey quickly came up on the couch to get petted and to get some attention from both of us. I sat there stroking Chauncey on the back, and Suzi on the neck.

About fifteen minutes into the nine o'clock show, Suzi stood up and pulled on my arm.

"Come on, honey. Let's have our dessert."

We walked back to the bedroom, and as soon as we got inside the doorway, Suzi pulled off her blouse. She had already removed her bra, and I just looked at her firm, creamy breasts like a kid looking at an ice-cream cone. When she pulled off her shorts, I decided right there that I must have gone to heaven. Suzi has the most exquisite figure, and yet, her personality outshines her figure. *I really am one lucky man!*

And that night, for the first time, we didn't even shut the door to keep Chauncey out! Go figure.

· 21 ·

We woke up fairly early the next morning, just after the first long and bright rays of the sun pierced our linen shades and poked themselves rather pointedly into our eyes. So we decided to lie in bed a while together since neither of us had any important early meetings on our schedule.

"So, how's the Black Bear case going, honey?"

"Officially or unofficially?"

"Since we're in bed in your cabin, unofficially, of course."

"Well, we're getting some good information here and there, but we're not ready to claim anyone yet as a specific suspect in the case. We do have two strong people of interest we need to locate and get more information about."

"At least you're making headway, then?"

"Oh yes, I'd say we are. Just not there yet."

After snuggling a while and just enjoying being with each other talking about various innocuous subjects, we got up and showered and dressed for the day. I cooked up some bacon and eggs in our cast-iron skillet, the only way to cook them right, I might add, and then we finished our breakfast and both took a cup of coffee for our respective rides to work. My travel mug had some beautiful Irish countryside scenes on it, while Suzi's mug had her station's logo on it.

As soon as I arrived at the office, Irish told me that Frank had called and wanted me to call him as soon as I came in to work. So I went in and sat at my desk and dialed Frank's number while Irish brought me a fresh cup of coffee. *I'm really going to have to cut down on my coffee!*

When he answered his phone, I asked Frank what news he had.

"I got a call late yesterday from a clerk I know in the judge's office down in Portland. She said she thinks the judge is going to grant our request to exhume Oscar Dillon's body, and she thinks the order may be presented and signed as early as this morning."

"Well, that's good news. What's the next step?"

"Once the order is signed and I get a copy, we can go ahead and have the job done. I've got a state medical examiner ready to review the body and see if they can make a definitive identification."

"Sounds like we're off and running on that front, then."

"Sure does. What about your investigation, Dell? Got any new information on Danny Windom?"

"I've tracked him from North Carolina selling cigars to Arizona selling guns. Now I've got him in Montana at a suspected survivalist group's ranch."

"Geez, the kid got around, didn't he, Dell?"

"He did. Now I want to call the ranch and see if I can get some more information."

"Well, that should be easy enough."

"Not really. These guys don't like cops talking to them. Hell, I had a hard time getting the gunsmith at the local gun shop in Billings to say much more than yes and no!"

"No kidding."

"In fact, the shithead basically told me to mind my own business!"

"A member of the survivalist group?"

"My thoughts exactly! Or at least a sympathizer."

"So are you going to call the ranch directly, Dell?"

"Yeah, thought I'd try to act like someone who wanted to get into their little group and see if I can get the person there to open up a little bit anyway."

"Geez, I hope we don't have to make a trip out there to interview anyone. My budget doesn't allow for too much travel, you know."

"Now, Frank, your state budget has to be bigger than my county budget. Anyway, I doubt if we'll need to at this point. I think I can get enough over the phone to satisfy our needs."

"Well, good luck to you talking to those folks. I'm assuming they're radical thinkers."

"My guess is that they are. Probably antigovernment. But, if they think I am too, they might open up a bit."

"Hell, Dell, if we weren't in the government ourselves, we would probably be antigovernment!"

"Who says we aren't, Frank?"

We both had a good laugh over our antigovernment within the government thoughts. But we both knew that government was essential; it just needed some revision and improvement now and then.

Frank and I agreed to speak again after I called the ranch in Montana and he got Oscar's body exhumed for identification. Our persons of interest seemed to be developing fairly quickly and on a parallel track at this point.

After I hung up with Frank, Berk stuck his head into my office to tell me that his cruiser would be back in service tomorrow from the accident. Luckily, there wasn't much damage, so the garage was able to effect repairs quickly.

I asked him how the day was going in the field, and he told me it looked like a quiet day thus far. He reminded me he had a meeting later in the afternoon with a couple of the Rome town selectmen, an assignment I'd given him a few weeks ago. Seems they had been having some minor traffic complaints, and I wanted Berk to brief them on our enhanced traffic control plans when they were applied to specific problem areas. It really was a longwinded way to say that we increased patrol and summons writing as well as making a review and assessment of the traffic patterns and any traffic control devices currently in use in the area of the complaints. I was glad Berk seemed to be prepared for the meeting, and I knew he would give our office a favorable impression to the selectmen. Berk was very professional and at the same time personable.

The remainder of my morning was spent reviewing the overnights and other reports from the past day or so and returning a few calls. Most of the calls were from citizens either complaining about traffic issues or loud music at night or similar things. One call, which as I returned it I expected to be yet another complaint, was from a woman who wanted to applaud one of our deputies.

"Mrs. Willingham. Sheriff Hinton. What can I do for you today?"

"Oh, Sheriff, I'm glad you called me back. I just wanted to tell you how pleased I was with your deputy, Anders Lowery."

"Well, thank you, ma'am. What did Deputy Lowery do for you?"

"Our son, Michael, took off the other night and got drunk at the bar. He apparently got in a fight with another bar patron, and your officers were called.

"They ended up taking both of the young men to jail for fighting and to sober up. When Michael called me, I realized he had taken his dad's truck when he left, and my husband needed it for work the next morning.

"The truck had been locked and left in the parking lot of the bar. So I asked the deputy, Deputy Lowery, how I could get the keys and the truck back."

"So, I guess he was able to help you, ma'am?"

"Yes, sir, he did. He got a hold of the other deputy and gave him the keys. Then, that deputy, I think his name was Wayne or something like that, he brought the keys here and gave them to me so we could get the truck."

"Well, I'm so glad we could help you, Mrs. Willingham."

"Oh and that nice Deputy Lowery said he would check in on Michael to be sure he was okay and slept off the liquor. I really appreciated how nice he was and how helpful, especially given the situation and all."

"I really appreciate that you called to tell me about this incident, Mrs. Willingham. As the sheriff, I'm frequently notified about actions my deputies take that upset citizens, but I so rarely get told about the good things they do. I really appreciate it."

"Well, we appreciated his actions that night, Sheriff. Can you tell him that?"

"Absolutely, ma'am, I will. In fact, I'll make some notes about it and be sure that a copy of those notes is placed in his personnel file. He'll get a good mark come evaluation time!"

"Thanks, Sheriff. You guys are doing a great job!"

"Thank you, ma'am. Thanks for the call."

It's always nice to hear something positive about our staff from our citizens. As the sheriff, it gives me the knowledge that our staff is doing their law enforcement job, but at the same time, continuing to foster good relationships with the citizens of our county. That is a true win-win situation for any sheriff!

I jotted down some notes about the call and handed the paper to Irish to file in Deputy Lowery's personnel file as I was walking out to get some lunch.

I walked down to the Woodburn Grill and had a lobster roll and some fries for lunch.

Some of the locals asked about how the Bear case was going. I told them that we were working on a couple of persons of interest and making a lot of phone calls and interviews. I know it wasn't much to give them, but I wanted them to know we were actively working on the case. With a multiple homicide like this, the worst thing that can happen is if the police department or sheriff doesn't appear to be hustling to solve the case. The citizens in a community need to know that their law enforcement officers are committed to solving crime and protecting the citizens. I just wanted to ensure they kept the faith.

After lunch, I went back to my office so I could call the ranch out in Montana. I knew this was going to be a chore; after all, I had to pretend to be a potential brethren. I decided it was best, under the circumstances, to use the cell phone we had purchased for undercover work; the caller identification was blocked so the receiving person would not be able to quickly ID the caller as being from the sheriff's office, or from Maine for that matter.

The phone rang about ten times, and just before I was ready to hang up, a voice answered.

"Hello, Patriot's Ranch, hep ya?"

"Yes, ma'am. My name is Drake Dawley," I said. "I'm scoutin' out a place to git some trainin' in fightin'."

"We ain't no place for boxing. We're more of self-protection type stuff."

"Yeah, that's what I'm lookin fer. I don't like the way our country is going right now, and I wanna be ready when the shit hits the fan—pardon my language, ma'am."

"Okay. Hold one a minute, and I'll have you talk to Lieutenant Commander Wilkie."

In a few minutes, a male voice came on the phone. He sounded to be in his fifties and rather gruff.

"What's your name, boy?"

"Well, it's Drake Dawley, but I ain't no kid."

"I know that, but if you're planning to come up here to the ranch, ya better be ready! It's like you're in the army now—just it's our army."

"Do I get enough trainin' to be ready?"

"What are you getting' ready for, exactly?"

"Well, I figure the way things is goin' in DC, it won't be long before they start sendin' out the black choppers to start takin' all the guns away. An' I'm tellin' you, ain't *nobody* gonna take my guns!"

"Well, now, you sound like a good candidate. Ever handled a gun in combat situations?"

"No, just hunting and target practice. You good at that combat stuff?"

"The best! I can teach anyone how to kill someone else in about fifteen different ways."

"Don't know if I could kill someone face to face though."

"You don't have to these days. Why, I could put a scoped rifle in your hands and train you how to put ten shots in a man before you can blink. And keep the shot pattern within the size of a quarter, if he didn't go down too quick."

I could really hear the pride in this man's voice as he boasted about how he could provide me with great training in killing. *What a schmuck. But a dangerous schmuck.*

"Well, I mostly use a handgun. I like a .40 caliber most."

"Okay, come out here, and I'll train you to kill three or four people in one quick move! Before they know what hit 'em, they'll be bleedin' out on the ground."

"Well, I've had some training. I can shoot pretty fair targets."

"That's good. Now we'll train you to handle the combat shooting and more."

"That's what my friend told me."

"Oh, who's your friend?"

"Danny. Danny Alexander. He said he stayed at the ranch a while. Said he liked it and learned a lot."

"Yeah, I remember that kid. Fast learner. Did he ever finish his mission?"

"Told me he did, but never told me what it was in the first place."

"Well, I figured he wanted someone out of the way, but he never told me either. So, Drake, was it? You want to come out here and see if I can make you one of the people this country's gonna be rebuilt upon?"

"Um, yeah, probably. Let me get my stuff together, and I'll call back for directions?"

"You call back, and we'll get you the admissions packet and directions and cost sheet and all."

"Okay, then I'll be ready to defend us and the Second Amendment."

"When you call back, just give Ellie your information. We'll see if you have what it takes, Drake, to be ready for the rebirth of our nation."

As soon as I hung up the phone on that guy, I felt like I needed to take a bath. He was just creepy and violent. But I knew if I worked it right, I could get him to tell me about their programs, and it worked. Guys like that are openly proud of their abilities and their political views and are not likely to keep them a secret. *Sounded like a blowhard braggart to me!*

I called out to Irish for a cup of coffee, lit a cigar, and sat back in my chair. It surely sounded to me like the PP Ranch training program could easily have made Danny able to kill all three people at the Bear. And Danny had told them he had a mission of some type. Unfortunately, what type of mission was conjecture at this point since Danny hadn't even told the lieutenant commander what it was. For now, I had a good bit of new information to mull over and another follow-up report to write in the case.

· 22 ·

I spent at least the next half hour going over the case in my mind as I was completing a supplemental report on what I had learned from my call to that ranch in Montana. *Those guys are really committed to their cause but are really out of the mainstream of our society,* I thought. My gut told me that many such people and organizations exist in America today and that if those people were not so paranoid about big government and some impending apocalypse, they would probably be pretty good soldiers and law enforcement personnel. But their commitment just seemed to be skewed from reality. It takes all kinds to be in this world, and some of those folks may have had some specific tragedy in their lives that skewed their thinking. *Who knows?*

Since it was getting late in the day, I decided to call Frank for an update. I wanted to see where he was on Oscar and to tell him about my call about Danny.

"Hey, Dell, I was just planning to call you. I've got the exhumation set for first thing tomorrow morning. Got the court order, and we're a go."

"Great, Frank. You going down to Portland to supervise?"

"Absolutely. I'll watch while they dig the grave up and go with the body to the state coroner's office. I want to keep chain of custody on the body so there are no potential complaints or challenges in court later."

Frank was referring to how we control all forms of evidence. Each piece of evidence, no matter the type or size, must be signed for at every place it goes. This signature list is called a chain of evidence. The chain of signatures allows the prosecutor to clearly show every person who touched the evidence until the time it is presented in court. By this chain of signatures, the prosecutor can show that the evidence never left the custody of law enforcement or the testing agency and, thereby, could not have been altered or contaminated.

Likewise, the chain of signatures allows the prosecutor to call into court as a witness every person in the chain who ever had access to the evidence so they can testify under oath about that piece of evidence. So the chain of evidence is a very important part of any investigation.

"Good, Frank, good. Sounds like we might get Oscar more definitely in or out of the case."

"Well, even if he's still alive, we aren't any closer to finding him."

"At least we'll know. Besides, we can go back to Boston and start from there."

"Good point, Dell. How are you doing on finding Danny Windom?"

"Danny Alexander right now, Frank. I called that suspected survivalist ranch in Montana. What a group!"

"Just like you thought, Dell?"

"Pretty much. I pretended to be a potential client, and the guy I talked to seemed to buy it okay."

"Did you get any good information?"

"The guy I talked to was Lieutenant Commander Willkie. He was kinda gruff, but once I played up to his pride in his abilities, he got boastful."

"Good work, Dell. What did he boast about?"

"For starters, about his training programs and his ability to train someone to kill people. He even boasted that he could train me to kill three or four people in one quick move. Sound familiar?"

"Sure does."

"And when I mentioned Danny as a friend of mine, he asked me if he had completed his 'mission,' which I found interesting."

"Yes, that *is* interesting. Did he elaborate on the mission?"

"No, I don't think Danny ever told him what it was, just that he was planning one."

"You don't think this commander knew more and was just keeping it to himself, do you?"

"No, Frank. I got the feeling that he was boasting earlier and was showing sincerity when talking about Danny. He didn't give me any indication that he had caught on to my ruse."

"Well, it still gives us thought, Dell. It surely does."

"I'd say so. At least it confirmed that Danny was there and that he received training on killing people. In addition, we can speculate that Danny had some type of plan in mind. Now we just have to get more to turn speculation into evidence."

"Yup, we can't take speculation to court."

"Nope, and we still need to locate Danny."

"Dell, have we run all his possible names in the computers for traffic tickets and arrests?"

"All the ones we know about, yes. But who knows what name he might be travelling under now?"

"Good point. Well, I've got to get home and see my wife, Dell. Haven't spent much time with her or the kids since this case started."

"I know, Frank. No wonder our wives and girlfriends think we're married to our jobs!"

"Well, Dell, we kind of are."

"We are, indeed."

After hanging up on Frank, I decided that I needed to update Berk on the case before I went home for the day. I really wanted to spend some time with Suzi as well.

I called Berk, and he arrived in my office about ten minutes later. I spent the next twenty minutes filling him in on Frank's planned exhumation of Oscar's body for identification and the information I had received about Danny and the Patriot's Progressive Ranch. Berk agreed with me about the potential of the comments made by the commander of the group referring to how Danny had a mission to complete. It would certainly fit our evolving idea that Danny might be a good suspect. But we still had work to do, and besides, we still didn't even know where Danny was living. Was he still in the west? Did he live somewhere or just float around the country? Where was he the night of the Bear murders?

Berk, Frank, and I all still had a lot of questions, and it seemed that each piece of information we got generated more questions. But that's the way investigations go. You keep getting new information, which brings up more questions, and it all kind of builds until you get to a reasonable conclusion. In the meantime, it's a lot like playing a game of dominos!

After Berk left the office, I called Suzi on her cell phone to see if she was going to get home on time that night. I thought maybe we could go out kayaking on the lake again and watch the sunset.

"We can't go kayaking, silly. Have you forgotten about the bean supper?"

"Oh my gosh, I did. Dex wouldn't be very happy with me for forgetting that, now would he?"

"I'm almost home, honey. You come home and change, and we can just make it over to the church in time to help Father Delaney with any last minute set up, okay?"

"I'm on my way, babe."

I was sure glad Suzi remembered that supper since it had completely slipped my mind. *Oh well, no sunset for us tonight!* But at least I expected the bean supper to be a nice break from thinking about work. It might just be relaxing for me anyway.

After going home and changing, and picking Suzi up, we drove over to Dex's church. In our area, bean suppers are fairly frequent. Besides being a nice way of getting many of the members of the community together periodically, they're used for other community needs as well.

Some suppers are designed to take donations for some charitable cause. Maybe an illness, maybe replacing home furnishings for a family whose house had burned down, or maybe a new building project for the town hall or a local church. Or in some cases, and this was one such case, it was just an event to get the community together to celebrate life and discuss the future.

Although often referred to as bean suppers, you might find the menu being spaghetti and meatballs. But in tonight's case, we could smell the aroma of beans and franks as soon as we entered the downstairs gathering room of Dexter's church.

As soon as we walked in, Dex came over and greeted us.

"Well, Dell. I'm sure glad you brought Suzi by for the supper."

"Dex, I could hardly miss it. I've had this on my calendar for two months!"

"Dell, I know better than that. I'll bet if Suzi hadn't reminded you, you'd never have shown up!"

"Okay, Dex, you got me. I've just been tied up working on the Bear murders."

"I know. It's okay, Dell. I won't take any offense at being forgotten."

"Well, now that we're here, do you need any help finishing setting up, Father Delaney?" Suzi asked.

Dex handed us some paper napkins with little flowers on them and asked if we would put a big handful on each table. So we went about doing as asked.

The gathering room in the basement of the church was a large, open area. About twenty small folding card tables had been set up. Each one had four folding chairs around it and a plastic tablecloth covering it. In the center of each table was a small potted plant of some kind.

Along the far wall was a group of larger tables with some warming pans on them. Once the food had been fully prepared in the small adjacent kitchen area, or brought in by the various people who had volunteered, each item would be placed in a warmer or on a plate on the large serving tables. Then everyone attending would simply walk down the length of the serving tables, get whichever foods they wished on their plates, and move to the smaller tables for eating. There was still a large, open area where people who wished to stand and mingle could do so.

The doors opened for the public at seven o'clock, and the bean supper began. Suzi and I got in line about fifteen people from the start. I never liked to be the first in line; I felt it might look like I had some priority over other folks, and I didn't want to give that false impression.

As the supper continued, I spoke to quite a few citizens. Many of them commented on the tragic losses in the Black Bear murders. Some asked me how we were doing trying to solve the crime. As before, I just tried to be sure they knew we were working hard to solve the crime without giving anyone actual details of the investigation. After all, giving out case information was Frank Bell's job, not mine, in this case.

Daisy Mae Toddle, one of our more elderly citizens, came by our table to share her memories of Betty Dillon and how much she liked her. I listened to Daisy Mae and tried to console her a bit, telling her that we really did have some leads and that we never forget the victims in such cases. I reminded her that we had solved the Billy Snow murder just last year, even though the case was some ten years old and cold. I'm a firm believer that we should never forget the victims.

A little while later, while I was standing in the open area talking to a couple of other townsfolk, Shelly Cooper came up to talk about the case. Obviously, when a case of murder strikes in a close-knit community, it becomes the daily talk almost everywhere in the community. It tends to affect everyone.

"You know, Sheriff, I feel so bad for the Windom family."

"Yes, ma'am. I think we all do."

"That Paul was such a nice man!"

"He was that, ma'am."

"Say, have you located Danny to tell him about his father?"

"Why, no, we haven't. Do you know much about Danny, Mrs. Cooper?"

"Well, Danny used to come by to see my daughter, Emily. He was kind of sweet on her at one time."

"Oh, really? I didn't know that."

"Oh, yes. In fact, I think she's gotten a card or two from him since he left."

"Well, it sounds like I need to talk to Emily then. Did she ever tell you anything Danny said about leaving or where he'd gone?"

"No, I try to stay out of her business. You know kids in their teens. They want their privacy."

"Yes, ma'am, I guess they do at that."

"I do hope you find him to tell him about his father. I know Danny and Paul used to argue a lot of the time, but I'm sure he really loved them both."

"What makes you so sure of that? I mean after their blow up."

"Well, Danny said in one of his cards to Emily that it was a mission of his to pay them back for all their kindness to him."

My attention to Mrs. Cooper's conversation now became a laser pointer. Her terminology about Danny's having a mission had just peaked my interest considerably.

"Mrs. Cooper, did Danny say it just that way? Did he write it was a mission of his or are you just paraphrasing what he wrote on the card?"

"No, no, as I recall, he specifically called it his mission. You know, like a mission in life to do something. He must have really loved them to say that."

"Yes, ma'am. I guess he must. You don't think you or Emily still have that card, do you?"

"I doubt it. I guess Emily could have kept it, but she usually threw out her mail after she read it."

"Thanks for talking to me, Mrs. Cooper. You've been a help."

Now my mind was really swirling. Was this the part of the puzzle I had been waiting to find? Did this now give me a reason to tie Danny directly to the murders? Could I now really consider Danny a suspect rather than just a person of interest? It seemed like a lot of decisions were based upon a simple word *mission*. But I quickly decided that it was a significant use of the word. And that word tied him ever so closer to the murders.

I tucked the information back in my mind for tomorrow and continued walking around with Suzi at the bean supper and talking to other citizens from the community. *Who knows what other interesting things I might hear?*

The rest of the bean supper went well, and there were no other comments by anyone that peaked my interest like Shelly Cooper's had. I was beginning to see a common theme from Danny Windom, né Alexander, with regard to having a mission involving his parents. And although Mrs. Cooper thought the comment derived from Danny's love of his parents, I knew that it could just as easily have been indicative of his hate for them having hidden his past from him throughout his childhood, coupled with his quarrelsome, if not violent, relationship with his father in particular.

After the supper, Suzi and I were both quite tired. We went to bed as soon as we got back to the cabin after, of course, petting Chauncey for a bit. He always demands some attention, especially before bedtime.

The next morning over breakfast, Suzi and I talked about the bean supper, and she opined that I seemed to have satisfied the people from the community who had asked about the status of the Black Bear murders. I was glad to hear her opinion, since I often feel that in having to restrict my comments, I might give people the impression that I'm either hiding something or not working the case as hard as I should. Suzi's opinion and support gave me some confidence in my approach. *She makes a good sounding board for me!*

On my way into the office, Frank called me on my cell phone.

"Dell, glad you're up early. Got some news."

"Oh, what's that, Frank?"

"I got a call from our medical examiner on old Oscar. Turns out he is about 75 percent sure the body in his grave isn't him!"

"Wow! Only 75 percent?"

"He won't be totally sure without the final DNA results. But his examination has given him lots of doubts."

"Well, well. Maybe old Oscar is still out there. Gives us some more possibilities, doesn't it, Frank?"

"It does. But we don't have anything other than hunches that might point to him."

"No, we don't. But it does give you pause to wonder."

"I haven't told anyone at Portland PD yet. Don't want to get anyone stirred up until the decision is 100 percent."

"That's probably a good idea, Frank. I'm guessing that they won't particularly like knowing that they blew the ID."

"Would you, Dell?"

"No, but I would have relied more on facts to make the confirmation in the first place."

"Point taken, my friend. I would have done likewise."

After a bit more discussion, Frank hung up, and I was just pulling into the parking lot at the office. *Boy, doesn't this information about Oscar potentially being alive make me consider some new options!*

As I walked in, Irish greeted me with a smile and a cup of coffee. I told her about the call I had just received from Frank Bell and that Oscar being alive added a new dimension to a potential suspect list. I had figured there was at least a fifty-fifty chance that he was the person in the grave and could therefore be excluded permanently from our list. But not so.

I also realized that I had been so busy yesterday that I had forgotten to call that friend of Danny Windom's at the sporting goods store in Arizona. I wasn't sure if he was even working today but figured I needed to try to contact him later. I wasn't sure if he could provide any additional information, but I don't like leaving any reasonable contacts and interviews undone.

I sat down in the office and pulled out the case file on the Bear murders. I looked through the notes and follow-up reports I had made on the various interviews, looking to see if we had missed any information or failed to ask any key questions. The review took about an hour, so I was glad it was a quiet morning in the office.

As I lingered on the interview material of Elizabeth Tressman, Danny Windom's aunt, when we visited her at Greene's Pineywoods assisted living unit, I had noted that the attendant had mentioned Elizabeth had a visitor. I did not, however, see any notes containing names. The note just listed that the home thought the visitor was a niece, maybe. *Now let me see, what was the name of that attendant? Oh yes, here it is. Dominique.*

I decided to call the Pineywoods home and see if I could get a name.

"Hello, is Dominique there? This is Sheriff Hinton from Castaway County."

"Yes, I'll get her for you. She's dealing with one of our clients now."

"Thank you, ma'am."

I was on hold for about five minutes, while the other attendant had Dominique relieved so she could come to the phone. Their phone system had classical music playing for the callers when they were on hold. It was actually quite relaxing.

"This is Dominique, Sheriff Hinton. How can I help you?"

"When we interviewed Mrs. Tressman, you spoke to her about a visitor. I'm afraid we never asked you if you had a name for that visitor."

"I'm sure she signs in on the visitor's log at the front desk. Can you wait a minute and I'll check for you?"

Before she put me back on hold, I could hear a loud commotion in the background. Dominique quickly told me she had to call me back and hung up the phone. Obviously, something had happened with one or more of their clients and she had to respond. In my business, I completely understood that, so I made a note to myself to call her back later, if she didn't call me back first.

It was still too early to try to make that call to Arizona, so I decided to walk down to the jail to see how things were going.

When I walked in, I noticed that Winston Call was working the booking desk. I always enjoy seeing him since he's one of our most jovial deputies.

"How's it going this morning, Winston?"

"Pretty good, boss. Had a few drunks to release this morning. One guy was kind of funny."

"Oh, how's that?"

"Well, he was a real terror when they brought him in last night, as I understand. He was fightin' everyone. And a spittin' and a cussin'."

"So what then?"

"Well, you should have seen him this morning. He walked out and made a formal apology to all our staff!"

"Guess he knew he'd been a wise-ass last night, huh?"

"Guess so. But this guy is a regular. Does that every time he's in. All kinds of problems coming in the doors, then meek and apologetic when he sobers up."

"Sounds like the kind of guy who shouldn't drink at all."

"Yeah, and the dumb thing about it is *he obviously knows it!*"

"Guess he just can't help himself, Winston. He's got the disease."

"Yup. It's a shame though. If you catch him sober, he's really a nice guy. But when he drinks, look out!"

"Anything else going on, Winston?"

"No, just the normal daily things. Are you going on a walk through, boss?"

"Maybe a quick one today."

I walked through the inmate housing areas, checking the conditions and speaking to a few inmates here and there. I didn't talk to anyone very long since I wanted to get back to the office to work on the Bear case some more. But, regardless of the case, I still had a jail I was responsible for, as well as the other sections of the office, so I had to be sure to fit my administrative duties as sheriff in with the investigative responsibilities that the murder case dictated.

When I arrived back at my office, Irish told me that Dominique had returned my call and asked that I call her.

When I got her back on the phone, she apologized for having to hang up on my initial call, but she had an emergency in the dining room area: apparently two of her clients had been involved in a physical altercation. I assured her that I understood about having to attend to emergency situations.

"Now, Dominique, were you able to check the sign-in book?"

"Yes, sir, I was. The young lady who has been visiting Mrs. Tressman is Alexandra Smith."

"And what about her boyfriend? Did he sign in as well?"

"No, I'm sorry. She just lists her name and beside it notes 'boyfriend.'"

"Have you ever heard her call him by name?"

"I have. It's something like ... David, I think."

"Could it have been Danny or Daniel?"

"I don't think so. Those names seem too long, maybe. I think it was David, could have been Dave, Dan, or Dick, but I'm really not sure. I'm sorry, but we see so many people come in here to visit. I'm just not sure about the boyfriend."

"Well, you've still been very helpful. If those two come in to see Mrs. Tressman anytime soon, pleased try to ask the boyfriend's name, if you can do so without being too obvious."

"Okay, Sheriff, I'll be glad to do that. If they come in anytime soon."

After I hung up with Dominique, I started thinking about this couple that visits Mrs. Tressman. Could the boyfriend be Danny Windom? But if it was him, who was the girl? Was she really a relative of Tressman's or was she just posing as her niece? I certainly couldn't ask Mrs. Tressman any of these questions and expect that I would get the true story. In her condition, she might have only known this couple by having them identified by staff members like Dominique.

I decided to go have some lunch, and when I returned to the office, I would continue making more phone calls. I still had David Wimbley, Danny's friend and coworker in Arizona, to contact, as well as setting up an interview of Shelly Cooper's daughter, Emily. But first, I had to call Mrs. Cooper to locate Emily, Danny's good friend and possibly his girlfriend. I had not met her daughter, even though I'd seen Mrs. Cooper at quite a few civic functions, so I assumed she did not live in the immediate Castaway area.

After a quick lunch, I returned to my office to find Irish waiting to speak to me.

"Sheriff, I've been conducting my monthly review of our budget, and I wanted to talk to you about some overages."

"Sure, Irish. Bring your materials in. I'll get a cigar, and we'll sit at my table and look over the budget."

While Berk and I, with Irish's help, drafted the yearly budget for our office, I had assigned Irish to conduct a monthly evaluation on the budget to be sure we were sticking to it, as best we could. When she located a problem, then we got together to discuss it and make any changes to our spending that we could. I also asked her to call Berk to see if he was available to attend this little impromptu budget meeting.

My office has, besides the large executive desk and the two leather chairs, a smaller wooden table with four straight-backed chairs. This table I use for budget meetings and other projects. It keeps my desk from getting all cluttered up. I just hate a desk so cluttered with files and stuff that you have no room to work. And, if it's too cluttered, it makes it difficult to locate important items and files. *Clutter breeds chaos,* my mother used to preach. And I had come to know that Mom was always right!

In about twenty minutes, when my cigar was about half finished, Berk arrived, and we set to work. Irish began by identifying the problem.

"Dell, we're only about three and a half month's into our budget cycle, and we've already spent over half of our overtime and staffing budget."

"Berk, why have we used so much already?" I asked.

"Well, boss, we had that rape trial that came up right at the beginning of April. It took extra manpower. Remember? The families began a brawl in the courtroom that had to be sorted out."

"Yeah, I remember, and then too, we've already spent a good bit of overtime on this Bear case."

"And what about the extra duty when those hikers got lost for three days out by Rome?" Irish asked.

"Yes, we did use some overtime there as well, boss."

"So," I said, "it appears that we may well go above our overtime allotment for the year. Unless, of course, there are no major crimes, lost hikers, major trials, severe weather, or other reasons why we utilize more overtime."

We all looked at each other and smiled. Budgeting for an agency whose primary responsibility is keeping peace and responding to every emergency situation imaginable is a little difficult. Being a weather forecaster is easier, yet the public expects us to get it right every year.

"Okay, how are we doing in some of the other line items of the budget, Irish?"

"We're good, Dell. Actually, Berk, can we get away with our current prisoner photography and fingerprint equipment for another year?"

"Oh, I think so. We just put in for the next generation to enhance our capabilities. But our current equipment is still in pretty good shape. Should last a while yet."

"Okay, we could do a budget adjustment and move some of that money into the line for overtime."

"Good thinking, Irish. What else can we look at?"

We kept at it for another half hour or so. During that process, we identified several other lines where we could move money to put in the overtime budget. When finished, Irish had all the information she needed to file the budget adjustments with the board.

As Irish headed out to her desk to work on the budget paperwork, Berk headed back out on day patrol, and I sat behind my desk again so I could begin some of the phone calls that were waiting. All I could think was, *Thank God for a great administrative assistant. Don't know what I would do without her!*

· 24 ·

decided to try to call David Wimbley at the sporting goods store in Arizona first. When the phone was answered, I asked for David, and to my good luck, he was at work. I had been afraid that by not making the call yesterday, as originally planned, I might have missed his scheduled workdays, and it might take longer to contact him.

David came on the phone after about a minute. He sounded to be in his late twenties, by voice.

"David, this is Sheriff Dell Hinton from Castaway County, Maine. I just wanted to ask you a few questions about a former roommate of yours, Danny Alexander."

"Yeah, my boss told me you might call. Said Danny was a person of interest or something."

"Well, I'm trying to track him down so I can ask him some questions as well."

"I don't know where he is now. He went to a ranch in Montana for training. Last time I heard from him was a call when he was leaving there."

"When was that?"

"Maybe, oh, six weeks ago by now, I'd guess."

"Can you tell me, David, what type of person Danny was when he was rooming with you and working at the sporting goods store?"

"He was very nice. He's a good shot with a handgun. He and I won a couple of local pistol firing tournaments. And he was a good salesman at the store. He's very charismatic. You know, I think he could have sold a gun to a priest."

"David, did he ever talk about his parents with you?"

"Yeah, once in a while, but not often. Usually when we were drinking a few beers or something, he'd start in on them."

"Oh? Did he speak badly about them?"

"Oh yeah, especially his father. He didn't seem to have anything good to say about him. He was real bitter. Something about his being adopted, but they never told him that, and suddenly he found some document that related to the adoption. Said he and his father really got into it after that. He sure took it hard, I guess. Like I said, he didn't talk about it unless he had been drinking a bit."

"Did Danny ever indicate that he wanted to go back to his home and discuss the issues with his parents?"

"Not exactly. He just said that it was his mission in life to pay them back for what they had done to him."

"How did you interpret that when he said it?"

"Well, like I said, he'd been drinking. But he was clearly pissed at his parents, so I thought it was one of the threats you make about someone when you're drinking that you wouldn't make if you were sober."

"And Danny used the term 'mission'?"

"Oh yeah. In fact, that was what he said when he told me he was going to the ranch in Montana."

"What did he say, *exactly*?"

"He said he was going there to get more training so he could complete his mission at his parents' place."

"And did Danny call or write you while he was in Montana?"

"He called once to tell me his training was going well. Said he had a great teacher who knew more about combat fighting than anyone he'd ever met before, and said he liked some of the speeches he'd heard from the guy who ran the whole operation. He seemed to be impressed with the ranch."

"Sounds like it. Have you heard from him since he left?"

"No, like I said, he called right before he left the ranch. Told me it would be a while before I heard from him again, but he'd call when he could."

"Did he say where he was going after the ranch?"

"Nope. Just said he wanted to put his past behind him and get on with his life."

"What did you think he meant by that, David?"

"Well, I thought he had maybe given up on being so mad at his parents and was planning to move on. I really didn't think any more about it. Guess he could have planned to go home and talk to them, or maybe he was just going to forget about them and move on."

"Is there anything else you can think of that might help me locate Danny?"

"Not really. He talked about some girl a few times. I think her name was Elise or Emily or something like that. It began with an E. Anyway, he only spoke of her a couple of times, but I think he called her a few times while we were rooming together. I'd walk in, and he was on the phone and acted like it was a girl-type call, you know?"

"Like he was hiding her from you?"

"Yeah, like a hidden girlfriend. But I don't have any idea how to find her."

"Well, David, you've been very helpful. Thanks for talking to me."

"I hope you do find Danny. Like I said, he's a good guy, and I enjoyed having him as a roommate. And I could use him again as a partner for pistol competitions!"

"Good luck on that, and if I find him, I'll suggest he call you. By the way, if he happens to call you, please give me a call. I really want to ask him some questions, if I can find him."

"Sure thing, Sheriff Hinton."

After hanging up the phone with David Wimbley, I decided that we could now put Danny Windom on our suspect list. David was the first person who Danny seemed to have really opened up with about his feelings toward his parents, especially his father. Most people assumed that he still loved them, but Danny had been more forthcoming with David. He clearly hated the Windoms for having kept him in the dark about his being adopted, and it sounded like that, in turn, increased the problems between him and his father. And his use of the terminology "mission" seemed to tie all the parts of the puzzle together. We could now surmise that Danny Windom's mission was to get back at his parents for their perceived transgression of not telling Danny he was adopted.

And now I could also surmise that Danny may have still had contact with Emily Cooper. That made it a priority for me to locate her, and for Frank and me to go interview her.

But one thought still crept in my mind: it is now quite possible that Oscar Dillon is alive, so he may also be a viable suspect. I had to be sure I didn't get tunnel vision with regard to Danny Windom. While he seemed to be the stronger suspect, I didn't want to forget about dear old Oscar. For now, we just had to keep working on them both as suspects and follow the evidence we got from interviews and other investigative tools.

I quickly dialed up Frank on the phone to tell him about my phone interview with David Wimbley. Frank agreed that we could now feel safe calling Danny Windom a suspect, although we had no intention of letting the press in on any identities of suspects. Frank would be making another weekly press release on the case tomorrow, and in that release, he would simply state that we now had several suspects. If asked, he would still allow the press to think we also had additional persons of interest. We didn't want to give too much away to the public at that point. But we both felt that we were really making some headway on the case. That was important for us!

My next call was to Mrs. Cooper. I needed to get her daughter, Emily's, current location and contact information. As it turned out, Emily lived in South Freeport, not far from the Lunch and Lobster, two streets up and one block south of the main street into town.

I called Frank back and asked him if he wanted to meet me in Waterville again so we could go down and interview Emily Cooper.

"I take it you don't want to just call her, Dell?"

"No, Frank, I'm thinking she may be right in this whole mess, and I want to be able to observe her eye contact and body language while we ask her some questions."

"Well how about this, Dell? How about you and Berk head down to interview her this evening, and I'll handle the press conference in the morning, and we'll touch base by phone after that?"

"That works, Frank. I'll call you around eleven?"

"Press conference may not be done by then. Make it eleven thirty or a quarter to noon, Dell."

"Okay, I'll call you then."

"Hey, Dell, are you and Berk going to stay in the area overnight?"

"Yeah, we probably will since it's as late as it is already."

"Okay. I'm hoping to get the final results of the DNA testing tonight or tomorrow morning. If Oscar is still around, we might need to go back to Big Eddy again."

"You think he'll say anything to us?"

"Probably not, but it would be good to rattle his cage so he knows that we know."

"I suppose it could get some movement from him, but I doubt it, Frank. He seemed to me to be really old school. That type of criminal doesn't roll over or make many mistakes, especially the mistake of talking too freely with cops."

"You're probably right, Dell. Anyway, we have to wait for the final DNA. So just call me around noon."

I hung up on Frank and called Berk on his cell. I asked him if he had someone to cover him tomorrow morning for roll call and told him I needed him to go with me on an overnighter to South Freeport. He was fine with that assignment and told me he would go home, get some stuff packed, and be back to the office by about five thirty.

I had Berk set for the trip, so now I had to call Suzi and tell her she was going to have another night alone at the cabin, or her place. I wasn't really sure why she still kept a place of her own, since she mostly stayed at the lake with me, but I guessed she still liked to be able to have her own space to go to. *After all, it isn't like we're married or anything.*

I called her, and to my surprise, she was already home for the day.

"No meetings this afternoon, baby?"

"No, honey, came home about a half hour ago. What's up?"

"Well, I hate to be the bearer of bad news, but I need to go down to the Freeport area to conduct a very important interview. Since it's this late, I just figured we stay overnight."

"Oh? Frank going with you?"

"No, he has a press conference tomorrow he didn't want to reschedule, so I'm taking Berk with me."

"Okay, honey, you boys have a good, safe trip. I assume this might be a break in the Bear case?"

"I don't know as I'd call it a break, just someone I think might be a step closer to one of our persons of interest." Even with Suzi, I had to try to maintain the integrity of any press release material. It isn't that I don't trust her to keep stuff out of her reporting, but I know how easy it is to allow something to get out if it's in your head, even by accident. So I try not to give her any information I don't want to release so she doesn't have to decide which parts are to be kept secret and which ones can be released; it's my way of protecting her and the integrity of the investigation.

"Well you boys just be safe then, honey. Will you be back after work tomorrow?"

"That's the plan, baby. Maybe if I'm early enough, we can kayak some on the lake."

"I'd love that, honey. See you then!"

I always keep a "go-bag" in my office closet for just such occasions. In the bag are clean clothes for at least two days, a pair of hiking boots, a toiletries pouch, and a handful of organic power bars/meal replacement bars. I like to be prepared for whatever the job holds without having to go home each time to pack.

I got my bag and told Irish about the impending trip. She said she would take messages for me as always and call if anything really big came up.

While I was waiting for Berk to return, I pulled a couple of cigars out of the humidor and located my four-hole cigar case. I threw the case with the cigars into my go-bag and zipped it up. I sat there thinking about the information we now had before us.

Oscar was likely to be alive, but we didn't have anything suggesting that he was involved at the Bear, other than maybe the professionalism of the shots. True, he was an ass to his former wife, but that didn't translate into any evidence that he may have wanted her dead and then done something about that. At this point, he was still interesting, but not a viable suspect really. We would need to find him to get more information, and that was if he was really still alive.

Danny Windom, now, was a viable suspect. Although he had clearly moved around the country, and it had taken days to track him, some of the interviews were paying off in spades.

Danny had worked at a sporting goods store in Arizona where he became good with a handgun, even winning competitions with his roommate, David Wimbley. He had opened up to Wimbley about his hatred for his father and disillusionment with his parents in general and having a mission in regards to them.

After that, he had attended a survivalist ranch in Montana where he clearly obtained additional combat shooting training. And while there, he had made the same comment about having a mission to complete.

Now, I found that Emily Cooper might be, or at least had been, a girlfriend of Danny's. She was clearly someone we had to talk to about Danny. Maybe she knew his current location. Maybe she knew a lot more than that. Who knows?

But it was imperative we interview her, and do it in person. You can ask questions on the phone and get answers. But the only way to evaluate those phone answers is by the tone of the person or how quickly they respond. Did they give you an answer quickly without thinking about it or take time with the answer like they were making it up or trying the answer on for size before verbalizing it?

When you ask questions in person, you have the additional tools of being able to see the responder's eye contact and body language. You can tell more easily if they're being evasive or if the question bothers them in some way. You can see if they're uncomfortable or sweating. Are they fidgety? Are they avoiding eye contact? The in-person interview is much more favorable, but the phone interview can be helpful, especially when there are great distances involved.

But for suspects or potentially closely related individuals, nothing beats a personal interview.

Now I just had to wait for Berk to get back with his overnight bag, and we would be off to South Freeport.

· 25 ·

Berk and I had a fairly uneventful ride out the Airline Road to Bangor and down I-95 and then I-295 into the Freeport area. On the way, we discussed the case and also how our office needed to continue growing and planning for the future of Castaway County.

While our population is not significant, like many rural coastal counties in Maine, there are pockets of more dense population throughout the county, and these are separated by vast wilderness. While forests and wild animals comprise the majority of the county, the small towns have population centers, and when tourist season arrives, each of them may swell to four times their normal size in population, or more.

Berk and I have had many discussions about the need to somehow cultivate responsible candidates as deputies who can accommodate a seasonal position into their lives. In the winter, when there is little tourism in our county, we need half the deputies that we need during the tourist season. But it's difficult in the current economic times, not to mention the depressed state of Maine's economy overall, to attract qualified people for part-time seasonal positions.

We discussed the potential to try to attract individuals from other localities, such as Boston or Philadelphia and their suburbs, where the economy is somewhat better and we might find more success in making seasonal positions attractive. But we had two primary problems with that concept. The first was a simple matter of training and certification. All persons performing law enforcement services in the State of Maine have to be trained and certified at the State Police Academy in Vassalboro, just south of Waterville. Persons from outside Maine would still need to be trained and certified.

Additionally, and this was an issue that I brought to the table, persons hired from outside of Maine might not have the community compassion and development attitudes that I wanted to provide to our citizens. Especially those who came in as seasonal employees. They would likely not ever feel a part of our community. And for me, as an administrator, one of my goals is for the sheriff's office to be an integral part of the community. And to do that effectively, I need the deputies and civilian staff to be part of the community and have that "buy in."

Now that doesn't mean I wouldn't hire someone from another state as a deputy, but when I do, they will move into the state and become a citizen of Castaway County or a neighboring county; either way, they will become a Mainer, even if "from away." A sense of community is important to me and, I believe, to running an effective sheriff's office.

So between Berk and me, we never came up with the best solution to our needs for some seasonal positions. We currently had only one part-time sworn deputy position, and that was Eli Samples in Court Security. We normally used him for big trials and for inmate transportation needs. We had no seasonal positions in Field Services, and that was where we wanted to provide more staffing during tourist season.

Well, luckily for us, the next budget cycle in which to make requests for additional positions was not any time soon, so we had time to formulate ideas. Talking about the future as we drove to Freeport passed the time and got us started in the planning process.

It was nearly eight at night when we arrived in front of Emily Cooper's house in South Freeport. She lived on a quiet side street in a small, white, Cape Cod style clapboard house with black shutters. The grass hadn't been mowed in the front yard for at least two weeks, and there was a push mower sitting near the driveway. The exterior of the house was neat enough but appeared to be lacking in maintenance, such as shutter repair and general painting. The house bespoke of a woman living alone and working to pay the bills. There were no outward signs of anyone having been around doing work on the house or a vehicle. In fact, the only vehicle in the driveway was a blue Volkswagen Jetta, and it appeared to be an older one.

As we approached the door, a young woman in her mid to late twenties opened the screen and asked who we were.

"Ma'am, I'm Dell Hinton, sheriff of Castaway County, and this is my chief deputy, Berkley Smith. We just came by to ask you a few questions. We're trying to locate someone and give them information about a death and potential inheritance. May we come in?"

After we showed her our official identifications, she stepped back and invited us in to talk. She walked us into a small living room, just off the main entrance hallway. We sat down in two chairs while she sat on a small sofa.

"As I said, Miss Cooper, we're trying to locate Danny Windom."

"Oh, Danny. Yes, I remember him from my days growing up in Castaway County."

"Well, unfortunately, someone killed his father, and the family attorney is also looking for Danny to claim a small inheritance."

"His *step*father," she corrected me. "And I'm sure he wants nothing from him!"

"Aw, yes, it was his stepfather. Do you know where Danny is these days?"

"Um, no, I don't. I haven't seen him for years."

"Oh, when was the last time, ma'am?"

"I'd say it was about the time he went out west."

"Oh?"

Emily related how she had kept in touch with Danny during the time he was working at the cigar store in North Carolina. She had actually visited him there a couple of times, as well as taking a short vacation with him in Myrtle Beach, South Carolina, about an hour farther south.

"So, did you lose track of him when he moved out west?"

"No, he sent me cards and a few letters, but we didn't see each other after he went west."

As I watched her face, Emily broke eye contact quickly as she was saying they hadn't seen each other since then. I got an immediate feeling that she was not being truthful.

"You were friends, if not a couple, prior to his moving out west then?

"Well, I guess you'd say he was sweet on me. I always liked him. He was a good friend and all."

As she was telling us this, I could see a passion in her eyes that belied her claim of Danny just being a friend. *This girl clearly cared about him, then and maybe still now.*

I asked her why they hadn't seen each other since he went west, and she said it was because the trip would be too costly for either of them, and they wrote to each other occasionally, just to keep in contact.

"Besides," she said, "I kind of felt like he ran out on our friendship when he took off for the west."

Once again, her eyes did not speak of any madness or ill feelings toward Danny as she said that, but rather still hid the emotion of love.

"Did Danny ever tell you why he was going out west, ma'am?"

"No, he just said that he was taking a new job that had better prospects for him than selling cigars."

"Sounds like he was on a mission to improve his career possibilities."

"I don't know as it was a mission, but I think he wanted a better life for himself."

Well, I had hoped for Emily to pick up the term of "a mission" and maybe confirm Danny's drive in that respect, but she didn't do it. I'll have to try some other questions, I thought.

"So, did Danny ever talk about his father the game warden?"

"His *step*father, you mean?" *Again, the stress on "step."*

"Yes, ma'am, sorry, his stepfather the game warden."

"Yes, he did. I knew Mr. Windom when I was growing up. Nice man toward me but tough on Danny. I never liked how he treated Danny. Sorry to hear he's gone, though."

From her body language and eye contact, I felt that she was being truthful about her feelings toward Paul Windom. *I think she may actually have liked Paul in a general way.*

"Did Mr. Windom and Danny fight a lot, ma'am?"

"Mr. Windom was pretty hard on Danny. He couldn't do anything as good as the warden wanted him to. Yeah, they argued all the time, I'd say."

"Did the arguing increase after Danny found out he was adopted?"

"I don't think they ever spoke a normal word to each other after that. Danny and his mom were more cordial, but he was pretty pissed at them both over the adoption thing."

"When was the last time you heard anything from Danny, Miss Cooper?"

"Well, I think it was when he was in Montana. Yes, that's it. He sent me a birthday card from there, Billings I think."

"So did you two just gradually lose contact with each other over the time?"

"Yes, pretty much. We stopped seeing each other due to the distance, and the letters and cards grew fewer with time. I just assumed he'd moved on. Guess he'd lost being sweet on me. We just sort of lost touch, you know."

While she was saying this in a fairly dramatic way, much like you'd see in an old movie, her body language seemed off. She appeared to be fidgety and somewhat nervous. *Lots of folks get nervous talking to the cops,* I thought. I shot a quick glance over at Berk, and I could tell he had also noticed her body language.

"So, I take it that Danny hadn't gotten over the fact that his parents hadn't told him he was adopted? I mean, by the time you all stopped talking to each other?"

"Would you? I doubt he'll ever get over that. He felt betrayed by his own parents. He didn't like to talk about it much, but when he did, that was the word he used, 'betrayed.'"

"Well, I guess I can understand that."

Just before I could ask her another question, her cell phone rang. She looked at the screen and then excused herself to take the call in the adjoining room. I think it was the kitchen, although I couldn't see clearly through the doorway.

Keeping quiet ourselves, Berk and I could hear a small portion of Emily's side of the conversation. It was mostly muffled, but at one point she repeated something to the caller in ever-increasing loudness, as if the caller was hard of hearing. We clearly heard the second and third times Emily said, "Yes, Auntie, on Sunday. Sunday!"

After a few more words with the caller, Emily apparently hung up on the call and came back into the living room with us.

"Sorry about taking the call and interrupting. Old Aunt worries about me a lot. You know how it is."

"Oh, I sure do. Your mother's or father's side?"

"Oh, Dad's side of the family. Lives in the Midwest. Calls a couple times a week to check on me. Gets her days mixed up."

"Well, we really need to locate Danny. We don't even know if he knows about his stepfather yet. If you hear from him again, would you please give me a call?" I handed her one of my business cards.

"Oh, sure. But I doubt he'll call or write me again. Like I said, we've sort of lost touch over time. I hope you all find him to tell him."

Emily had taken on a whole different attitude now that she knew we were leaving and the questions would stop. *Why she's almost cheerful we're leaving,* I thought. She had definitely brightened her face, and she looked less nervous than before.

Berk and I said good-bye to Emily, and I asked her if I could give her a call if I had any further questions, and she reluctantly said that would be fine. I knew she didn't mean it. And in fact, I really doubted I had any other questions to ask; I just wanted to see her reaction when I asked her. She didn't disappoint me either; her cheerfulness seemed to change in an instant to dread.

But just before we went out the front door, she said, "I'm always glad to help in any way I can. Call if you do have any more questions I might be able to answer."

There it is, I thought. *She wants to be sure we think she's being helpful and cooperative.* I thanked her for seeing us and telling us what she knew about Danny. She feigned interest in hoping we found him to notify him of his stepfather's fate.

Berk and I got in the Tahoe and drove about a mile up the road to Freeport and pulled in behind L.L.Bean's in one of their huge parking lots.

"Are we going shopping, boss?"

"No, Berk, I just thought we could get a nice dinner before we head back."

"Head back? What'd I pack a bag for?"

"Well, I had planned to stay tonight, but I think Frank and I might be coming back down here the day after tomorrow. So I see no need to stay tonight."

"Okay, can you tell me about it over dinner?"

"Sure I will. Let's go to Jameson Tavern and get something."

Jameson Tavern, a very old and historic pub, is situated just beside Bean's flagship store, across a small alleyway. It was built in 1779 and considers itself "the birthplace of Maine," because the final papers giving Maine its independent statehood status were signed in that building. Today, it serves great food, including lobster dishes, other local seafood, and traditional pub fare.

I figured we could get a good dinner, and then with both of us refreshed and willing to drive, we could make it back to Castaway County by about one or two in the morning, assuming there were no other problems.

As we sat in the pub waiting on our dinner, I started to discuss our interview of Emily Cooper with Berk.

"I don't know about you, Berk, but I think Emily is still Danny's girlfriend."

"Yeah, I'm with you, boss. Her eyes and her body language told me the same thing."

"Yup. And I don't for a minute believe that she and Danny have lost contact, do you?"

"Nope. She was way too nervous, I mean, even for being interviewed by cops. Why are you thinking you and Frank Bell will be back down here on Sunday?"

"Well, I have a hunch. I think that phone call she got may have been from Elizabeth Tressman."

"And what made you jump to that?"

"Danny was close to his Aunt Elizabeth, right?"

"Yes."

"And we know that the only visitors Mrs. Tressman gets is someone they think is her niece, and the niece's boyfriend, right?"

"Yup."

"Well, how about if Danny is the boyfriend, and he's having Emily pose as the niece? That way he can still stay in contact with the only relative he still likes and at the same time not have anyone notice he's around?"

"So, he's hiding in plain sight!"

"Well, that's my theory. We'll have to wait for Sunday to see if it pans out."

"So you think Emily was setting up a visit with Mrs. Tressman on that phone call."

"Well, it sure could be. I know she said the aunt she was talking to lives in the Midwest, but I'm thinking it was Elizabeth Tressman. And Mrs. Tressman is a bit hard of hearing, and then the Alzheimer's makes conversations more difficult."

"It fits, Dell, it fits!"

"I think so, Berk, I really do. Let's eat and get back on the road. I need to make some calls tomorrow and check a couple other things so I can set up with Frank for Sunday."

"Any chance I can come along too?"

"Sure, Berk, you're in this case right along with me and Frank. I'd keep that overnight bag ready for Sunday, though. If we get lucky, we may have to stay a day or so down here."

"Sounds good to me. Let's eat!"

As I had anticipated, Berk and I didn't make it back to Castaway County until nearly two in the morning. We'd had a very nice dinner in Freeport at the Jameson Tavern, and the traffic up I-95 and out the Airline wasn't too bad, even for a Friday night, Saturday morning.

We did, however, have to dodge a cow moose when we were rounding a curve on the Airline, just past the snack bar about halfway in toward Castaway County. I suspected that the moose had been grazing by the side of the road, and it was loping across the road toward a small pond on the other side when we came around the curve. Berk was driving at that time, and he simply swerved a bit to the right onto the shoulder, and we went easily around the moose without any problems for either the moose or us.

We got to the office parking lot, Berk got his cruiser, and I headed back out of town toward the lake. While I was traveling along Route 901 toward the lake, my eyes were really starting to droop; I was really tired. It had been a long day but a fruitful one.

I saw something moving in my headlights fairly far up the road on a straightaway, about three or four miles from the Route 901, Route 121 junction. As I got closer, I realized that it was a large black bear lumbering into the woods on the left side of the road, after having crossed the road. By the time my headlights lit the black form up enough for my tired eyes to be able to focus on it and identify it, I realized it was just the hindquarters of the bear going into the woods. *A minute earlier, Dell, and he would have been right in the middle of the road!* One thing for sure, living in this part of Maine, you get to see your share of wildlife. I think that's one of the things that always appealed to me and made the decision to live here so easy.

By the time I finally walked into the cabin, the clock on the wall said 2:43 a.m. I kept very quiet as I came in so as not to awaken Suzi. Chauncey was in the kitchen eating at his bowl of dry cat food and immediately came over and did the kitty-flop right at my feet so that I would be sure to see him and pet him. Of course, I complied with his wishes. *Don't all cat owners?*

I opened the bedroom door carefully, went into the bathroom, and closed the door so I could wash my face and brush my teeth without waking Suzi. After, I slipped quietly into the bed and rolled over to put my arm around Suzi to snuggle her.

She woke up enough to push farther back against me to snuggle and then said, "I thought you were staying down in Freeport tonight, honey."

"I was planning to, but things changed. I'll be going back down on Sunday, so I decided to come home tonight."

"Get some good leads then?"

"Officially, no. Unofficially, yes."

"Okay, I get it. Think you're getting close to solving the case?"

"Well, I'm playing a hunch right now. If it pans out, yes. But like anything else, I could be reading the tea leaves all wrong."

"You have the best intellect I know, honey. It will be fine."

"Thanks, baby. I missed you today."

Suzi just responded by pushing even closer to me in the bed. By now she had turned to face me, and I could feel her breasts rub up against my chest, and I could feel the light breath escape her lips as she sighed with arousal. I'm sure my heart had already begun beating faster as well.

"You know, if we get any closer in this bed, I'm not going to be able to control myself, baby."

"That's what I'm counting on, you silly man!"

★

Since it was Saturday morning, and neither of us normally worked in the office on the weekends, we didn't get up until about eight thirty. Suzi got up first to get a shower, and she left me in bed. I just lay there enjoying the sunshine flowing through the window and caressing my side of the bed, making it warm and pleasant just to stay there. A couple of squirrels were out in a nearby pine tree, chasing one another around the trunk and chastising one another over the nuts in the feeder. It was always a hoot watching them as they carried on a war to see who got to the feeder first and who maintained control of the feeder. Sometimes one would just sit on the top of the feeder like he was playing King of the Mountain or something. They were very comical, and when I wasn't too busy to notice, I could spend hours watching them cavort about the trees and the porch areas.

After Suzi finished dressing, she went out to start the coffee and breakfast. I took a leisurely shower, dressed, and joined her in the kitchen by about nine thirty. She handed me a cup of coffee while she was finishing up some bacon, eggs, and toast for our morning breakfast. *She knows what I like, and that applies to breakfast too!*

After breakfast, Suzi said she wanted to go out and work in her vegetable garden. Suzi had a small garden for things like cucumbers, squash, and corn that I had built for her. It was located down our driveway a bit, in an open area I had cleared for storage of a boat trailer and snowmobile, and it gave me somewhere to pile snow in the winter. It was fairly large. I had used large timbers to make a rather nice raised-bed garden to accommodate her green thumb. So Suzi went out to weed and care for her garden, and I decided it was a good time for me to make a few calls.

First, I called the home where Mrs. Tressman was located. I found that Dominique was on duty, so I asked for her. When she came on the line, I asked her if she could check the logs for me and see what days of the week Mrs. Tressman's "niece" and her boyfriend usually came in to visit. She told me she would call back in a few minutes, after she had time to locate and review the sign-in logs.

I waited about twenty minutes, and Dominique called me back. She told me that although the visits varied some over the past year or so, it appeared that a slight majority of them were on Sunday afternoons. She said the times varied as well. I asked specifically about the Sunday visits, and she said that they were mostly in the two o'clock to five o'clock bracket of the day. I thanked her for the information and told her that I would likely call her back later in the afternoon. She said she worked until six and was off on Sundays and Mondays.

The next call was to Frank Bell.

"Hey, Frank, just wanted to update you on our trip to South Freeport."

"Good, Dell. What came of it?"

"We interviewed Emily Cooper. I think she was lying and covering up. I think she knows where Danny is."

"Couldn't get her to open up?"

"No, but I think I've got an idea. I think she's still in love with Danny, and I think she might be the girl visiting Mrs. Tressman at the home."

"Oh? So what are we going to do about her?"

"Well, Frank, while we were there, Emily got a phone call. We could overhear a part of her conversation when she said something about Sunday. She claimed she was talking to her aunt in the Midwest."

"Ah, but you think it was Mrs. Tressman?"

"Well, it could easily be. I called the home and talked to Dominique, and she checked the sign-in logbook for me. She said the visits from Mrs. Tressman's 'niece' vary, but that a slight majority happens on Sundays. Afternoon, between two and five."

"Well now, that *is* interesting, Dell."

"I'm thinking that Danny has been keeping touch with his aunt all the time. I'll bet that Emily, being his girlfriend, is taking him in to the home to visit her. In the old woman's condition, it would be pretty easy for Emily to pass herself off to the staff as Tressman's niece, since Mrs. Tressman would not be likely to refute that."

"And even if she did, Dell, who'd listen to her anyway?"

"Good point, Frank! So, maybe the 'niece's' boyfriend is actually Danny Windom, Tressman's nephew."

"Sounds like a real good hunch, Dell. Guess we need to get down there tomorrow."

"That's my thought exactly, Frank. I'll bring Berk; I know he wants to be there if we find Danny is the boyfriend."

"Okay, and I'll call someone at the Cumberland County Sheriff's Office and see if they want to go along to assist."

"That is a good idea. We may have two individuals to follow, especially if either one tries to run."

"And it's always good to include one of the local guys since we're in their area."

"Better make sure whoever you call, Frank, knows we're just playing a hunch. There may be nothing to it in the end."

"I will. I'll call one of the guys I've worked with before. Detective Sergeant Rawlings. He's a good guy and works well with me; at least he has in the past."

"Want to meet me and Berk around eleven o'clock at your office?"

"That works for me, Dell."

Before I could say anything else, I heard some clicks on the phone and realized that Frank had call waiting and there was another call coming in on his line. He told me to hold on so he could answer it. In a minute or so, he came back on the line.

"Dell? You still there?"

"I am."

"That was my guy at the coroner's office. We got a confirmation on the DNA ID of the body in Oscar Dillon's grave, and it ain't Oscar."

"Well, well. Any idea who it was?"

"Yeah, some guy named Reggie Downs. My guy said he remembers Downs was a town drunk in Portland years back."

"Well, that's pretty interesting. Kill off a town rummy and use his body in place of Oscar's?"

"Guess whoever did that assumed no one would miss the drunk, Dell."

"I'm thinking you're right, Frank. So we now know that old Oscar Dillon is alive out there somewhere."

"Well, at least we know he wasn't buried in his marked grave anyway, Dell."

"That makes things more interesting, indeed."

"Indeed it does."

We both agreed that knowing that Oscar Dillon was likely to be alive was a very interesting fact. But in the long run, we still didn't have anything to link him to the Bear murders, with the exception of his ex-wife and how he used to be physically abusive with her. Other than that, we had no known threats or any evidence that might suggest he was the murderer.

In Danny Windom's case, we at least had some circumstantial evidence that might suggest he was interested in killing his father and had been trained in how to do it. Now it became a matter of trying to locate Danny and interviewing him.

We were going to play my hunch out, but I was a bit worried that if Danny and Emily saw us approaching them, they might run. I figured if they did, we had to make Danny the priority since this might be our only chance to get him for an interview for a long time. And I felt that our current evidence was so circumstantial, it would not support a warrant without some additional evidence. I felt that our best chance was to take him into custody for questioning and then try to break him and whatever alibi he tried to present. In my experience, you often get to a point in a case where you actually *know* who committed the crime, but it still takes a while to develop the evidence to get a warrant, and yet more to get a conviction.

While I was still pondering the case information we had, Suzi walked in and asked if I wanted to go out kayaking.

"It's a beautiful day, honey, and the lake is quite calm. We could paddle our thoughts away out there in the sun!"

"Okay, babe, I'm in. Let me get my bathing suit on."

The reality was that I needed a little while to decompress, and going out on the lake in our kayaks was a great way to forget work for a brief time and relax.

We put the kayaks in at the end of our floating dock and started out. I told Suzi I wanted to go back into Bear Cove. There was a bald eagle that had a nest in a big pine tree toward the back of the cove, and I wanted to see if he was there.

As we rounded the point and started paddling back into the cove, I noticed the eagle sitting up in another pine tree, a bit taller than the one with the nest, on a limb bending out over the water. We stopped paddling and just floated so we could watch the magnificent bird.

As we watched, the eagle quickly took flight and swooped down over the lake about eighty feet away, toward the opening of the cove. In an instant, he grabbed a fish in his beak and returned to the air, carrying the fish back toward the tree he had initially been sitting in. He landed on the same branch and was only about forty feet from us as we watched. We could easily see him pulling apart that fish with his beak, and we could hear the ripping noise as his beak pierced the scales of the fish's side and crushed its bones. It was an amazing and wonderful sight! *Nature in front of our eyes.* Such a scene can be found on nature programs on cable television, or maybe old shows like *The Wild Kingdom.* But I'm sure many Americans have never even seen our national bird, let alone seen it in its natural habitat as the king of the lake.

We paddled our kayaks around the parts of the lake nearest our cabin and Bear cove for about two or three hours. It was so relaxing out there in the sunshine, with the cool water lapping against the hull of our kayaks. Sometimes I forget for a moment just how beautiful and serene the lake can be, and for that matter, how rejuvenating it is for me to be out on the lake. It's just gorgeous!

After we returned to our dock and I pulled the kayaks out of the water and stored them up on shore, Suzi suggested we take a swim. It was warm out, and the sunlight on the lake had been bright, so the act of paddling around tended to make us sweat.

We jumped right in off the end of our dock and swam around for a while. Then I grabbed the life preservers we had worn on the kayaks, and we strapped them on. This allowed us to just "sit" in the water and float around like we were sitting in a chair. We must have bobbed around in the water, about twenty feet away from our dock, for at least another hour. I was so relaxed when we got out that I was afraid my legs wouldn't hold my body up!

So, we went inside to have a snack of veggies and fruit. *What a day! That girl certainly knows what I like and what I need!*

Soon enough, I'd have to go back to reality and start planning our efforts for tomorrow. *Soon enough!*

· 27 ·

By late afternoon, I was ready to get back to work on our case. I'd taken all morning and most of the afternoon to relax with Suzi on the lake. That had given me the chance to clear my mind for a while, which often allows me to gain a better perspective. It seems that just clearing my mind almost always lets me return to a case or a subject with both a renewed effort and a more objective mind. While that might seem strange to some, I mean, taking time out from a big case to go out and enjoy the quiet of the lake, it really is a good process in the length of an investigation.

Probably one of the largest detriments to solving a case is tunnel vision. It's far too easy for a law enforcement investigator to set his sights on a specific suspect, then to actually ignore or discount evidence that's not directly associated with that suspect. Frankly, I always worried if there seemed to be one and only one suspect in a case and that suspect came up immediately near the beginning of the investigation. I found that reduced my objectivity, and I had to really push myself to consider that there might be alternatives to my suspect. At least push myself to look at the evidence more critically to be sure there wasn't another suspect I might be missing by jumping to the first, direct conclusion.

Objectivity is critical to performing a good investigation. That can be seen in the amount of cases in our country that have been adjudicated in past years where new evidence, especially DNA evidence, has determined that the person jailed did not commit the crime. If you look at some of these cases, as they have been reported on such television shows as *60 Minutes* and *Nightline*, you hear an all too familiar story: the evidence in the case that would have suggested a different suspect was there all along; the investigators had just zeroed in on the one person, and the other clues were not followed up upon. In some cases, it's a tragic mistake that has caused someone to serve a long sentence or even be executed, having been innocent of the charges.

In our immediate case, I wanted to be sure that while we were following the tracks we now thought led to Danny Windom, I didn't want to overlook Oscar Dillon as a suspect, or anyone else for that matter. So taking the day on the lake with Suzi to clear my mind was actually a very important step in the investigation.

Since it was getting later in the day, I called Berk at his home and asked him if he could come over so we could discuss the case and do some planning for tomorrow. He arrived at 5:25 p.m., and we sat down at the kitchen table. I had my files spread out all over the table so we could examine everything again.

"So, what are you thinking, boss?"

"I'm liking Danny pretty well. But I think he's going to be a hard nut to crack, even if we find him tomorrow."

"How's that?"

"Well, he's held this grudge against his parents for a long time now. And he's been pretty good at covering up his ultimate intentions from some of his friends and coworkers, at least the specifics of his plans.

"He's taken a good, long time and moved a considerable amount of times to obtain the training and the equipment to carry through his plans. That takes a lot of effort. He's very calculating."

"I agree, boss. He's pretty good at concealing his thoughts."

"Exactly, Berk. And that's why I think he'll be hard to break when we talk to him."

"So how should we go about it?"

"Well, I've been thinking, and there's something bothering me about Danny. He has been carrying this grudge against his parents for many years now, but he only killed his dad. Why not his mother?"

"Hey, I never thought about that, but you're right. If he was so upset about his parents not telling him he was adopted, shouldn't he be mad at them *both*?"

"I would be, if I were him. So why is he more upset with his father? Is it that they already had a volatile relationship before he found out, and that exacerbated it? Or is he simply less upset with his mother than his father for some other reason?"

"There's something about his mother, boss. "

"I think we need to go talk to Mrs. Windom again, Berk. Maybe if we can figure out why Danny doesn't seem to be as mad at her, we can use that to our advantage when we finally catch up to him and get an opportunity to break him."

I called Mrs. Windom and asked if it was too late for Berk and me to come over to ask her a few more questions. She said it would be fine, and I also asked if she wanted me to see if Father Delaney was available to sit in. She said he was planning to visit her around seven o'clock to read some scriptures with her, so our paths might cross anyway. I told her we would be there shortly after seven.

Before we left for Mrs. Windom's, I asked Berk if we had anything in the way of evidence to implicate Oscar Dillon, now that we had confirmed he had not died in that shed fire in Portland.

"Not really, boss. Oscar was apparently a violent guy, and he and his wife had split up, but we don't have anyone who spoke of threats being made or placing him in the Castaway area on the night of the Bear murders."

"In addition to that, Berk, I just don't think that Big Eddy would have permitted one of his guys to go off script and kill someone for their own personal reasons. Eddy seems to rule with an iron fist, and his guys act accordingly, as far as I could see."

"Well, you and Frank talked to him, boss, so you would know his style better than I. But it sounds from your descriptions of Big Eddy that you're right. I wonder where Oscar is and what he's doing?"

"I suspect he'll turn up somewhere. My friend, Brendan, in Boston seems to think he pulled a job down there. That's how we got onto his possibly being alive in the first place. So my guess is that Big Eddy is going to keep him hidden and just use him sparingly for specific jobs."

"Guys like that always seem to turn up eventually."

"They do."

"So right now, we just have one suspect? Danny Windom?"

"That's the way it looks to me, Berk. Let's go see Mrs. Windom and try to find out why she wasn't targeted by Danny."

I asked Suzi to hold something for my dinner, and Berk and I went out to my Tahoe and headed down the roads toward Weaverton Port, to the Windom residence.

When we arrived, Mrs. Windom answered the door and showed us in to her sitting room where Dex was already sitting in one of the chairs across from the sofa. Dex had his Bible in his hand, open with a small notepad beside it on the chair's arm. I guessed that we had interrupted a Bible study session.

"Hi, Dex. Sorry if we interrupted your Bible study tonight."

"Don't worry for a minute, Dell. We will continue after your visit. More questions?"

"Just a few. I think we're getting closer on the case, and I need to do some follow-up with Mrs. Windom, here."

"All right, Sheriff. What questions can I help you with?" Mrs. Windom asked.

"Mrs. Windom, we're still trying to locate Danny for you, and I wanted to ask about your specific relationship with him."

"Well, we had gotten along fine until he found out about his being adopted."

"By fine, do you mean you had a typical, loving, mother-son relationship?"

"Oh, yes. He used to make me cards for special occasions that he had drawn himself. He was a very loving child, although he grew a bit more distant as he grew up. I think all kids do that to some degree."

"Absolutely, ma'am. Now, how did he change toward you after he found the evidence that he was adopted?"

"Well, he got really mad at us. He would cuss his father out over almost anything. If any little thing happened that upset him, he would fly into a tirade toward his father. They had their problems before that, though. Paul was pretty strict with Danny."

"But, Mrs. Windom, how did Danny react with you specifically, not your husband?"

"Well, he never cussed me out, if that's what you're asking."

"Were his reactions toward you always better than his reactions toward Paul?"

"Now that you say it, I guess they were. He and Paul fought each other verbally and physically until Danny left. But he never got really nasty with me, he just stopped being friendly and loving."

"Danny and your husband had physical fights?"

"I say that, but they were never more than just shoving each other. I didn't see either one ever throw a punch or anything. As I said, Paul was a bit strict."

"So, Mrs. Windom, the biggest change you saw in how Danny interacted with you was that he grew less loving and was withdrawn?"

"Yes, I guess that would about summarize it. He just stopped talking to me and became remote."

"Which was clearly different from how he reacted to Paul, right?"

"Yes, it was. I really didn't realize that until now, though. I guess when you've been married as long as Paul and I, you just start thinking about yourselves as one person or unit. I suppose that's why I never saw that Danny was treating us as differently as he was. I guess he just never got along with Paul as well to begin with. I mean, before he found out about the adoption."

"Well, thank you, Mrs. Windom. You have been very helpful. Dex, I'm sorry to have interrupted."

"Oh, it's fine, Dell. Hope you can solve this case soon and that everyone in the community can move forward."

"Me too, Dex, me too!"

Berk and I drove back to the cabin, and thankfully, Suzi had some dinner still heated on the stove for us both. As we were eating, we continued talking about the interview with Mrs. Windom.

"I think we may have a small opening now, Berk. I think Danny still has feelings for his mother. Maybe it's the nurturing that mothers provide their children or some other reason there's a bond, but I think that's what kept him from going after her."

"Well, he sure hated his father, but seemed to just be ambivalent about his mother."

"I think it's more than that. I think he still loves his mother. And if he does, we may be able to exploit that to our advantage to get him talking. At least it's worth a try."

"Are you going to call Frank Bell now to fill him in?"

"It's getting kind of late, Berk, I think I'll wait until tomorrow morning. Let's plan on leaving the office at, say, 6:00 a.m., okay?"

"I'll be there ready to go, boss."

I smiled at Berk and said, "And don't forget your overnight bag. If we do get lucky and the boyfriend is Danny, we'll take him into custody and start interviewing him. I expect it might be a late night for all of us."

"Okay, boss. I'll be ready to go."

After Berk left, I made sure all the doors were secured and the lights were off in the cabin, and then I walked into the bedroom. Suzi and Chauncey had both fallen asleep waiting for me to come to bed. I got ready and then slipped in beside them to get some sleep. I knew I had a big day tomorrow, and I wanted to be properly rested.

28

Berk and I met at the office as planned and left for Frank's office in Augusta by 6:20 a.m.

As usual, while we were driving, along the way we talked about the case and continued planning how to approach Danny Windom, if we located him. As we talked, I realized that we were going to have to work to get someone as steely as Danny to break. And, in truth, we only needed to get him to crack one little bit to give us the leverage we would need to get the truth out of him. But it wasn't going to be easy.

By the time we reached Frank's office, I had a pretty good idea of how I wanted to try to back Danny into a corner. Now I just had to convince Frank to let me take the lead on questioning Danny. Obviously, if my hunch didn't pan out and Danny wasn't the boyfriend, all the planning in the world was for naught. And, for that matter, Emily might not be involved either. I was making a calculated guess, but I thought it was a reasonable one, given the facts we knew.

I told Frank my idea as we headed down I-95, then I-295. Although I think Frank felt a little left out, especially given that he was the lead investigator of the case by law, I think he thought my plan was sound.

"We don't want to put all our eggs in one basket, Frank, and we do want to be able to use any information that we've withheld from the press during the investigation. I think I can soften him up with one line of questioning and then finesse him with the withheld facts. Between the two, maybe I can crack his armor a little."

"Okay, Dell, it sounds like a plan. But I'm in the room with you."

"Of course, Frank. We have to maintain the investigative process for the state."

"We're a team."

"Absolutely, Frank."

Frank had already contacted his guy at the Cumberland County Sheriff's Office, Detective Sergeant Steve Rawlings. He had given Sergeant Rawlings a briefing on the case and told him we were going to sit at the Pineywoods home to see if this couple was Emily and Danny. We met with Sergeant Rawlings in his office in Portland.

"Steve, this is Dell Hinton, sheriff of Castaway County," Frank said by way of introduction.

"Pleasure, sir," he said as he reached out to shake my hand.

"And this is Chief Deputy Berk Smith," I said.

Then Frank continued, "Now, Steve, we want to keep a low profile around the home so as not to scare our couple away from the place."

"Do you have any contacts inside the home we can use?" he asked me.

"Not today, I'm afraid," I said. "I've been talking to Dominique in the past, but she's off on Sundays and Mondays."

We drove over to the Pineywoods home in plenty of time to get settled to wait for the couple to arrive to see Mrs. Tressman. The way the building was designed, it had two entrances. One entrance was off a parking lot on the lower side of the building and accessed the bottom floor where the Alzheimer's care unit was located. The other entrance was located off another parking lot to gain access to the top floor of the building where the assisted living unit was located. The building sat on the corner of two streets, so you entered each parking lot from a different street.

From going in the building to interview Mrs. Tressman on our prior trip, I was aware that the entrance into the Alzheimer's unit coming in from the lower parking lot was not a secure entrance. There was a second, internal entrance to the unit, and that door was a secure door to be sure none of the patients inadvertently walked out. Staff going to work used the entrance off the lower parking lot; I had noticed a time clock just inside that door.

The other entrance from the upper parking lot was actually the main entrance to the building. Patients in that unit were allowed to go in and out at their pleasure, and there were benches located outside the entrance on either side. After entering the main doors, there was a nice parlor area, the information and sign-in desk, and behind that the dining room.

Frank and I decided that we would go inside the building. I would go into the Alzheimer's unit and sit down at a table as if I were visiting someone there, and Frank would go into one of the adjacent office spaces to await the couple's arrival. We thought that two men would look out of place, and as most cops know, we tend to stand out like a sore thumb anyway, especially to those who are looking for us. But we hoped that if it was Emily and Danny, they had no idea we might be there.

We had Berk posted in the lower parking lot behind the dumpsters and between them and the wooden-slat fencing around them. From that vantage point, he could keep an eye on the entrance as well as most of the parking lot.

We asked Steve to cover the front entrance on the upper parking lot. He planned to sit on one of the benches and converse with one or two of the patients sitting there enjoying the sunshine. He should also look like a visitor to anyone scanning the area for police.

We all had our badges and guns, but none were displayed in any fashion. We wanted to be sure to keep a low profile. We also had communications between us with portable radios and earpieces for private listening.

After about an hour, Berk radioed that he had just seen a blue Jetta pulling into the lower parking lot.

"Looks like two people in it, one male and one female, female's driving."

"Okay, everyone, hold your positions. We don't want to scare them off until we can ID them and take them in for questioning," Frank said.

Berk told me later that the two got out of the vehicle and looked around the parking lot once, the male dropping a cigarette on the ground, and then they walked directly to the entrance of the building. It didn't sound as if they were very edgy or concerned about being seen.

I was still sitting at one of the tables interacting with one or two patients over some type of card game. I'm not really sure if either one of the patients knew they were even playing cards, but they appeared to be content.

The entrance door to the Alzheimer's unit had a lock that made a buzzing sound when someone was allowed to enter or leave, so I heard the buzz just before I saw Emily and a young man I suspected to be Danny Windom enter the unit.

If it was Danny, and I presumed it was, his looks had changed quite a bit since the photo we had been given of him standing in the cigar store some eight years or so ago. His hair was cut in a short military style, he had a scruffy-looking goatee, and was wearing some type of commando style pants and a white T-shirt. In a pinch, he could pass as either a woodsman or a commando.

I waited a minute or two to be sure they were fully in the unit and the door had locked behind them, making sure that I didn't look directly at either of them. Danny wouldn't know me, but Emily would recognize me immediately, so I wanted to be careful.

As they both walked toward the center of the living room area of the unit where most of the patients were watching television, I stood up and called out, "Danny Windom!"

Before I could take another step, Danny broke into a dead run and headed for the door to the unit. Just as he went to push on the locked door, I heard the buzzing sound and realized that someone was coming in the door at the same time from outside the unit. Danny took full advantage, almost bowling over the woman coming in the door as he slipped through it and out into the hallway.

I called on the radio that Danny was running and told Berk I expected he would be coming out the door into the parking lot. I then turned to notice that Emily had also taken off somewhere. She hadn't gone out the door, so I knew she was still in the unit somewhere. Frank came out of the office where he had been waiting and came over to me. I told him Emily was still in the unit, and Frank proceeded to start searching for her while I went out of the unit and to the parking lot entrance. I met Berk just as I opened the door, and he said Danny had never come out the door.

I ran back toward the Alzheimer's unit and noticed an elevator on the left side of the hallway. Since this was the staff entrance as well, I was sure the elevator was for their use to get up to the assisted living floor.

I radioed to the others that I suspected Danny had taken the elevator to the upper floor and that I would follow him up there. I told Steve and Berk to stay at the doors in case he doubled back to get out. These were the only outside doors that we knew of, so Danny had to be trying to head for one of them.

Once I got off the elevator upstairs, I asked one of the staff members if they had seen a guy running from the elevator or in the housing areas.

"Saw a young man get off the elevator, and he went down this hallway, but he wasn't running."

"Okay, where does this hallway go?"

"It just goes all the way around the housing area and ends up right back here beside the dining room, like a great big horseshoe."

"Are there any other doors out of the building other than the main one and the Alzheimer's unit?"

"Why, no, sir, there ain't."

I called on the radio again and told everyone that Danny was trapped somewhere on the top floor and Emily was in the same predicament in the Alzheimer's unit. With Berk and Steve covering the only doors in and out, we just had to take some time and find these two. They were there, somewhere.

About seven minutes passed as I walked down the hallway and began checking each room with the help of a staff member when Frank came on the radio.

"Okay, I've got Emily Cooper! Found her hiding in a closet in one of the patient's rooms. She's in custody. I'll bring her out to you, Berk."

"Good job, Frank. I'm still searching for Danny on the top floor."

"I'll be right up, Dell, as soon as I give Emily to Berk."

"Make sure you stay until he gets her in the cruiser, Frank. We don't want that entrance exposed, even for a minute."

In a few minutes, Frank radioed that he was on the elevator coming up, and I suggested he get a staff member and start down the far side of this horseshoe-shaped hallway.

The staff member assisting me was opening the doors to rooms and, if they were occupied at the time, the staff member would interact with the patient while I made a search of the room.

Most of the rooms were actually quite small; they had a bathroom, one large, open room for sleeping and living areas, and a decent-sized closet for their clothes. It only took a minute to search each room for something as large as a person.

When we entered a room with the name Griswold on the door, the staff member with me said that Mrs. Griswold appeared to be sleeping in her bed. I checked the bathroom and then the closet, and we turned to leave.

Just as we walked out of the door, the staff member looked at me with a blank stare and said, "You know, I thought I just saw Mrs. Griswold watching television in the main room when we started checking rooms."

I immediately turned around and walked over toward the bed. The covers were all the way up so there was no portion of the person in the bed visible. I motioned for the staff member to stay away by the doorway and drew my weapon. I held the weapon pointed directly at the body under the blankets and ordered, "Danny Windom. I have my gun trained on you. Come out from under those bed sheets, *slowly*, and with your hands up!"

Danny did as he was told. He used one hand to remove the covers and put both hands in the air in plain sight while he stood up. I had him turn around and put his hands on top of his head, then holstered my weapon and handcuffed him. I then searched him to be sure he had no weapons on his person.

I radioed the others to tell them that I had Danny in custody and that I would bring him out the front, main entrance so he could be placed in Steve's cruiser. I wanted to be sure that both Danny and Emily were kept completely separate from each other until we could interview them back at the Cumberland County Sheriff's Office.

Frank came around the corner and walked out with me to put Danny in the vehicle.

Danny looked dejected and asked, "What do you have on me?"

"Well, for starters, we were taking you in for questioning in a case. But now we can add a fleeing charge. Why did you run?"

"I don't go by Windom no more, so I knew you were a cop when you called my name out. Figured you had something trumped up to talk about."

"Well, let's not talk anymore until we get back to the office. Detective Sergeant Rawlings, here, will give you your Miranda rights."

I handed him off to Steve to put in his vehicle.

"Okay, Frank, I'll ride with Berk, and you ride with Steve?"

"Works for me, Dell. By the way, good work in there."

"You too. We each got our man, as it were. Now let's see if we can break one or both of these two and get the full story."

"Okay, Dell, and we'll play it your way. I think it might work."

29

We had transported both Emily and Danny back to Cumberland County Sheriff's Office and placed them in separate rooms for interviews. The primary interview room is large and has a two-way glass in one wall, much like the ones depicted in police shows on television, and it was ideal for talking to Danny Windom. Emily Cooper was placed in another room, much smaller, more resembling a typical closed-office space with a desk and two chairs.

Frank and I took our time before talking to either of them; I wanted to give them time to think and to wonder if we were already talking to the other one prior to interviewing them. Providing time like this is critical to being able to use information that *could* have come from one of the individuals against the other one. Sometimes a good bluff is the best tool you have in law enforcement. But you have to set the appropriate elements up for the bluff to be believable. To work, it had to be logical, and it had to be timed correctly. You couldn't very well try to bluff about someone having said something specific during an interview if there hadn't been enough time to have held an interview in the first place. *The setup and timing are very crucial to running a good bluff.*

So, Frank and I shared a cup of coffee and talked to Berk and Steve about the case. We took our time. We let Emily and Danny sweat. Then Frank and I went in to interview Danny. Berk and Steve went to the area behind the two-way glass so they could observe. There was a small speaker in the wall, so they were also able to hear the interview.

"Okay, Danny, you have been read your Miranda rights and signed off on them. We wanted to talk to you about the robbery and murder at the Black Bear Truck Stop in Castaway County."

"I wasn't there, so go ahead, talk."

"Were you aware of the fact that your father was one of the victims in the case, Danny?"

"*Step*father, and yes."

"How did you know about it?"

"Em called me and told me."

"Emily Cooper?"

"Yeah, Em!"

"Okay. How did you feel about your father being killed?"

"*Step*father," Danny said with more emphasis and a sound of distaste in his voice.

"Okay, Danny, stepfather."

"Didn't feel nothing. I hated the old bastard."

"Why was that, Danny?"

"He was a mean bastard, and he destroyed my life, that's why!"

"You said he was mean, Danny. How?"

"A strict SOB. We fought a lot."

"What do you mean by strict?"

"I could *never* do anything the way he expected me to. I was always wrong or incompetent."

"And you hated him for that?"

"I hated him for that and for destroying my life."

"How did he do that?"

"Didn't tell me I was adopted. Had to learn it from some old papers."

"How did you find out, Danny?"

"I was looking through some stuff in the attic when we were cleaning, and I saw some adoption papers. They had my name on them. Well, both names I guess."

"So that made you mad at both your parents?"

"Yeah, I was pissed. But I know it was my stepfather. Wasn't Mom, I don't think."

"Why do you say that?"

"He ruled the house. What he said goes. She always did as he said. I told you he was a strict bastard."

"So, you think he made the decision, and she just went along with it?"

"That's about it, I guess."

"Did that make you even more upset with your stepfather? I mean the fact that you thought he was solely responsible for misleading you about your adoption?"

"Damn, straight. He fuckin' ruined my life!"

"Well then, Danny, you must have felt betrayed by your parents."

"Not Mom, I said. Just the old man. And yes, he betrayed me. He acted like I was his son, all the time hiding the fact that I wasn't even a blood relative of his!"

"So, is that why you left Castaway County in the first place?"

"After I found the paper, it was just the last straw. I didn't want nothing to do with that old man. I couldn't wait until I could get away from him."

"That when you went to North Carolina to the cigar store to work?"

"I went down to Carolina and bummed around a while. Wasn't able to find a job until the cigar store took me on."

"So, Danny, when was the last time you were in Maine?"

"Me and Em come every so often so I can see Aunt Elizabeth."

"When was the last time you were in Castaway County?"

"Not since I left out."

"Let's go back to the robbery/murders. When was the last time you were at the Black Bear?"

"Wasn't ever, really. When I left out, it was an Irving Truck Stop."

"Oh, so you've never been to the Black Bear, then?"

"Nope, never in my life!"

"So you couldn't describe how it looks, inside or outside?"

"I'm guessing they changed it some since the old Irving. Ain't seen it since."

"Do you ever talk to your mother these days, Danny?"

"Nope, I left out and left those two people behind. They aren't my real parents anyway, so why should I care?"

"Well, Danny. They did raise you like their own child, didn't they?"

"I guess."

"Was your earlier childhood nice, Danny?"

"I guess it was."

"Did your parents, I mean stepparents, treat you well?"

"Pretty good, yeah."

"Geez, Danny, how do you think your mom is handling having her husband murdered?"

"Better off probably."

"Come on, Danny, you can't mean that. Maybe you think you're better off since he's dead, but you can't think she is."

"Well, maybe not. I guess she misses the bastard. I don't."

"I get it, Danny; while you still love your mother, you hated your stepfather and are just as glad he's gone."

"Yup."

"But I notice you don't call your mother a stepmother. I mean in reality she's not even your mother, is she? Why is that?"

"Leave Mom out of this! She was a good person, not like him!"

Clearly I had touched a nerve. Danny hated his father a lot, but he still seemed to love his mother. I decided to continue talking about her and her feelings to soften Danny up a bit more.

"Well, Danny, I spoke to your mom right after the incident at the Bear. She was very upset about your stepfather. Since you left, he was the only family she had."

"Well, I'm sorry for her."

"You know what else she said? She wanted me to find you. She was worried about how you're doing."

"Really?"

"Yeah, of course she was crying a lot, but I think the tears were for both your stepfather and for you."

"Aw, I don't know about that."

"Well, Danny. Your mom clearly loved him, that's for sure. She seems devastated by the loss."

"Well ... maybe."

"And she was the one who wanted us to find you so you could get your inheritance. Said she thought you could use it."

"Nice of her, but I didn't want anything from him."

"Your mom even said that I shouldn't tell you to contact her. She wanted you to be able to make your own life choices. She was still thinking of you before herself and her worries."

At this point, Danny just dropped his head a bit and didn't answer me or say anything else for a minute. He really seemed to be considering his mother's feelings about her husband being killed and not knowing where Danny was to be able to talk to him.

I decided it was time to bring in my personal experiences to the conversation to continue breaking down the barriers in Danny Windom's mind.

"You know, Danny, I was adopted myself."

"No, I didn't know."

"My parents couldn't have children, so they adopted five of us. I'm the baby of the family."

"Then you understand how I feel?"

"I understand about being adopted. However, I can't identify with your feelings of being betrayed because my parents told me I was adopted from an early age. I always knew."

"Well, Sheriff, just think how you would feel if they hadn't told you, and you found out by accident like I did."

"I've tried to see your side, Danny. And while I would feel betrayed, I would also feel thankful."

"Thankful? Are you kidding?"

"No, I'm not. In my case, I always knew I was adopted, so I knew that my parents really wanted me. I mean, some kids might grow up not being sure if they were a 'mistake' and weren't planned for, you know. But in my case, I always knew I was wanted, almost like I had been selected by my parents."

"Well, I guess I could see that since you always knew."

"But don't you see, Danny, regardless of when you found out about being adopted, your parents obviously wanted you. They selected you and made room in their lives for you. You were wanted!"

As Danny looked me in the eyes, I could see a swell of tears building in his eyes. I don't think he had ever considered just how much and how important it was that he was wanted by his parents. Even if they hid his past and the fact that he was adopted, they wanted him.

"Danny, I can tell you that when I spoke to your mother, she said that they had made a conscious decision when you were adopted not to tell you because they were afraid you would look at them differently. They feared you might not look at them as your parents and might just want to seek out your biological parents."

"Did you, Sheriff? Did you ever try to seek out your biological parents?"

"No, I never have. I don't hold anything against them though. They made what they thought at the time was the best decision for them and for me, to give me up for adoption. And my parents, the ones who raised me, I would never discredit them by leaving to 'go find my *real* parents.'"

"Weren't you interested in them?"

"Who are parents anyway, Danny? They're the ones who take care of you: clothing, feeding, supporting, educating, and nurturing. Well, my adoptive parents did all of that, so in my mind, they *are* my parents. And they dearly earned that right to be called my parents. I'm sure I was no easy child to raise."

"Yeah, I guess you're right."

"You know I am, Danny. And both of the Windoms loved and cared for you, even if your stepfather was overly strict. Regardless of that piece of paper, they were your parents in the true sense."

"I suppose."

Danny was starting to sound a little shaky in his voice and answers. I knew I was getting to his inner soul. I hoped that would soften him up a bit, as well as relax him. I continued talking to him about being adopted and how tough it must have been to find out about it the way he did. I emphasized the feelings he might be having and tried to bring out as much emotion in him as I possibly could. I also wanted to make some reasonable comparisons between Danny's life and mine. I wanted to develop a feeling of kindred spirit between us. *The setup is critical*, I reminded myself.

I felt like I had begun to build a rapport with Danny, and now I wanted to see if we could exploit it. We just had to switch topics.

"It really is a terrible thing about your stepfather being killed like that."

"How'd it happen, Sheriff?"

"Well, that's a slightly controversial issue, Danny. Frank and I, we seem to have differing ideas about the whole case."

"What do you mean?"

"Well, I've said all along that it was a case of a botched robbery at the Black Bear. But Frank, here, he thinks it was a professional hit. Don't you, Frank?"

"That's the way I'm leaning, Dell."

"Why is that?" Danny asked.

"Well in looking at all the physical evidence," Frank said, "all the shots that were fired seemed to be extremely accurate and well placed. That speaks of a professional killer to me."

"But, Frank," I said, "you're forgetting about all the money that was taken. Why would a professional hit man take money?"

"I can't explain that, Dell. Guess he just wanted some additional money above what he was paid by whoever wanted one or more of those people killed."

"No, Frank, I think you're wrong about it. I think it was a case of someone entering the truck stop to rob it, and then Paul showed up or something else happened, and the perp just took off after shooting them all."

By this point, Frank and I were carrying on a discussion of the case between ourselves, and we weren't letting Danny interject, nor were we trying to get him to talk. We wanted him to hear our discussion and start to get into our differing opinions about the case. We wanted him to take sides in the issue so we could see where that might lead him.

"Come on, Dell, there's nothing to point to a robbery attempt except some money being taken. Really. What are you thinking?"

"Well, Frank, I know most of the evidence points toward a contract killer, but I really like the botched robbery idea."

"Well, Dell, I guess that's why you're just a local sheriff and I work for the state police; you just don't have a head for big cases!"

"That's not fair, Frank. You still can't account for the missing money, if in fact your hired killer did the job."

Now, Frank and I were deliberately starting to get personal about this case. We both had raised our voices a bit, and our faces had turned a slight crimson color. We wanted to sell to Danny that we were having a genuine argument.

"Now look, Dell. There's simply no evidence to substantiate your claim that this was a botched robbery. None! Sometimes I think you local sheriffs just invent stuff: you don't seem to have the intellect to follow simple evidence!"

Frank had made these comments sound exactly like a strict father might as he chastised his child for not measuring up. *Frank's a pretty fair actor, I'd say*, I thought.

"Damn it, Frank!" I then let my shoulders slope down and looked at the table as if in defeat. I wanted to sell my dejection to Danny.

After a few seconds, Frank pressed on. "Okay, Dell. I'll give you a chance to try to redeem your reputation. Give me just one shred of evidence that this could have been a case of a botched robbery, and I might not think you were just dreaming."

Frank had presented the challenge in a fierce and authoritative way. He almost sounded like he was gloating as he said it.

Before I could make any response, Danny, who had been watching us argue the points of the case, spoke up.

"Well, Mister State Police, what about the cash left in the register? It wasn't *all* taken, now was it?"

"Thank you, Danny," I said. "I appreciate you helping me out." I turned toward Frank. "There you are, Frank. What about that money left in the register?" Then I turned directly toward Danny and asked him, "By the way, Danny, how did you know about the second cash register?"

"I ... um ... well you know that was in the news report, and I think Em told me anyway." Danny's faced looked like he had just had his hand caught in a cookie jar.

"No, Danny, I'm pretty sure you didn't read it or hear it from Emily. In fact, that was our ace in the hole. We always keep a piece of evidence out of any papers and reports on the news so we have something that will tie a person directly to a crime scene. You were there that night, Danny. And the only person who would know about the second cash register having money left in it would be the killer."

"Well ... I'm sure I heard it from Emily or somewhere else."

"You couldn't have, Danny; that fact was completely withheld. You might as well get it off your chest and tell us what happened that night. We know you were there, and you have to be the killer, Danny. What we don't know is why."

It was done. Danny had fallen into our trap. Frank had done a great job selling our argument, and after I had built a rapport with Danny over being adopted, he had quickly come to my rescue in defending my theory of the case. He just didn't realize that it meant his ultimate confession.

Frank and I got a full statement from Danny about how he had gone to the Bear to kill his stepfather, and the other two clerks had essentially been collateral damage. He had nothing against them; they were just in his way, viewed as disposable witnesses to his crime. So they also had to go.

Danny confirmed his attendance at the training facility in Montana and the other places he'd worked. After breaking, he was fairly forthcoming and appeared truthful about his crimes. I'm not sure, but he seemed to show some small signs of relief that it was all over.

After the interview was over, Frank and I prepared the documentation necessary to place formal murder charges against Danny Windom for his father's murder, and those of Betty Dillon and Mary Watson.

It had been a long few days, but the rewards for Frank and me had been great. We had our multiple homicides at the Bear solved and a killer in jail. Next we would need to see just how far Emily Cooper had been involved in Danny's crimes.

· 30 ·

onday morning proved busy for Frank and me. We had to meet with the prosecuting attorney and file additional court documents in Danny's charges. We also conducted an interview with Emily Cooper. We needed to determine just how far she had gone in helping Danny.

After about two hours of interviewing Emily, we both realized that her only connection to the crime was assisting Danny after the fact. She had been with him on numerous occasions after the crime had occurred, and she was aware that he had committed the crime. She had also not been truthful and forthright when Berk and I interviewed her about Danny. She knew where he was, and she was covering for him. She even facilitated his visits to his aunt at the home.

But we were not able to dig up any evidence that she knew about the crime before it happened, nor had she played an active role in the crime at the Black Bear. We presented all of these facts to our district attorney, and he decided to file charges against Emily for being an accessory after the fact of the murders. Better that, for her, than being culpable for the murders themselves. While she would definitely do some time, I suspected it would be far less than Danny was facing.

Emily's defense was that she and Danny had been life-long friends and she couldn't find it in herself to betray him. And she seemed to have felt some understanding of Danny's great feeling of betrayal by his parents, step or otherwise. Unfortunately for Emily, the law does not provide deference for family or friends, especially in cases of murder. Maybe she would be lucky and get a sympathetic jury.

I couldn't help but think about Danny's situation. Even though his parents had failed to tell him he was adopted, he *was* adopted. He was wanted and had been selected by the Windoms. And now, he had totally ruined the Windom family, as well as the Watson and Dillon families. It seemed such a pity that Danny wasn't able to see the positive side of his being adopted—only the dark side of it.

Frank and I left both Danny and Emily incarcerated in the Cumberland County Jail, pending transfer back to Castaway County. Now we had to go back and speak to the victims and their families.

Our District Attorney, Josh Beldings, requested to go along with us to speak to the families. So the three of us went to break the news, before Frank and I held any press conferences.

The worst notification, of course, was to Paula Windom. She had the mixed feeling associated with knowing that her husband's killer had been caught, but that it was their estranged adopted son, Danny, who had killed him and the others. She was horrified, as you might expect.

I had called Dex and asked him to come over, when we were on the road heading toward Mrs. Windom's. He had arrived about five minutes after we did, so he was able to try to assist her with her outpouring of grief. *We were able to provide her with closure, but at what cost? She needed to hear the truth.* They all needed to hear the sad truth of the case.

Notifying the family of victims in a case remains the hardest part of a law enforcement officer's job. Often it just tears your heart in two having to tell folks that one of their loved ones has died or been the victim of a brutal crime. If you could, you'd just cry along with them. But you can't. Your job is to be sympathetic and helpful, but also to remain strong and maintain your composure. The victims and their families need that. They need to know you are steady, composed, and ready to be leaned upon if necessary. Like one of my old training officers told me years ago, "A cop can't go all blubbery and expect citizens to have faith in him to do his job." Maybe that's why so many cops drink, to deaden the pain they feel for others they came into contact with in their work. I don't know.

Frank called a press conference for three o'clock, to take place in front of the Black Bear Truck Stop. He asked Josh Beldings and me to attend.

I had promised Suzi I'd be sure she had immediate knowledge when we made an arrest, so I called her and told her we had and said to be at the press conference.

"I'll be right up front, honey. Was it the Windoms' son, Danny?"

"It was. See you at the press conference, babe."

I drove to the Black Bear by a quarter to three, and we started promptly at three.

"We would like to announce that we have arrested Daniel Paul Windom on three counts of first-degree murder in connection with the shootings here at the Black Bear

Truck Stop. Mr. Windom is the adopted son of Warden Paul Windom, one of the three victims in this case.

"Another individual was taken into custody and charged with being an accessory after the fact to the murders. Her name is Miss Emily L. Cooper. Both individuals are being held in the Cumberland County Jail without bail, pending transfer back to Castaway County.

"I would like to thank Sheriff Dell Hinton for his tireless assistance in solving this case and locating the perpetrators. I would also like to thank District Attorney Beldings for his assistance and his continued prosecution of the persons arrested. Dell, have you anything to add?"

"Just one thing, Lieutenant Bell. I want to thank all of the citizens of Castaway County for their help in this investigation and for the community support given to the families of the victims. Homicide is devastating in any community, but in one such as ours, it is particularly devastating. It is my hope that everyone in the community can move on, and I will continue to do my best as your sheriff. Just as Lieutenant Bell has done his best as the primary investigator in this case."

Following our brief presentation, we took questions from the press. As you might expect, many of their questions could not be answered, and we found ourselves referring to "an ongoing investigation" as our answer to most of them. We knew that over the following weeks and months there would be more interviews conducted with both Danny Windom and Emily Cooper. And other evidence might come to light. And to the primary point, we were not about to try the case in the press, so the facts and evidence would be held for the trials.

After the press conference, Suzi walked over to Frank and me.

"Well, you boys did a great job on this case. Frank, are you coming out to the lake to fish with Dell?"

"No, got to get back to my family. But I might be talked into bringing them out with me one weekend. Maybe a fishing day with a grill out in the evening?"

"That sounds good to me. How about you, honey?"

"Sounds good to me too, Frank. But for today, I just want to go home to the lake and get some relaxation and maybe some sleep. I can't remember the last time I was this tired."

"Suzi, you'd better get the old man home and in bed. He needs his beauty sleep, you know!"

We all three laughed, and I realized it was the first time in a while I really felt like laughing out loud. Actually, it felt really good!

Epilogue

By Friday evening, most of the dust had settled from the Black Bear murders. Danny Windom and Emily Cooper were secure in our jail, in separate housing areas. Their defense attorneys had met with them, and it appeared, thus far anyway, that they were star-crossed lovers who would never turn evidence on each other. *I guess only time will tell on that one.*

Frank told me he was planning to bring his wife out to the lake, maybe next week, so we could fish and have that cookout we'd talked about. I figured that made good sense since our ladies probably already thought he and I were the couple since we spent so much time together the last week and a half.

I had spoken to Brendan Murphy on the phone on Thursday, and although we had been able to resurrect Oscar Dillon for him, his department had not yet located him. He seemed to be like the wind, blowing from place to place while never being seen. Guess that's the way Big Eddy wanted Oscar. My guess is that he still has him on his payroll.

If so, it's only a matter of time until he turns up again. Maybe Brendan and his guys will get lucky.

Suzi and I were sitting out on the dock having a nice glass of wine, and a cigar for me, before dinner. The sun was still at least an hour from setting, so Suzi said, "Baby, you want to go kayaking? Or maybe we could go over and see Darby Webb, see if he has any new stories to tell us?"

I looked out at the lake, the water growing smooth as glass, and heard a loon calling to others farther up lake. I smiled and took a sip of my wine and a puff on my cigar.

Then I closed my eyes and raised my head toward the clouds. I must have let a huge sigh escape from my lips because Suzi immediately spoke.

"Everything okay, honey?"

"Why, yes, yes it is, sweetie. Let's just stay right here on the dock and wait to watch the sunset."

"That works for me. Then I'll go in and make us a nice dinner."

"How about we just skip dinner and go right to dessert?"

"Oh, Dell, you silly man!"

About the Author

John Lindsey Hickman was raised in a farming community in south-central Pennsylvania. He began his career in Law Enforcement as a Deputy Sheriff in Hagerstown, Maryland.

John spent the majority of his twenty-eight year career in law enforcement with the Loudoun County Sheriff's Office in Virginia. His varied experience includes serving ten years on the Sheriff's senior staff with responsibility for daily operations of the corrections and court services division of the sheriff's office. He was one of the first nationally certified jail managers. During his tenure he published various articles and training documents for the American Jail Association and the National Sheriff's Association magazines.

John continues to live in Northern Virginia with his wife, Jennifer and spending summer vacations on a lake in Maine. He is a third-generation owner of property on the lake and has summered there since age 5.

Ingram Content Group UK Ltd.
Milton Keynes UK
UKHW041114050623
422887UK00004B/84